THE FALLING GIRLS

Hayley Krischer

RAZORBILL

For my parents

RAZORBILL

An imprint of Penguin Random House LLC, New York

First published in the United States of America by Razorbill,
an imprint of Penguin Random House LLC, 2021

Copyright © 2021 by Hayley Krischer

Visit us online at penguinrandomhouse.com.

LIBRARY OF CONGRESS CATALOGING-IN-PUBLICATION DATA

Names: Krischer, Hayley, author.
Title: The falling girls / Hayley Krischer.
Description: New York : Razorbill, 2021. | Audience: Ages 14 and up . | Summary: Seventeen-year-old
Shade learns that friendship can be toxic after she joins the cheerleading team over her best friend's
objections. Identifiers: LCCN 2021027519 | ISBN 9780593114148 (hardcover) |
ISBN 9780593114162 (trade paperback) | ISBN 9780593114155 (ebook)
Subjects: CYAC: Best friends—Fiction. | Friendship—Fiction. | Cheerleading—
Fiction. | High schools—Fiction. | Schools—Fiction. | LCGFT: Novels.
Classification: LCC PZ7.1.K748 Fal 2021 | DDC [Fic]—dc23
LC record available at https://lccn.loc.gov/2021027519

Printed in the United States of America

1 3 5 7 9 10 8 6 4 2

CJKV

Design by Tony Sahara
Text set in Walbaum MT Std

Also by Hayley Krischer

Something Happened to Ali Greenleaf

"Heather, why can't you just be a friend?
Why are you such a megabitch?"
"Because I can be."

—*Heathers*

"Even as [she] is for your growth
so is [she] for your pruning."

—Kahlil Gibran, *The Prophet*

PROLOGUE

"YOU GUYS, something's not right," she says, her voice shaky. "Something's not right."

Just minutes before, she was saying how beautiful it was. "Isn't it, Shade? Isn't it so beautiful?"

Lights flashing pink and green. The three of us. Sweaty bodies pulsing. Music beating. The vibration through your feet, up through your skin. Faster and faster.

She's a whirlwind, spins in the center between us all, dripping in a pink iridescence, like candy, in rainbows. She's so radiant. Like nothing existed before and she was born right here. Our arms reaching to the pink lights, all of the lights, the whites, the golds. How the pinks and purples stream across her face, a mask of pastel streaks through her hair.

"What's happening to me? I can't breathe," she says. Her electric-blue cat-eye liner and long fake eyelashes, blinking too fast. She wrenches back, wobbles, and stumbles into Jadis.

"Get her to the bathroom," Jadis says.

"What's happening? What's happening to her?"

The music pumping too loud and too fast now, my body covered in sweat.

But her convulsing body slips out of Jadis's arms, her locks of hair right through Jadis's fingers, the weight of her body, this fit cheerleader, her body on the wooden gym floor. Her mouth spitting, bubbling.

"What's happening? What's happening?" they're shrieking.

One sits down on the ground next to her, that terrified look on her face, shouting, *My best friend, my best friend,* but the music drowns her out.

A circle forms. Kids crowd. A teacher hollers over that deep pulsing bass vibrating through the floor, *Put away your phones! All of you, put away your phones!*

I kneel down, my mouth close to hers, push her locks away from her face, that ashen face. I whisper, but I don't even know if words come out. Then her eyes. Those wide-open eyes, the purple lights flashing over her blank stare. And those eyes, with no life behind them.

Part

I

Chapter
1

THE PEP RALLY. I wake up before Jadis this morning because I don't want to be late. Jadis Braff, my best friend, says pep rallies and organized sports are archaic. But I keep us on schedule because I don't miss pep rallies. No matter how Jadis complains.

Jadis and I have been best friends since the fourth grade, since she moved into the big-walled castle down the street from me. She's the person I wake up with almost every morning with her arm across my chest. Her blue veins are translucent through her pale skin. Her light-brown eyelashes. Her newly dyed black hair like the color of tar over her face, that sandy brown, her natural color, the last strand of her childhood and who she used to be, gone.

Jadis, who tattoos drawings on my body and hers. She taught me how to do it to her too, but I'm not as good. We mark each other because we own each other. Just two weeks ago, we tattooed two tiny hands on each other's forearms. Inked on our skin forever. Pinkies entwined.

I shake her lightly and whisper, *Wake up, sunshine*, to her, but she pulls the covers over her head.

"Saccharine devil!" she cries. "Make it stop. I curse you back to your virginal hole."

"Hey, don't virgin-shame me," I say, and throw a pillow at her.

She climbs out of my bed and rifles through my clothes like they're her clothes, and they might as well be. In the bathroom, I swipe deodorant under my arms, then she swipes. I squirt face wash in her palm, then in my own. I brush my teeth and then hand the toothbrush over to her. She pees. I pee. We share everything except bras. She swims in mine. She's flat and I'm wider, more fleshy.

We stare at ourselves in the mirror. We heard this line in a movie once where a woman described her relationship with her best friend: "We're the same person, but with different hair." That's me and Jadis. We're the same person, on the inside at least. On the outside, I'm curly and frizzy. She's straight and geometric. I'm olive-skinned. She's ghostly. My wide, dark eyes. Her deep-set, ocean blues.

Except Jadis is the better, cooler, more interesting version of me. The person everyone stares at when they walk in a room. Like no one else is there. She's been the coolest girl in our school since . . . forever. Not the most popular or most feared. Just the most brazen.

■ ■ ■

At the pep rally, we stand out like two sore thumbs. I grab Jadis's hand, and we stare at the wooden bleachers filled to the brim. Because we're late, there's no room except for the front.

"Take a seat, girls," Mr. Falcone, the oldest teacher on earth, says to us.

"Just trying to find a spot," I say, and then he points to the front row. We stare at him in horror.

"I'm not sitting here," Jadis says. "I'm sure there's a place in the back." Because the front row is an unthinkable gesture. I want to be here probably more than anyone else, and we *never* sit up front. It's way easier sitting on the last bleacher against that cold wall because there, no one looks at you. Up there you have a vantage point. You can see everyone below. You get the best view of the cheer stunts from up top. I can watch their moves with my mouth agape. I can gasp or be critical at the back and no one notices how into it I really am. Up front, you're left on display.

"Would it hurt you to smile, girls?" he says, his greasy comb-over like an animal's nest. "When I was a kid, girls used to smile."

I promise you that girls his age didn't smile. Especially when they were talking to him.

So we sit down because we have no choice. The pep rally is about to start, and the place is packed. Say what you want about the cheerleaders, but they always get a crowd. Down in the front, you can feel the pulse of the room. You get the full view. We're so close to the cheer squad I can see the hair on their arms. The clogged blackheads on their noses. The stubble in their armpits. Rashy thighs. Their coach, pacing back and forth. All those cheer championship banners from twenty years ago filling the gym walls like ghosts.

"I can't wait to get waterboarded by pom-poms and the Three Chloes," Jadis sneers.

The Three Chloes are Chloe Orbach, Chloe Clarke, and Chloe Schmidt. The in-your-face tight circle that heads the squad. They're all juniors, like me and Jadis.

Their uniform tops cropped a little shorter than everyone else's, their tight cheerleader stomachs and glossed lips glinting under the gym's dingy lights. They're ferocious about their bond, the way they grip each other's hands in the hallway, making a wall so you have to walk around them. They've been doing it since middle school, so everyone is used to it.

Except for Jadis.

Jadis, of course, has to make a point that this is not 1958 and you can't just *rule* a hallway, so she forces her way between them until they split apart.

The Three Chloes are the reason anyone comes to the pep rally.

The blaring dance party music starts as the cheer squad and their hyperfocused faces, their eyes wide, jaws clenched, take their places. There are only five of them out there; they're a skeleton of a team. The Three Chloes and two seniors, Gretchen Paley and Keke Achebe. There's a desperation. No giggling on the side. No tightening each other's bows.

During a graduation party in June, two girls from the cheerleading team, Randi Schaffer and Isla Davidson, went to the hospital for alcohol poisoning. The year before that, one girl broke her collarbone trying to do a stunt. Another girl needed knee surgery. There were endless school meetings about the number of concussions cheerleaders were getting. Football players had helmets and precautions. They had a concussion expert on the turf. Cheerleaders, on the other hand, had two-inch-thick gym mats separating their heads from the ground. That was it.

Right away, the focus is on Chloe Orbach. Her wild, blonde ponytail tied back in a giant white bow. The other girls shaking their gold pom-poms in a line, in formation, waiting for their leader.

Chloe Orbach sprints into a roundoff and then hurtles her body into three backflips, one exploding after the other.

That's all it takes. Three perfect backflips, and I'm in a trance.

Spread out in a line. Clap, thigh slap, head nod. All of them, grunting, "We. Will show. Who's best." And they hurl their bodies into perfectly synchronized back tucks.

Four of the girls turn in to make a circle. Their bodies in a blue-and-white blur. White bows clipped in their ponytails, their arms up to the sky, those pom-poms whizzing.

Then on Chloe Orbach's *one, two, three* count, they rocket Chloe Clarke, dark hair, big brown eyes. They propel her up to the gym's rafters, her long, tan legs in a wide V, arms out to the side, huge smile on her face, all that glitter sparkling in the light. Then she comes down as hard and as quick.

And they catch her, and somehow she rises again and does a tight scorpion, one leg above her head, the other straight as a pin, and she spins in a double down back into their arms. (I watch competitive cheer videos incessantly on YouTube. I know the terms.) The three of them, Chloe Schmidt, Gretchen, and Keke, catch her like she's nothing.

The crowd screams and the girls, in sync, drop to their stomachs. Except for Chloe Schmidt, who flips her body backward and then lands hard, two feet planted on the ground. Like it's nothing. Like she didn't just lift Chloe Clarke seconds before that flip. If that's not enough, she jumps up with her knees to her chest, then one leg stretched out, then down again, rounding her arms up, and explodes into a spread eagle.

It's everything I want.

I was a mini gymnast. For a little over a year when I was eleven and twelve. Twice a week. Splits and handstands and roundoffs and back handsprings. "She's a natural," the coaches told my mother. And wasn't I? My little tween body, so skinny and malleable, so flexible, just weirdly flexible, that I could do all of these routines so easily. I never got my mother's jokes when I was little. "Being flexible runs in the family, honey," she'd guffaw. How embarrassing.

The Three Chloes were there too. They were equally as assertive then as they are now. Just as aggressive, with Chloe Orbach as their leader.

They played this game where they'd rate us, all of us. It

was the beginning of middle school, that time when girls like the Three Chloes delight in punishing other kids. Their little squeaking voices. "You get a four. Bad form." Shit like that. They were gymnastic terrorists.

A parent complained that the Three Chloes were intimidating her daughter. But the gymnastics coach, a beast of a man, tiny, a powerful chest and spindly legs, said it was good for competition. So the ratings went on, and I'd watch girls get ripped apart, waiting for it to be my turn.

And then I learned how to do a back tuck on the balance beam before Chloe Orbach, and this became a problem. I could feel Chloe Orbach, her eyes on me while I was up on the beam. She screamed, "*Five!*" right there in front of everyone, and I tripped off, landing on my bottom and falling to my side, something I had never done.

I wanted to kill Chloe Orbach, because I knew I was better than her. But she had what I didn't have: discipline. And a mother who wouldn't let her quit. A mother who talked her up, who made sure she made it to the gym on time, who bought her real competition leotards, not the cheap black ones from Target I wore.

I was humiliated and I refused to go back to gymnastics. My mother was relieved when I quit. She didn't want to drive anyway, and she always said gymnastics would stunt my growth and that the costumes were tacky. "I couldn't stand doing small talk with those mothers," she said, "especially Chloe Orbach's mother. Jesus. What a maniac."

And so that was the end of gymnastics.

Watching them now at the pep rally reminds me of how still, all these years later, I can go right down into a split without even trying. Some people run to relax. I do handstands in the middle of the room. Back walkovers while I'm watching a show. Competitive cheer documentaries. Gymnastics qualifiers. They say our muscles remember. And mine never forgot.

Jadis nudges closer to me just as the squad breaks. "Well, that was jam-packed with energy," she deadpans. "Did you get your cheerleader fix?"

"For five girls, they're really good. They're tight."

"Oh, please. You're just as good as they are, Shade. I've seen you backflip off a fence. You can do a split without even stretching. Those no-handed cartwheel air thingies."

"Aerials."

"Right. So don't tell me you're not as good."

But she's wrong. I can't do that. I can't fly.

The squad lines up, everyone back in formation. Everyone together. Hands over thighs. Faces smiling. Shoulders back. Shoes gleaming. Chloe Orbach commanding them into the next drill.

That fire. That drive to keep going. And that's when something in my brain clicks. Because Jadis is right. I'm watching them, but it could be me. It's so clear that I belong out there. That my body is throbbing to be on the gym floor. Then there's a deep rush up my chest and into my throat, an excitement. The way it feels the first time you kiss someone. Taking your breath away.

And that's when it really locks in.

I want to do that.

Imagine me. Off the ground. Into the air. Flipping like that. Flying like that.

I can do that.

But I could also think of a million reasons why not.

For one, the cheerleaders had traditional mothers. Even if they were drugged up on their Vicodin or drunk on merlot. Even if they were lawyering all day, or outsourcing their pajama fundraiser duty, sending their daughter's uniform to the dry cleaners along with Mommy's designer suits. These moms filled out forms on time. They showed up to PTA meetings. They had husbands at home. They had calendars they checked. Cheerleaders had someone, a housekeeper, anyone, making them lunches every morning or the night before so they didn't have to eat the tater tots at the cafeteria. Their mothers did *everything* for them.

My mother bought me pencils with sayings like *Little Miss Hard-Core Feminist.* I don't have a curfew because she wants me to make the judgment call on my own. She wants me to rebel. To try new experiences and take chances. That's my mother's big theory about parenting, that it's her job to push me to experience life, not wander through it following someone else's lead.

My mother smokes hash with her friends. Most of them don't have kids—they aren't chained to the suburbs—so they read poems together long into the night because my mother thinks she's Gertrude Stein, hosting literary salons in Paris for fledgling artists.

These girls, they would never understand me.

Except I can't stop watching them. The way they flip casually on the mat. The way they lifted Chloe Clarke up so easily.

What do I even want with cheer?

I want to go up high.

Backflip into it.

I want them to lift me up to the sky, above all of them, so that I arch my leg out like a goddamned angel's wing.

The Three Chloes and their tight flips, the way they exploded into synchronized spread eagles, pom-poms flying, all that glitter sparkling as the light peeks through the gym windows.

I can do that.

I just have to admit it to myself. The decision is already made.

I can do that.

Chapter 2

THE THREE CHLOES tower over the sign-up table like interchangeable dolls. Their gold pom-poms stacked on top of each other.

One Chloe drapes an arm over another Chloe. A knee close to a leg. Head resting on a shoulder like a weird experimental fashion shoot.

Chloe Orbach stares at me from her little circle behind the sign-up desk. Then it's a ripple effect. One Chloe stares, then they all stare. Chloe Orbach waves, her face lighting up. Then the other two wave, their faces not as excited as Chloe Orbach's, sure, but it's mechanical. They fall in line.

I wave back because I don't know what else to do. It would seem rude if I didn't at least move my fingers. I'm staring directly at Chloe Orbach. *Staring* staring.

So I force myself to look away, pretend like I'm looking at anything else, anybody else. Jadis has trailed over to Emma Scanlen, who she dated over the summer while I was at a writing camp my mom forced me to go to in Vermont. They broke up because Emma hadn't come out to her parents.

It's better for me to do this without Jadis, and I watch her sneak off with Emma inside the locker room.

I stroll up to the sign-up desk, the Three Chloes hovering, watching me. And I walk like I deserve to be there, like they need me. And they *do* need me.

"How do you sign up?" I say, but it comes out more like a whisper, because there's such a buzz around the table, because I'm speaking too softly. Usually Jadis is my loudmouth microphone.

So I blurt it out this time. "How do you sign up?"

Chloe Orbach locks her eyes on me. "Shade Meyer? You're signing up?" She practically chokes on her words. Her hair out of the bow now. Like a crown, those blonde waves framing her face.

Their faces erupt in sly grins. Scanning my outfit: Overalls and a white muscle tank. The tiny rings on my fingers. Broken-in combat boots. Their eyes shift to my face. How my hair is long and curly, but not like Chloe Orbach's kempt waves. The messy kind. My curls are the kind of curls for girls who have zero control. The kind of girl who has no structure. No discipline. No hair products that work right.

I rub my hand across the back of my arm, scratching it. Better than playing with my hair. A nervous tic.

"Shade Meyer is here to sign up for cheer?" Chloe Schmidt says. "You're kidding me."

"Shade Meyer, former gymnast, you mean," Chloe Orbach says.

"I remember how good you were in junior gymnastics. You had a killer back handspring," Chloe Clarke says.

"I was so angry that you could do a back tuck on the balance beam before me," Chloe Orbach says. "I was stuck on back walkovers and you landed it like it was no big deal. You had some weird, natural agility. I really hated you for it."

"Yeah, well, it seems like you caught up," I say. Not mentioning that it was her fault, all of their faults, that I quit.

They smirk at me. Their feral grins. Eyes blinking madly.

What am I doing here?

I look behind me to see if Jadis has reappeared from the locker room, but she's nowhere.

"What do I have to do?" I say.

"Nothing. Just sign your name on the line," Chloe Orbach says.

"Literally, nothing?"

"Just show up. Just come to practice. You can come to practice, can't you?" That's Chloe Schmidt. The meanest one. With her tiny waist and her angry pout and her Instagram account. I heard she pays for followers.

After Jadis picks herself up from the ground once she hears that I've up and joined the cheerleading team (will they have to restrain her?), she'll preach some lecture to me about how I'm signing my life away, that I might as well be joining a cult.

"What else do I have to do?"

"You have to commit," Chloe Orbach says, tapping at her skull. "In your mind. You have to put everything to the side. Everything. Are you ready to do that?"

Everything. What does everything even mean? If Jadis was standing here, she'd be the first person to ask that question. *Define everything*, she'd say. Surely they don't mean I should give up the rest of my life for this stupid team.

But maybe they do mean everything. Maybe that's exactly what they mean.

"We were wondering," one of them says, her tone softer. More curious than defiant.

"Can you do it?"

"You know. A back handspring? We could use some more tumblers."

"I thought back handsprings weren't a prerequisite?" says Sasha Chandler, a sophomore with big shoulders like a swimmer. She's standing to the side, her lips trembling. I want to shake her. Don't you know not to ask questions like that? Don't you *know* worrying sparks weakness? She doesn't know that the Three Chloes were once eleven-year-old vipers.

"Yeah, I can still do it," I say. Of course I can do it. I've been waiting years to do it.

"Can you show us?" Chloe Orbach says.

"Now? As in right now?"

"Well, not *later*. We're all here now. Now is as good a time as any."

It's a dare. And if I don't take it, I'll look cowardly. All of them staring at me, waiting for the magical back handspring.

But I'm not warmed up. I'm not stretched out. I'm in my overalls. Combat boots and rings. Jesus, I'm going to crack my head open on the gym floor, aren't I? I don't need to prove anything to anyone and I know this. But I want to do it. Just to show them I can.

Slip off rings. Untie boots. Socks off. Bare feet on the ground.

I'm fine. *I'm fine.* I mean, I'm not fine at all. But I'm going to tell myself that I'm fine. I suddenly feel this rush of energy, and I'm hopping up and down on my toes the way I used to.

I stretch my arms out straight in front of me. Rock my hands down to my sides. And then propel my arms up to the sky, my back arching and my legs firm until I feel so much power in my thighs, so much power in my calves and in my feet that my body can't do anything else except spring backward so hard, so fast, like a rush, until my hands are down on the ground behind me, my legs up in the air and then over my head. One time, two times, three times. My feet stick down hard onto the gym floor. Breathing heavy.

I turn to Chloe Orbach, because she's the only one who matters, and she's walking toward me with a slow clap.

"Damn, girl. Damn," she says. She turns to the small group who have lined up to sign their name on the dotted line.

"You bitches better buck up. Because here's what you're going to have to work toward. *This* girl. Magic. Here she is. In flesh and blood." She rolls out her hands like she's rolling out a red carpet.

Then Chloe Clarke, the flyer with the dark hair, the one who is more talented than any of them, takes a few steps toward me. "Impressive," she says.

Next comes Chloe Schmidt with her bitchy tone. "I'm not sure I could do that in overalls," she says, wincing. Like it hurts for her to say it.

Suddenly, I feel silly. Happy even. Not self-conscious or awkward, like I want to crawl to the back of the room. *I rocked it.* Those flips, my body up in the air like that. I could still do it. I could still own it.

I slip my socks back on, my boots and my rings. Proud of myself for the first time in a while. Beaming inside.

And then it hits me, that sinking feeling. I'm going to have to tell Jadis.

Chapter 3

I'M WAITING OUTSIDE by Jadis's car, my muscles still shaking from those back handsprings. My arms feeling strong in my muscle tank. I tighten up my boots and I can't get the Three Chloes out of my mind. The way the three of them stood there like one person, chained to each other.

Something about that loyalty reminded me of Jadis, specifically this time in the eighth grade when Fiona Campbell told everyone I stole one of those fuzzy pink wallets you get at the mall out of her locker. *Me*. With a fuzzy pink thing? It was ridiculous. Jadis went after Fiona, dragging her by the hair into the bathroom and telling her she was going to scratch her eyes out if she ever said anything about me again. During lunch, Fiona Campbell apologized to me in front of a crowd of people, tears streaming down her cheeks.

I never felt so loved and protected. Having someone like Jadis on my side, as my family, meant everything to me. It still does.

Jadis drives us to the diner with the neon sign that says EAT HEAVY, and I don't say anything about cheerleading or the fact that a stream of frantic texts about the practice schedule light up my phone because Chloe Orbach added me to their group chat.

Jadis and I crawl into our favorite big booth with the old jukebox from the 1980s. You have to put in a quarter, but only one song plays. Elvis Costello's "Alison," and it skips three times on the line *Alison, I know this world is killing you.* So we hold each other's hands across the table and sing the line over and over into each other's eyes. We order black coffees and disco fries, and I watch her as she draws with her mechanical pen on the white placemat.

"This is the new tattoo I want to do for us," she says, and shows me two sparrows. One for her and one for me. We'll put them on our hands, right between the thumb and forefinger, she tells me.

Another text from Chloe Orbach comes in, buzzing against my thigh: *Be there at 8am bitches.*

And then one after that, just to me: *Don't wear overalls to practice, Shade.* ☺

The disco fries come, and the hot gravy and mozzarella cheese shimmy all over the plate and we tear it apart like vultures.

"So are you gonna tell me who's texting you or what?" Jadis says, her mouth full of fries.

"Group project," I tell her. And that stops her from any

more questions. Everyone knows how irritating group project texts are. It gives me a little time until I can figure out how to handle this.

■ ■ ■

After disco fries we go to Dave Sozo's garage to play Ping-Pong. Even though he's captain of the wrestling team, he's also a big fan of Sylvia Plath and somehow he and Jadis bonded in AP English Language. We play doubles against Sozo and Trey Wheeler. Trey stands for the third of something. I have no idea what his real name is. Trey also has this never-ending crush on me. He's a cute boy with a sweet face and blond, nicely cut hair, and I'm sure some girl somewhere will fall in love with him, but I'm not at all interested.

Sozo asked me about it once, why I wouldn't give a nice guy like Trey a chance. *All the girls like Trey*, he said. How do you explain it when someone isn't your type? How do you explain it when you don't like guys who stare longingly at you in the hallway like stalkers?

I told Sozo that I don't date country clubbers.

And now look at me. Cheerleaders are basically honorary country clubbers. They belong in the same animal genus. My stomach turns thinking about it, or maybe it's the disco fries, and I completely miss an easy point.

"Wake up, Shade," Jadis snaps at me, "you want to lose to a couple of boys?" And then I serve an ace. Sozo and Trey scream at the top of their lungs, doing some weird rage thing because they've been beaten by a girl.

Jadis and I leave when the rest of the wrestling team shows up. Sozo tries to get us to stay, but Jadis answers him in a typical Jadis way. "Too much toxic masculinity in this place, sorry, Soz," and she blows him a kiss.

He laughs and yells across the room. "Love that girl."

This is why it's not always easy being Jadis Braff's best friend. She's everything for everyone. She hangs out with the jocks and the punks. She can cut school and still get a 1400 on the PSATs. She can draw the most delicate art on paper, or tattoo it on your arm.

Sometimes I want to eat her alive.

Sometimes I want to build a wall between us so I can breathe.

Sometimes I hunger to be defined as more than Jadis's best friend with the curly hair.

■ ■ ■

Outside it's chilly, and I'm still just in a muscle tank and my overalls.

"Let's walk," she says. She wants to leave her car here at Sozo's and get it tomorrow.

"I'm so tired. It's been a long day," I say, and I think about all of the group texts piling up.

"It's a full moon," she says, and pouts.

So we walk, just two girls strolling down a dark road, past

the old willow trees, past the FOR SALE signs, past the old metal windmill and the crumbling garden apartments.

"One day they'll knock it all down and build more garden apartments," Jadis says. "And we'll never remember what this place looked like. At least I hope I don't."

"Yeah."

"Why are you so out of it?" she says.

How do I tell her that something major in my life happened today and I haven't even shared it with her? Where do I even begin? I just shrug as we stomp through the dried-up grass at the old farm, and it crunches under our boots. This beautiful wasteland, just abandoned here by the town because someone said they'd do something with it, donate it to an open-air project, but no one's done a thing.

It's so bare in the moonlight and all of the energy I have today just takes over, so I race into the field and flip into three back handsprings in a row. Jadis watches me, her vape cloud rising into the sky, clapping and whistling.

"It's like watching a beautiful angel soar," she shouts.

"So I have to tell you something," I say.

"That's good, because you've been acting like a weirdo and I have to tell you something too." She lights a cigarette and hands it to me because she knows I won't inhale any of that toxic vape.

"You first," I say. "Did you and Emma talk?"

"We did more than talk. We had a full on make-out." She dances around in a circle.

"Wow, does that mean you two are back together?"

"You know how lesbians are," she says. "We're not good at breaking up."

Emma apologized for not telling her parents about the two of them during the summer, Jadis says. Apparently she came out to them recently.

I was allowed two phone calls a week while I was up at camp and I used them to talk to Jadis. During those calls, I got all sorts of details about their sex life. And while I was happy for her—because you're always at least supposed to act happy for your best friend when they're falling for someone, aren't you?—I worried that when I got home from camp, Jadis and Emma would still be tied together in their perfect love match. It started to make me sick to get her phone calls. I even considered scheduling a phone call with my mom, and I never want to talk to her.

I hated the way Jadis talked about Emma. How Emma's so good at surfing. How Emma's got an art studio in her basement. How Emma is so easygoing. Was that her way of telling me I wasn't easygoing? Was it her telling me that I didn't do anything adventurous or athletic? What *didn't* she and Emma do together? Ms. and Ms. Perfect.

I became distracted, writing short stories about jealous best friends and dramatic fights between lovers. I wrote a poem about a lizard that I thought would never hurt me until one night it hurled itself out of a cage and bit my neck. After class, my poetry teacher asked me if I was dealing with anything abusive at home or in a relationship that I wanted to talk about. The lizard poem, he said, was so symbolic of deception.

I felt ashamed. My best friend had a girlfriend. How do you admit that's what's wrong with you? That's what's making you unfold from the insides?

And then it happened, right before I came home. Like a gift from the gay heavens, the three-week whirlwind with Emma was over. Jadis was devastated and I was a terrible, shallow best friend because I was so happy that they broke up.

We made a pact to just date people (though I never really dated anyone—too many daddy issues) and never commit to any one person except each other. It was too painful to be apart, and it was too painful to be broken up with. We'd simply avoid heartbreak altogether.

That was the first time Jadis did a stick and poke on me, the two of us in my bed, her clothes and my clothes mashed together. Each of us with one half of a tiny jagged heart on our ankles. Puzzle pieces that would fit each other forever. Best friends for life.

But now it's different. Now I'm relieved. A rekindled relationship with Emma means maybe it'll soften the blow when I confess to her about cheer.

"Good for Emma for coming out," I say.

"Okay, yes, but what took her so long to come out to her parents?" Jadis says.

"Don't be so judgmental, Jadis. We don't know what her parents are like."

"Her mom is a *therapist.* They're close."

"I don't know," I say, "sometimes it's hardest to tell the truth to the person you love the most."

I suddenly realize that I could just as easily be talking about myself.

"So what's *your* secret?" she says.

I imagine the Three Chloes taunting me in the hallway if I don't show up to the practice tomorrow. Their arms folded across their chests, shaking their heads. Hissing *loser* under their breath.

"I think I'm going to stop by the cheerleading practice tomorrow," I say, feeling myself blush.

Jadis stares at me, holding the cigarette in her hand so elegantly, her mouth wide open in disgust.

"You can't be serious," she says. "I went to the locker room to make out with Emma Scanlen for, what, all of ten minutes? And within that time you not only got sucked into the cult of the cheerleaders, but you've committed to practice on a Saturday morning?"

"They didn't *suck* me in. You know I've wanted to do this for a long time. Why do you think I drag you to all these pep rallies?"

"Liking a pep rally is one thing, but to be down there with them? Clapping? Smiling? You don't even know how to smile, Shade. Your mouth doesn't work like that."

"Oh my god, I can learn how to smile," I say, though I doubt I really could.

"You're an artist, Shade. Not a cheerleader. You're nothing

like those girls. They're cookie cutters. They're dolts. They're robots. And what? You're going to change your name to Chloe too? Because that seems to be a requirement."

When Jadis is angry, her face has a particular glow. It's as if her insides are exploding, all the fireworks—the blues, the reds, the pinks—translucent through her white skin.

But I'm angry too. I'm angry that she's dumping on the one thing I want. Because this is something I *want*. Or at least I want to try. It's something I've wanted for a while, but I've ignored it. I've pushed it down. And I don't want to ignore it anymore. I want to prove to the Three Chloes I can do it. I want to prove it to myself. And now I want to prove to Jadis that I can accomplish something without her. That I don't need her inflating my ego. I don't need her holding my hand.

"You're the artist, Jadis," I say. "I'm just the artist's muse."

The smoke cloud hits the night, weaving between us, and she tosses the cigarette butt down on the sidewalk, crushing it under her foot.

"You could come if you want. Like sit on the side," I say, and try to laugh. "You know, cheer me on."

"Uh, no thanks," she says. "The Three Chloes . . . and Shade. It has an interesting ring to it."

"It's just one practice," I say. But we both know that's not true. I know joining the cheer team is like a shot through the heart. It's like I severed a limb.

"If you really don't want me to go—" I say.

"What? Please. What, am I in charge of you?" She gazes down at the cigarette butt and instead of picking it up and putting it in her pocket she smashes it until it's in tiny particles, mostly disappearing into the sidewalk.

"Soon you'll be sipping tequila at the country club, saying, *Those were the good old days.* Maybe you can finally date Trey. Maybe you and Trey will get married and in twenty years, you'll be at the country club chasing after a kid named Trey IV and then a kid named Trey V. Botox between the eyes, fillers. All of it."

"And where are you?" I say, quietly.

"That's a good question," she says, and looks away.

I hold my pinkie out for her to clasp on to it. She hooks it lightly. I look down at the matching tattoos on our inner arms, perfectly mirroring our fingers.

"It's not going to change anything between us, Jadis. It's just a practice."

"Those are some famous last words," she says, laughing, throwing her head back. "*Nothing will change* means that *everything* will change. You've sealed our fate with those words. I hope you know that."

She stares at me blankly, and I don't know if she's serious.

Jadis and Shade, the two of us against the world.

"Our fate was sealed a long time ago," I say, and embrace her, hug her tight, feel her bony shoulders against mine.

■　■　■

That night at home, I do about an hour of reps that I find online. I google cheer conditioning drills and find fit women who train you to do the hardest cardio kicks, handstands, push-up holds, bridge holds, and squat jumps that you've ever seen. Engage the core, squeeze the glutes, arch the back, lower the shoulder blades.

I look down at myself, my little paunch belly, and squeeze it, making tiny dimples in my skin.

Chloe Orbach texts the whole team: *Go full Rocky. Run stairs. Get your abs Gabi Butler rock solid.*

I'm on my fifth set when my mother bangs on my door. She and her friend Esthere, who is in from Paris (but not exactly Paris, as my mom says, thirty minutes just *outside* of Paris, which is not the same thing, according to her), are playing Donna Summer records and dancing in the hallway. She wants me to come out and dance with them.

My mom is very beautiful and very young-looking, to the point that once a supermarket clerk looked at us blankly and said, "Sisters?" This wasn't a flirtatious gesture. My mother looks that young. It's not something I'm exactly proud of, that she's more beautiful than me. Just something else I have to contend with.

I walk out there with my little sports bra and sweats, and she instantly stops dancing and stares down at me. I know she's high, I can see how glossy her eyes are.

She told me when they made weed legal in the state that she was no longer going to hide it from me. That she was going to openly smoke or eat gummies or do whatever she wanted to because she was an adult. She said it was just like drinking a few glasses of wine, like the rest of the mothers do around here. The country clubbers are *all* alcoholics, according to my mother.

Everything she does in her life is in spite of the country clubbers.

She and Esthere twirl toward me in white caftans. "Esthere brought back caftans from Morocco, aren't they wonderful?"

"Wonderful," I say.

"Esthere," my mom says. "Did you know Shade decided to become a cheerleader?"

Esthere practically chokes. "A what? Like a *sis-boom-bah* cheerleader?" She laughs. "That's so American. So quaint."

I think about how my mom showed up to back-to-school night once with *fuck you* painted on her stiletto nails because she said she was just too tired to scrape the glue off.

"Jesus, Mom, can't you just be a normal person?"

"Normal is about fitting in with the crowd," Esthere says. "You know your mother does not fit in with any crowd, my darling." Esthere reaches in and gives me a kiss on both cheeks.

"I think it was Maya Angelou who said, 'If you are always trying to be normal, you will never know how amazing you can be,'" my mom says.

She's one of those people. Filling up her social media with quotes she swears people love to read.

"I'm going back in my room," I say.

"What *is* a cheerleader anyway?" my mom says as I turn away from her, but I'm familiar with these kinds of open-ended questions from her. It's one for the wind and the sky, her exaggerated opinions about my life and the world. "If they had a dance team. *That* I could see. A dance team would make sense."

"I thought too many eating disorders come with dance, Mom," I say, and she sneers at me. Esthere tries to get her off the subject. Go back to their little disco party. To let me live my life. *That's how the French do it*, she tells my mother. *The children have to be themselves.*

I go back in my room and slam the door. She shouts from the hallway, "I watched that cheer documentary, Shade. The girls were unnaturally obsessed with their bodies. I'm *sure* the girls in your school are nothing like that."

She waits for a response. I can't tell if it's a dig or if she's being sincere. So I say nothing, letting her walk away.

Chapter

4

IN THE LOCKER ROOM, all the girls are wearing booty shorts and sports bras. Their tiny waists wafting in the air. Everything, arms, belly, legs, all of it on display. Tanned and oiled. Scrubbed. Smooth, supple skin over bulging muscles. So comfortable with their bodies. How do they know how to do this? To be so tanned and manicured? Did their mothers teach them? An older sister? Did they study magazines? How did they get their elbows to shine? Their eyebrows in a perfect arch?

What am I doing here?

This is the biggest mistake of my life.

There's a strict school dress code where they send you home if you're not wearing a bra. If the vice principal measures your shorts and they're too short, you get sent home. Just last year, you couldn't wear leggings to school. Too provocative, they said. But over here, in the locker room, there are different rules. Everyone is on display.

I'm wearing my old sports bra that barely holds me up. A

pair of gym shorts rolled over two times. My mother's black T-shirt that says CLUB MED 1993. She got it from Goodwill because she believes in sustainable fashion. The T-shirt covers my ass; I'm swimming in it. It's 85 degrees, and I'm baking. The hot sun plows through the jail cell–like window.

Standing in front of the hazy glow, the rays of light streaming around her, is Chloe Orbach. Her hair in a high bun. Booty shorts and a purple tie-dyed sports bra. A lapis heart necklace lined with diamonds gleaming in the light.

"You can't wear that T-shirt, Shade," she says. "It's not part of the uniform."

"You just said not to wear overalls," I say.

Just as I think Chloe is going to tear into me about not being a team player, she softens, exhales like she's a flower opening her petals to me.

"We have to see your body, Shade. How can we see you move, and correct your positions, if you're wearing enormous clothes?"

Her face is so gentle and kind now. Sweeter than I ever thought she could be. This is the girl who destroyed my gymnastics career. The girl who tormented other girls just for shitty cartwheels. For sloppy dismounts. Who humiliated girls in front of an entire gym while coaches watched in glee. She scans my body. Her eyes all over me. "You're a little powerhouse, Shade."

And something lights up in me. Maybe it's just shock that she's not trying to harass me right off the bat. But I sink into it, feeling fuzzy and warm in my chest.

"You have a sports bra on under there?"

"Yeah, of course."

"Then take your shirt off." She doesn't stammer.

"Right here? I'm not taking my shirt off right here."

"Do you have like body dysmorphia or something? You have a great body. Big boobs. Tiny waist. What's your problem?"

My problem is I'm not used to being the center of attention. I've always reserved that spot for Jadis.

So I hold in my stomach and pull my shirt off. I feel like I'm being inspected by my Jewish grandmother who always wants to see how "skinny" I am when I visit her.

"You don't have to suck it in so hard. You're tiny. Just get used to it."

"I'm really out of my comfort zone here, you understand that, right?" I say.

"I know," she says, and takes my hand, guides me through the locker room like I'm hers. Her face straight ahead, walking me toward the five other new girls. Kaitlyn Frazier, Priyanka Laghari, Olivia Cohen, Sasha Chandler, and Zoey Potter. There's eleven of us on the team in total. All of them screaming over each other, with Chloe Schmidt and Chloe Clarke sandwiched between them all, their bodies so muddled and tight together like they know how to do this. They know how to be a group of giggling girls, happy and cute, the kind of girls you walk past and wonder what they're whispering about.

Chloe Orbach turns to me. "Loosen up," she commands.

It makes me more tense.

When Chloe Schmidt and Chloe Clarke see Chloe Orbach,

they abandon the new girls and march over to us, like soldiers.

"Tell Shade she looks amazing. Tell her something nice," Chloe Orbach says.

"You're not very tan. You should probably sit out in the sun," Clarke says, and grins.

"That's not a compliment." Chloe Orbach sneers and flicks her arm. "Be nice."

"Isn't that what a cheerleader is supposed to be?" I say, taunting. "Aren't you all nice? Aren't you all sweet?"

"I don't know what we are," Chloe Schmidt says, her eyebrow arching. "But we're not sweet."

Chloe Clarke rolls her eyes. "Okay, I'll go first," she says. "You have a great body, but you slouch your shoulders too much."

"Thanks?" I say, sending my shoulders back. Every part of me wants to crouch down and crawl out of here. But that's the point of this little game, isn't it? To test me. For me to wilt. I don't wilt.

"You need new shorts," Schmidt says. "Those are too loose. You need cheer shorts."

"Chloe likes 'em tight," Orbach says, and Chloe Schmidt smirks.

"I like your tattoo," Clarke says. "It's pretty."

My tattoo. The pinkies intertwined. Two delicate fingers. Me and Jadis. What would Jadis think of this, them undressing me? God, she would hate it so much.

"Who's the other pinkie?" Chloe Orbach says. But she knows exactly who it is.

"Jadis Braff."

"Are you together?" Chloe Schmidt asks.

"No, she's with Trey Wheeler," Chloe Clarke says.

"I am *not* with Trey Wheeler," I say; it's the only thing that comes out of my mouth with clear intention.

The question about Jadis, on the other hand, isn't so unusual. People ask me this. Jadis's private art teacher and even Jadis's brother, Eddie, recently. My own mother asked me; she was excited to tell her friends that she had a queer daughter. They would have been so impressed, she said, because in her day, that sort of thing was so taboo. *It's such a beautiful thing, how inclusive your generation is*, my mom always says. I know, I told her, *I know*.

But Jadis and I have never been together. Plus, I'm straight. We're best friends, and that's it.

When Chloe Schmidt asks me about Jadis, that twinge in my stomach comes up, the nervous tightening of my belly. I would hate it if Jadis joined the landscape photography club, or if she decided to be a stagehand for the school play. I would see it as her choosing something over me.

I'm a terrible person.

"No," I say to the Three Chloes. "We're best friends."

"Jesus, Chloe. Really?" Chloe Orbach says. "Shade's personal life is none of our business."

"She didn't seem to mind that I asked," Chloe Schmidt says.

"I don't care. It's rude," Chloe Orbach snaps, and then she smiles at me contentedly and blows a big bubble with her pink gum, before it cracks across her lips.

Chloe Clarke grabs booty shorts from her locker. "Put these on," she says, and chucks them at me.

"We'll wait while you change," Chloe Orbach says.

"You ready to do this, Shade?" she says.

Suddenly everything seems so hopeful—and I almost forget that five seconds ago I felt guilty about joining the team. About leaving Jadis. I'm being included in something that's imperfect and filled with sexist stereotypes, as my mom would say, but it feels good to be included.

"Uh, sure?" I say.

The three of them laugh, groan.

"Oh, my god, this is going to take so much work," Schmidt says. "She needs an entire transformation."

"Let's try it again," Clarke says, her body solid in front of me. Arms down. Shoulders back. Then, in a peppy cheer command: "You ready to do this?"

Their eyes. Heavy on me. Peering into me. I know what they want. They want some corny drill sergeant *YES MA'AM* out of me. I have to decide if I'm too cool to give it to them or if I'm going to jump into this role, because here I am at cheer practice. What have I got to lose?

"I'm fucking ready," I say.

We walk out of the locker room, the four of us together, and I pass the mirror, slow, like it's watching me. A panicked little girl's voice in my head, *I don't belong here. I don't belong here.* Yet here I am, my curls, my bare stomach, my legs, my shoulders. All of my body on full display. My belly button, for

the first time in years, seeing daylight. The little pooch underneath it. Here with all these girls and their tight abs, their
stand-up postures. I want that to be me.

■ ■ ■

Coach Demi wants us to warm up with leg kicks and thigh
stretches. Her full name: Demi Alvarado. She's a local girl
who went to the state college. She's not very sporty, with
her long straight black hair and tight jeans and her cropped
T-shirt.

I heard she's going through a divorce from a lacrosse player
who also went to our high school. It's so messy that she had to
get a restraining order. Coach has us running laps to warm up.
Twenty minutes later, I'm so covered with sweat I don't notice
anyone else. Then a deep stretch and it feels so good to spread
my legs and hips. To pull my muscles apart because I haven't
in so long.

"Let's get into a rhythm first," Coach says. "Let's get into
a beat. Rhythm. Beat. We have a lot of new girls here, but
we're one person. We're one unit. Unity. We're a team. Get on
the same period schedule so you can share tampons and Advil
and borrow underwear. If I see one girl with Thinx or pads,
I swear to god, I'll cut it up in front of you. Understand me?
No pads. You don't know how to put in a tampon, one of these
girls will teach you. We're all the same. We all do the same
thing. Do not break from the team."

Clap. Tight. Elbows tucked. Clap. Tight. Unity. Elbows tucked. Clap.

My eyes on Chloe Orbach, her hands clasped together. Her elbows close to her ribs. Each clap with sharp precision. Her body locked in. Coach struts between us as everyone follows Chloe.

Everyone bouncing, clasping, bouncing, clasping. Elbows tucked. Tight. Don't lift your elbows. Don't move your body. Just the hands. Clap. Bounce. Clap. Until my hands tingle from all the clapping, my palms slapping against each other. My fingers cramping up. Who knew so much would go into a clap?

I stop for a second because my hands are so tired. Imagine stopping because of your hands?

"Shade? What are you doing?" Coach says. She's so tiny, so muscular, like she could punt me with one baby kick.

"My hands," I say, but they're all staring at me. Laughing at me.

"Her hands," Chloe Clarke says, the words dripping from her tongue.

"Her poor little hands," Chloe Schmidt squeals.

While the newbies are practicing basic cheer moves, the Three Chloes work on load-in drills and toe touches. I hear them whispering about intermittent fasting and reminiscing about their last three summers in hardcore cheer camp. I watch Chloe Orbach tuck Chloe Clarke's dark hair behind her ears and massage Chloe Schmidt's thick shoulders with arnica. The three of them an impenetrable unit.

Coach has us do fifty push-ups and one hundred and fifty crunches. My body aches like it's never ached before.

■ ■ ■

After practice, I limp out of the locker room with jelly legs, dragging my bag over to Jadis's car.

"Oh my god. What have they done to you?" she says. "You're wearing booty shorts. I'll kill them. I swear I'll destroy them."

I ignore her. This is just Jadis, her drama.

"Watch this," I say.

I show her a toe touch, even though I didn't get to try it at practice. I clap first, jump up, and graze at the tip of my sneaker.

"Impressive. By the way, your whole crotch is sticking out."

I stretch the booty shorts down. But they pop back up.

5

IT'S A LITTLE LESS than four weeks to homecoming, and I know this because Gretchen, the senior who I've heard drinks a glass of whole milk every morning with her breakfast, has made an Advent calendar for the big day. Instead of a Christmas tree with little numbers on it, she brings in a cut-out poster of a cheerleader from the 1950s piking in the air. There are little flaps with numbers peeking underneath up and down the poster.

Gretchen rips the first one off. "Twenty-six days!" she says, hopping up and down.

Homecoming has always been one of those town-wide events Jadis and I avoided. Too Americana. Too *Friday Night Lights*. Too parochial. Boys home from college with their red Solo cups filled with beer from kegs their parents secured for them. Their catered parties after the big game with an endless supply of Mike's Hard Lemonade.

The worst part, or the most atrociously entertaining

(depends on how you look at it), is the homecoming court. The girls and their hair and their gowns parading around in cars with sashes like the Miss America pageant.

I didn't factor in homecoming.

My brain hurts from the thought of it.

Coach starts us out in a power circle outside. We need a second flyer, and she wants a volunteer. So many of the new girls cower, shoulders hunched, timid and embarrassed. No one takes the plunge. But me, I have no excuse. This is why I'm here. Because I watched Chloe Clarke fly up to the rafters that day at the pep rally. If I don't raise my hand, then what am I doing here?

So I raise my hand. Gingerly.

"If you want to be a flyer," Chloe Orbach spurts out, "then you have to raise your hand a lot higher than that."

I reach my hand all the way up and wiggle my fingers around in the air.

Chloe nods in approval. "Good," she says. "Good. We can work with this."

Coach wants us to pair off and attempt something new: stretches, stunts, flips. Anything. She wants to suss us out, see what we can do before she deems positions.

Chloe Orbach takes my hand to partner off with me. I just assumed she'd work with the two other Chloes—it's impossible for me to hide my surprise. My big eyes have always been a giveaway.

"What?" Chloe says to me. "I can't pair up with someone new?"

"You absolutely can," I say. But it makes me uneasy.

Because the rest of them are going to wonder why she decided to shine on me.

"Okay," Chloe says, giving me her most golden of Chloe Orbach grins, her whole face lighting up. The way she looks at me with so much promise, like I'm a jam-packed football field on a Friday night. I'm a U.S. All Star Federation. "What you got for me?"

I tell her about my scorpion, how I can stretch my body into a standing split. One leg solid on the ground. Back arched. Other leg high above my head, hands stretching so that it reaches up to the sky. I used to do scorpions when I was a kid and I know I can still pull one out now.

On her count, I climb up on a short cheer box. Lift my left ankle and stretch my leg up. My standing knee starts shaking, my thigh muscles twitching.

"Break that shit apart," Chloe Orbach's saying forcefully. "There's no buckling in cheer."

And I want to do a perfect scorpion. I want to show her I can. To show her, and myself, that I deserve to be here. Of course, this isn't something I need to do. The other new girls are barely able to get their toe touches down.

I start again. Do a couple of quad stretches. Get my muscles hot. Back up on the cheer box, praying that I don't lose my balance. The two other Chloes make their way over, and I try not to pay attention to them. I stare into the rickety wire fence on the hill. *Focus, Shade. Focus.* Tunnel vision. Spread my body. Grab my back heel. And I can feel it's not right. My body imbalanced, my knee buckles, just like she told me not to, and I fall over, my shoulder crashing into the mat.

Suddenly there's a group of them around me. Studying me. I stare up at Gretchen, who's the closest, my face in line with her pale-white, bruise-adorned legs. I reach my hand out to her, thinking she's going to pull me up.

"Nah, you help *yourself* up on this squad," she says.

"Just remember, Shade, that falling is not failing," Keke says, projecting her staunch military vibe from behind Gretchen, her dark skin gleaming in the afternoon sun. "Falling is part of what you do if you're going to be a flyer."

"When we were freshmen, they threw flyers for fun, re- member that, Chloe?" Chloe Schmidt says to Chloe Clarke.

"Oh yeah, they tossed me without a mat once," Clarke an- swers, picking a hangnail. "Landed flat on my back. Knocked the wind out of me so bad I thought I broke a rib."

"I think all of you need to back off and give her a chance," Chloe Orbach says.

I dust myself off. I remember this from gymnastics, that everyone expects our bodies to be made of armor. We're not allowed to get hurt. We're not allowed to cry out in pain. You *take* it. You pretend like falling on your shoulder doesn't matter. You hold back those tears and you don't shed one single drop from your eye.

Everyone's crowded around now. The new girls take notice when you fall because they're happy it's not them.

So I get up there again on the box. My third time.

"You can do it, Shade," Chloe Orbach says. "This is what the town wants. And you have to give them what they want.

They want cheerleaders up high, waving to the crowd. So that the football moms in their sweatshirts will post it on their little community Facebook page where everyone pretends to like each other and root for the cheerleaders because we're so fucking cute."

Chloe is talking about something everyone wants but doesn't have the guts to say: celebrity. That's what she expects, small-town celebrity status. To bask in that glory. To command the crowd's attention.

"You can do that, Shade. You can all be superstars," she says.

Chloe Orbach turns to the new girls, their blank stares, their baby faces, all of them hypnotized by her.

"What are you dolts waiting for?" she says to them, her words sharp and mean, a one-eighty from her encouraging tone a second ago. "Can we get some excitement here, Jesus. Your dark little hearts. Your fearful little faces. Be a fucking cheerleader, for god's sake."

The collective embarrassment. Getting called out by Chloe Orbach is not something to be proud of. So I get a few claps from them. But I can see their worry. They're scared Chloe's going to make them press their bodies into some unnatural position. That they're next.

"Dig deep in that grit, Shade," Keke calls to me.

I grab my foot, arching my back until I can lift my leg high enough and bring it to my other hand. If I reach forward any further, I'll either fall over or pull my quadriceps. It's not a great scorpion, but I'm doing it.

Chloe Orbach jumps up and flails around, screaming. "We've

got a scorpion! We've got a scorpion!" My back foot touching the sky. My chest out. My ever flexible body, perfectly still.

Coach tells us that she wants both me and Chloe Clarke to get geared up for one-leg extension stunts, then she wants me to learn a basket toss by next week. She says this as if it's completely normal to toss another human being up in the air, have her balance on one leg like a stone-cold bitch, and then catch her as she's racing back down to the earth.

"Yeah, it'll be a breeze."

Coach laughs, and it's the signal for everyone to laugh. Except I think she's serious, and maybe she thinks I'm serious too.

"How many feet do you throw someone in a basket?" I ask Chloe Orbach.

"Oh, about fifteen feet," Chloe Schmidt chimes in. "Twenty if you haven't eaten lunch."

Just a few days ago I was the girl who secretly watched YouTube videos of college cheerleaders at two o'clock in the morning, carefully rewinding the video as they flipped in the air, flying high enough to touch the gym rafters, free of judgments, while Jadis lightly snored next to me.

Here, I can be someone else. Here, I don't have to hide that want and that desire to go up high. Here, I can be that girl too.

■ ■ ■

At night, asleep with Jadis lightly breathing next to me, my eyes wide open, staring at the blank ceiling, I practice my routine with the tiniest of motions, trying not to wake her. I shut my eyes and I dream of my spine curling into a perfect scorpion, foot in hand, shooting up to the sky.

■ ■ ■

By midweek, Coach breaks up the pairings because it's good for the brain, she says. *It'll help broaden this new energy.* New girls, new partners.

Chloe Orbach works with baby freshman Zoey on toe touches and back tucks. I hear Chloe telling Zoey she's got to pull her locs back tight in a ponytail like everyone else with long hair. Zoey gives her a swift nod and wraps her locs in a bun. Sasha, the one whose shoulders could hold a Mack truck, will base me with Chloe Schmidt. Priyanka, who's got the thighs of a professional soccer player, will backspot me. Gretchen, Keke, and Kaitlyn will base Chloe Clarke.

But Chloe Schmidt doesn't want to base me. She doesn't think it seems fair to be held back by the new girl.

"I've always based Chloe, Coach. Why does that have to change now?" she says.

I want to speak up because I'd much rather Keke and Gretchen base me. The amount of trust that I'm going to have to put in Chloe Schmidt, I want her to *want* to do it.

But she's relentless. She rants about how she almost broke her arm last year when that cheer wannabe, Madeline Steiner, slammed on top of her. How she was in a sling for four weeks because that girl wasn't ready. She hurls her pom-poms to the ground.

"You'll get used to it," Coach says to Chloe Schmidt, and then points to the Three Chloes, who've somehow melded together again. "You will *all* get used to it."

Coach seems to have a plan. She's breaking up The Chloes.

"Thanks a lot, new girl," Schmidt says to me as she breezes by. Girls like her are always looking for scapegoats.

"Don't let her get to you," Chloe Orbach says, like it's boring to her. It reminds me of a Jadis tactic: If you pretend like you don't care, eventually you won't.

Coach heard Chloe Schmidt's snipe and now she's annoyed. She calls us back in a circle.

"Your bodies are at war. Do you understand? You're an army." She tells us that if we don't take care of each other, we'll get hurt.

Coach raises her right arm in the direction of the football players behind the fence in the upper field. Their shoulder pads and their helmets and their padded tight pants. All of their equipment. We're naked compared to them.

"You don't have gear like they do. But you have your strength. You have your skin. You have skill. But it's up to you. You want to play mind games?" She points to Chloe Schmidt. "Or do you want to take our team to the next level?"

"Yes!" everyone chants. She wants to hear it again.

"YES!"

"Then stop working against each other. Stop tearing each other down. You're allowed to be a masterpiece and a work in progress simultaneously," she says, and I think about what that means. What she's saying to us. That we're perfect and messy all at once. It's the first time I feel defined.

"Do you want it? Tell me you want it!"

"WE WANT IT," everyone screams.

She tells us we have to do a set of twenty-five push-ups and a four-minute plank, then run the track.

Everyone moans and hits the ground.

"You could say something to Coach about splitting up me and Chloe," Chloe Schmidt says to Chloe Orbach when we're facedown in our planks.

"I wouldn't let those girls lift me. Not if you paid me," Clarke says, adding fuel to the fire, then lowers her head, counting to herself.

"You were one of those girls once," Chloe Orbach says to her.

"Yeah, when I was a fetus," she says. "I came out of the womb doing a double down and you know it."

We're on minute two, and my thigh muscles twitch uncontrollably,

"It was my idea actually, you know, to change things up," Chloe Orbach says, so aloof. As if she hasn't just dropped a nuclear bomb between them.

You can see Chloe Schmidt's chest heaving up and down, her face reddening. "What? Why would you do that to us?" She breaks her plank and plops to the ground.

"Both of you have gotten too complacent," Chloe Orbach says, sweat dripping down her nose, then licks it away with her tongue without even flinching in her plank, not for a second. "It's not a good look."

Chapter 6

THE NEXT MORNING I make a beeline to Chloe Clarke's locker, and she throws me a bored stare as she shuffles through a binder. I instantly regret approaching her.

"Hey, I just wanted to see if we could practice a little together," I say. The truth is I want the Three Chloes to like me, not just one Chloe. It would make things a whole lot easier if I was less of a threat to them, which is how things seem to be right now. "I could really use your help. You know, so I don't fall flat on my face."

"I thought you were a natural, at least that's what Chloe says about you."

She shoves the binder back in her locker and slams it shut.

"You have no idea what you're dealing with, Shade. One minute Chloe Orbach will profess loyalty to you. And the next, she'll turn on you and cackle as blood seeps out of your crushed skull."

I do not expect to hear a *Macbeth*-level warning from her about Chloe Orbach.

"I thought she was your best friend."

"She is. And I would step in front of a train for her, don't you forget it. She's the reason I'm on the cheer team."

"Where else would you be?" I say, not understanding the seriousness in her voice. "Clown school?"

But Chloe doesn't think this is funny. As soon as I say it, I want to take it back. I don't want it to seem like I'm making fun of her. I want to tell her about those days I used to watch them with wide-eyed amazement, the Three Chloes, flying off monkey bars at the playground, their perfect landings. Everyone gawking at them like they were rock stars. Even Jadis was transfixed by their show.

"My mom thinks that this level of cheer is a waste of time. It's not going to get me a scholarship. It's not going to get me any sponsorships. It's not going to win me any awards. She thinks I should be doing competitive cheer and that she's spent enough money on camps, private cheer lessons, and pyramid workshops. Oh, and how can I forget the stunting camps? My mom's from West Texas, okay? This is a religion to her." Then she says, in a high-pitched voice that I take to be her mother's, "*And after all that dedication and money, you insist on being a lowly high school cheerleader.*" Chloe shakes her head and tsks. "All those expectations down the drain."

"My favorite hobby is tormenting my mother too," I say.

"Cheer is not a joke to me, Shade," she snaps. "I'm not doing it on a whim or a dare or to piss off my little rebellious best friend."

I blush. So this is how they see me.

"It's not clown school either, by the way," she says.

"I didn't mean it like that, Chloe——"

"I don't have to be at this school to cheer," she says. "I'm dedicated to my friends. I *choose* to be at this school to cheer."

I want to shrink away, pretend this conversation never happened. I just wanted some cheer tips, that's all. I didn't intend to dive into the psychology of Texas cheer moms. I apologize for the clown school comment.

"I just want to work with you. Because you're so good and I have so much to learn. There's no ulterior motive. I'm committed to the squad. I'm committed to being a cheerleader."

She gives me a long stare. Her eyes don't move from my gaze, not once.

"Then we have a lot of work to do."

■ ■ ■

Later that afternoon at practice, Chloe Clarke runs flyer stretches with me. Hold a hollow, legs up in the air, no room on the ground between your back, squeeze your core. Stand on one leg for five minutes with your eyes closed for balance.

Then she has me lean into the gate that surrounds the field with my leg up above my head for five counts of fifteen. The soccer boys stop their drills on the other side of the fence to gawk.

"They always watch," she says. "You get used to it."

But I can't even concentrate because they're pointing at me. My legs spread so far apart. They make it so obvious, so gross while Chloe Clarke attempts to tear me in two. She counts slowly, shaking out my leg.

"Get out of your head, Shade," she's saying even though my body's screaming in pain, my leg rising higher.

Chloe Orbach glances over at me as I'm hitched up against the fence.

"You gonna make her stand like that forever?" Orbach calls out to Clarke. "She's gonna rip her vagina apart, and we have our first game Saturday."

I give Chloe Clarke my sad eyes, and she tells me I can stop.

I bring my leg down slowly, crumbling to the ground.

But Coach wants us to build stamina. So she ends practice with five reps of toe touches into back tucks—only one of those is part of our routine for the game on Saturday. Most of us can barely get through three, so she cuts it short and sends us running. Two laps. My abs ache in pain when I breathe.

After practice, Chloe Orbach strolls over to me with baby Zoey trailing behind, panting and catching her breath. She signals to Chloe Schmidt and Chloe Clarke, who slowly jog from across the field.

She kneels next to me and opens a small bag. A bag of goodies, she says, and rubs my thighs with arnica. She tells me I'm going to take four Advil because two Advil is for pussies. She tells me to cut out dairy. Not to eat carbs. Everything is about protein. That's the only thing that'll strengthen my muscles.

She places the Advil on my tongue. "Now swallow."

I take a protein bar out of my bag, but Chloe throws it over by a tree. Too much sugar, she says. Too much crap.

She's got kombucha and five rolls of turkey. One for me. One for Zoey. One for her. And one each for the other two Chloes. She gives the turkey to me first. Chloe Schmidt sighs. "Be patient, Schmidty," she says, "or you'll get the turkey last."

"Not funny," Schmidt says, and snatches it out of Chloe's fingers.

They blow little kisses at each other.

"Love you, Chlo," Orbach says.

"Love you, Chlo," Schmidt says back.

Zoey crawls over and shoves the turkey in her mouth.

I savor my turkey. I'm starving.

Chloe Orbach opens the kombucha and sips it. Passes it to Chloe Clarke. Then to Chloe Schmidt. Then to me. I sip back the kombucha. It tingles in my mouth.

I feel so taken care of.

■ ■ ■

On Fridays, the day before a game, all of the athletes and cheerleaders wear their uniforms to school. Some school spirit bullshit. I show up with my legs shaved and oiled, traipsing through the hallway, my cheer skirt swishing over my thighs with every step, every bounce. The feel of my tight, sleeveless top.

Everyone else prowls the hall with their black leggings

and their hoodies, blending into the dank, unventilated high school air. I'm not like any of them. Not anymore.

I see Chloe Orbach outside the cafeteria, that big smile, all teeth, pink lips sparkling, the blue heart-shaped necklace with diamonds around it on a chain.

"Pretty necklace," I say.

"This?" she says, and rolls her eyes. "Thank Instagram." But I feel like I'm missing something. "Soooo first day wearing your uniform in school. How does it feel?" she says.

My instinct is to make some snarky quip, something Jadis would say, like, *Feels like I rule the school.*

Once, I would have been embarrassed by all this attention. But the uniform is a symbol for what I know deep down in my short existence as a cheerleader. That nothing can shake me. Not when I crash down onto the mat after they elevator me up. Not the sweaty hands grabbing at my body. Not the way my spine cracks if I land the wrong way in my tuck. Nothing.

"I feel like we're a girl gang, and we're going to torment some people and break some windows and smash some shit up," I say.

She starts to laugh uncontrollably, this intoxicating release, and tugs my hair close as I laugh too, our foreheads touching, our hair entangled.

She swipes her arm through mine and we stroll down the hall as she whispers to me, "Let's go smash some shit up."

Chapter

7

I'M UP EARLIER than I thought I would be on game day. That feeling so real now, more so than yesterday at school when we played dress-up in our uniforms. Staring in the mirror, fully outfitted.

Who is she, this girl with the uniform? With the biceps beginning to peek out? Who is this girl with this hair framing her face, the glitter lined below her brows, with this skirt and this tight-fitting cheer top?

Will anyone recognize that it's me? Do I recognize myself?

One thing I didn't expect: I like the way I look.

I prance into the kitchen, and my mother practically spits out her coffee.

"Your hair," she says, pausing, her mouth wide open, "is tied back in a bow."

My hair has never, ever been tied back in a bow. Not even when I was little. My mom had a thing against bows, particularly because there was a young television star who started a big bow sensation and so all of the girls at school wore big bows, in every color of the rainbow, in their hair.

I was maybe in the fourth grade. We were at Target, and I grabbed a yellow bow from the shelf. A life-size cardboard cutout of the television star with her curly hair messily pulled back stood in front of the display.

"You are not wearing one of those," my mother said, snatching it out of my hand and throwing it back in the pile.

"I want to wear a big bow, Mommy. Everyone has a big bow!" I cried. Other mothers surrounding the display stared at us in horror. I could hear one woman whisper to another, *Just let her have the bow. Isn't that why we're all here?*

"You look at me, Shade," she said, making sure all of the mothers heard her. "I'm raising you to be an independent girl. Not a girl who follows trends, unless Coco Chanel dictates them. You don't wear an ugly bow because some marketing person decided to stick a bow in some girl's hair. Do you understand me?"

I cried all the way home. I never wore the bow.

Except for today. And it feels good to wear this bow even though I, too, hate the bow. I despise the bow. But I get great pleasure in watching the color drain from my mother's face.

"Oh, stop being so dramatic, Mom," I say. "Think of it like a crown. We're all queens."

■ ■ ■

The sunlight shining on our cold faces, the hardcore dads in the stadium, staring at us with their beady eyes. Chloe Orbach told me it's going to feel like some of them want to undress you. The moms are either CrossFit rats with their hard bodies and tight warm-up gear, or they're trying to cover themselves with their big boyfriend jeans and oversized sweatshirts.

Chloe Orbach zigzags through the rest of the squad to check on me in the back.

"They're all staring at us," I say. The fans, the parents, and the kids running up and down the metal bleachers.

"Don't look at them," she says. "Keep your focus on me in front."

But that's when I see Jadis, her black hair, her white skin, sitting with Dave Sozo at the top of the stands, waving at me.

"Jadis is friends with Sozo?" Chloe Orbach says.

"She's friends with everyone," I say.

"Not *everyone*. Anyway, Sozo is a juicehead," she says, and marches back to her captain's spot. I wave back to Jadis, get Chloe's smack talk out of my mind.

This week is simple cheers. No scorpions or pyramids yet. Avoid concussions. Our voices fall into sync and vibrate together. *We are the tower of power, above all the rest! We are the tower of power, GHS!*

I feel it building in me, that excitement as everyone jumps up and down, toe touches and back handsprings and round-offs, the energy rising. And when our team scores, the crowd screeches and the squad goes bananas, all of us holding each other, and I get caught up in the excitement of it.

I've always been one of those people who hated sports. But when you're right there on the field, it's impossible not to feed off the energy of a winning team, all that testosterone and that manic spirit and the thrill of it all.

At halftime we run out to the field and do a version of that pep rally routine with Chloe Clarke exploding into the air, between all those shaking pom-poms. All of us in sync with a toe-touch back tuck. Zoey and I cross back handspring, then follow Chloe Orbach, who leads us in a V-shape across the field as we bleat out: *GHS has the fire, we will be, the best!*

I hear the high-pitched moms screaming and clapping from the stands. The marching band blares "Don't Stop Believin'." I'm dizzy from the coordination of it all, the calculating moves and the grueling practice behind it. I'm ashamed that I never saw it before.

■　■　■

After the game, Jadis meets me at the side entrance to the stadium. Sozo's gone off to hang out with the rest of the sweaty jocks.

"How did we look?" I say.

"You didn't even smile once," she says, and takes a long hit off her vape. "Not that I'm surprised. I mean, that cheesy face they all do is kind of gross." And she throws her head back, releases a wide, fake smile.

After working my body down to the bone for the past week, this is not what I want to hear from my best friend. But I have to remember that this is classic Jadis. She's learned to fill all her anger and her resentment with what she describes as "brutal honesty." I've seen her do it to lots of people, and now she's directing it at me.

"I was having a good time out there. Sorry you couldn't see that," I say, and shrug, pretend like she hasn't gotten to me. That's the best way to deal with her when she's like this. Be a brick wall.

"Are you though? Having a good time?" she says, her jaw clenched. She opens up her phone and flips through the photos she snapped of all of us. It surprises me how far she's taking this.

The rest of the girls with big smiles stretching across their faces. Me, my body in sync with everyone, but my expression is lifeless. I look like I'm in shock.

I push the phone away. "It's my first game. Gimme a break, Jadis."

"Yeah. Maybe you just need time to get used to it," she says, her voice all sweet and concerned. "Yeah, that's all it is."

But it's unsettling to see myself that way, which was her intention.

"No more pictures," I say. "I don't need a paparazzi, thanks."

She slips the phone in her back pocket, looking a little wounded. I stand there strong in front of her, no buckling. I see her taking it all in. My uniform. The glitter. The bow.

"You really want this, don't you?" she says.

"Yes," I say. "I do."

Chapter 8

WE SPEND MOST of our second week working on a pyramid and the new routine, loading me up into my scorpion. But just as I'm catching my foot in my hand, I wobble and fall onto Sasha and Chloe Schmidt.

"My shoulders are fine, they're fine. They can take a lot of pain," Sasha says as she barely catches me.

But no matter how many times I apologize, Chloe Schmidt charges away muttering, "Oh my fucking god, this is bullshit," like clockwork.

Friday night, Chloe Orbach invites all of us to her house because she says we need to bond before tomorrow's game. I get a text from Jadis as I walk over there.

Night swim? she writes. It's warm out. The kind of night where she and I would eat a little bit of a gummy and go skinny-dipping like we did most of the summer.

Have to go to Chloe O's sorry

She doesn't text me back.

Chloe's house is on the North End, the richer side of town. I expect her house to look like one of the Tudors with the big lawns, or like Chloe Schmidt's massive Victorian, but it's not that way. Chloe's house is an ugly ranch with paint chipping. There's leaves everywhere and overgrown bushes with long bare tendrils that no one has cleaned up or clipped in a long time. Scratches cover the front door like someone was desperate to break in. Their neighbors with their well-kept Victorian homes must hate them.

Everyone's there: Keke, Gretchen, Kaitlyn, Olivia, Sasha, Priyanka, Zoey, and of course the other two Chloes. We file into Chloe's bedroom, and she's filled up half a Hydro Flask with vodka. Poured water in her stepfather's stash to make it look full again. She says he never notices. Her bedroom is painted a sophisticated dusty rose. Everything else is pink. A faded pink blanket is thrown across the bed. Peachy pink carpet. Bright pink tattered chair. Tiny pastel garlands hang from the ceiling.

And then there, across the room, an entire wall slathered with messily taped-up pages from magazines. Pictures upon pictures of women and girls. All of them in some action shot. Walking toward the Eiffel Tower swathed in gold chains. In a fringe coat in a meadow. In a fancy convertible driving down a side street in New York. A gang of girls in virginal white flowing dresses. Women in sunglasses, women layered in silk pink blouses, draping fabrics and giant leather purses, girls with long wavy hair.

At the bottom of every single picture, the name in large white letters:

CHLOÉ

Chloé. Chloé. Chloé. Chloé.

"Where . . . did you get these?" I say.

"Oh, just from magazines. You know. From the fashion house? Chloé?"

I don't know Chloé the brand, but I don't want to admit that to her so I just nod. Anyway, I'm too stunned to say anything. Her name over and over, with these women, pale and rail-thin in layers of clothes. All of them, staring back at us, a hall of mirrors like in Versailles, but instead of images of Chloe Orbach herself, it's her name, with an accented "e," flashing over and over again.

She created a shrine to herself. A cult of Chloes.

I think of Jadis, the pictures of skulls and crows and tombstones and black-and-white pictures of Paul Newman and Liz Taylor, of Kristen Stewart (her favorite), the desert, Siouxsie Sioux and cemeteries, her Joy Division poster, all messily pasted up on her walls.

But this? Your own name bleating across your room? This, Jadis would die over. The *utter narcissism*, Jadis would cackle. I can hear her now.

"What do you think, Shade?" Chloe Orbach says to me.

"I love it," I say. Is there any other way?

"It's my favorite thing in the world," Olivia says. "My mother won't let me hang up any posters because she doesn't want me putting holes in the wall."

"Tape it up then," Chloe says.

"My mother also doesn't want me using tape on the walls."

"It sounds like you need some medicine, a little escape from all those rules," Chloe Orbach says. She shakes the Hydro Flask and pats the bed. Olivia crawls up next to her and takes a few sips of the vodka.

Tell us everything about the shrine to Chloe, we beg her. How long did it take? Did she do it by herself? Where did she find all the pictures? It's an invitation to cram up on Chloe Orbach's bed, legs and arms and feet, sipping vodka and rolling around, playing with each other's hair, softer than we are at practice.

It's like we've been close for years, even though we've only known each other for two weeks. Wrapping our bodies around each other at practice, spotting hips and backs, hands all over each other's thighs—it quickly fuses you.

"I found all these old *Vogues* online. Chloe helped me," she says, pointing to Chloe Clarke. "We started with just a few, right, Chloe?" she says, staring, fingering the edge of a page coming loose from the wall.

"Yeah, then we just started having fun with it," Chloe Clarke says, oh so proud. "It's a goddamned art installation."

She takes a swig of the vodka, points at a few of her favorites, the way their hair glows in the sunlight. Everyone oohs and aahs from the bed like it's the *Mona Lisa*.

"Art installation," Chloe Schmidt repeats.

Chloe Orbach turns the lights off, flicks on a disco ball, and throws on music. Little pink lights stream across the images. Across her face. Pink boxes with an iridescent glow.

And I sink into the night, the plush peach rug, one of her dusty pink pillows underneath my knees.

"You've been doing well this week, Shade," Chloe Clarke whispers, siding up next to me. "Don't let Schmidt get you down. She can have a temper sometimes, but she's a softie."

"What made you become a top girl?" I say to her.

"It was Chloe Orbach," she says, stretching up one of her weed-like legs. "She had this idea that she and I would be the best flyers. We used to watch all these competitive cheer videos and copy stunts." She fixes the pillow so it's under her head, crosses one knee over the other. "And all of a sudden, I became a flyer and she didn't."

"Why not?"

She laughs. Her face blank, like I've asked an absurd question. "She didn't like falling."

The vodka in us and the disco ball spinning, everyone else starts to open up. Keke's parents are from Nigeria. Her dad is a retired Marine, her mother in the National Guard. "You won't believe this," she says, taking a sip of the vodka. "Their last names had to be shortened for their army uniforms. Instead of Lt. Achebe, it's Lt. Ache." She has to have a 4.0 and not one dot less.

Priyanka's parents, both lawyers, are happy about cheer as long as it looks good on her college applications. Olivia's parents are happy that she joined cheer, but they're not happy about her missing family dinner.

"Wait," I say. "You have dinner together every night?"

"We did before cheer," Olivia says. "Don't you?"

"Almost never," I say. "It's just me and my mom."

"Then how do you eat? Just at the kitchen table by your-self?" Priyanka asks me.

"I eat in my bedroom. In front of my television."

They all look at me with sad faces. They don't know what to say about my confession. A mother who doesn't make din-ner for her teenage daughter? These girls have never heard of such a thing.

"I'm on a strict vegan diet. And my stepfather just built a whole CrossFit gym in our garage," Chloe Schmidt says. "So that would never happen. I would never have that luxury of sitting alone, eating, without my mom watching me. The two of them needling me."

This is the first time I'm hearing her talk about this. I knew Chloe Schmidt had a personal trainer. That she had a chef. She's very #fitnesschallenge #fitnessmotivation #fitspo #girlswithmuscles #eatvegan on Instagram. A thirty-day workout challenge where her trainer takes pictures and vid-eos of her. Schmidt's father died of cancer when she was young, and I think that has something to do with it, but I don't ask.

I don't want them to quiz me about my mom. I don't want to say that she doesn't even know where I am tonight. That I make up my own curfew. That the last time she checked my marks was when I was in the fourth grade and even then she ripped up my report card because she said fourth grad-ers shouldn't have report cards. Now I know it's not just them born with this drive, it's their mothers' drive too.

"Stop talking about all this depressing crap and especially stop talking about mothers," Chloe Orbach says, and jumps on her bed, wobbling, little obedient Olivia and baby Zoey at her feet.

"Don't let me fall, bitches!" she says.

"Never!" they yell, laughing.

She changes the track, grinding down hard to Latin trap music. We all follow, flowing back and forth like we didn't just push our bodies to the limit at practice a few hours earlier to be ready for our game tomorrow.

Chapter 9

AFTER, WE RACE into Chloe's kitchen like animals. Ravaged with hunger, all those burned calories searching for replenishment. Tearing apart her pantry for snacks, eating out of boxes and drinking sodas from the fridge.

Chloe Schmidt stuffs her face with diet potato chips, then turns around to everyone, her mouth full. "Don't any of you take pictures. Understand?" Everyone understands.

Suddenly, it becomes so wholesome and all-American and innocent. A perfect squad of girls, dancing and sharing secrets, the kind of girls you'd want to come and raid your pantry.

Then Chloe's mother walks in. She's beautiful like Chloe, except with a lot of eye makeup and lipstick. Her blonde hair, too brassy. A spray tan, too orange. Long white nails like she's trying too hard.

"Stuffing your faces with crackers and chips, girls? Really? Chloe, it's so unlike you," she says to Chloe Schmidt, who sinks back into her self-loathing, spitting chewed-up chips into her palm. "And so unlike the two of you," she says, pointing to the two other Chloes.

"You're all going to break out eating this crap. Cellulite on your precious thighs. Bloated for your game tomorrow. An away game too? Oh, the home team will judge."

Everyone backs away. Collective shame, fear of varicose veins and thoughts of strangers in bleachers staring us down.

Chloe's stepdad comes up from the basement, out of his slumber, and Chloe's two younger brothers follow. They all have the same sporty look. Track pants and hoodies. Hair shaved in the back, short on top. They're an athletic catalog.

Then something happens. Chloe's mother claps her hands, her legs firmly together. "Let's do a cheer," she says, and smiles at Chloe.

Chloe doesn't even blink. "Let's not."

"I was a cheerleader just like you girls. I'm sure Chloe's told you about me," she says.

Everyone shakes their head no. But I'm not surprised, because of course she was a cheerleader. These are the women my mom has warned me about. Chloe and her mother. Mommy and daughter in all their pageantry.

Chloe looks like she's been punched in the gut as her mother beams.

"Chloe hates when I make her do a cheer with me."

"I never said hate, Mom."

"I know, I know. I'm just the old-school cheerleader. I'm the cheerleader *has-been*. My daughter can't even bear to do one little cheer with me."

I cringe for Chloe. Her mom's desperate plea is so uncomfortable. She's too needy.

"I was on a competitive team too, did you girls know that?" She points to a photo on the wall, grainy, a squad of girls stacked into a three-level pyramid. "That's me at the top. We went all the way to the state finals. We worked as hard as you girls do. Maybe harder. I haven't seen your team make it to any state finals. I haven't seen your team at any regionals."

"We're doing a new routine for homecoming," Chloe says, and points to me. "Shade's our new flyer."

I wave awkwardly.

"Cute," she says. "I'm sure your routine will be adorable." Her husband takes her hand, gives her a little pull, but she doesn't take the bait. She's still waiting in her cheer clasp. Hands tightly squeezed together. "You can't do one little cheer with your mother? Just one little eensy bitsy cheer."

How do you back down from your mom . . . in front of all these people? You don't.

"Sure," Chloe says, with utter dread.

They stand together. Clean. Chloe's mom gives her a deep "Ready, go."

Arms up above their heads, then a switch to a K clap. "Let's go. Panthers, get psyched. Let's go."

Left high V. Clasp. Bend knees down.

"Let's GO. Groveton, get PSYCHED. Let's GO."

Tuck jump. Clean. Right there in the kitchen. Both of them exact. Like they've been practicing it forever. Chloe's mother rising high in the air. Higher than her daughter. She basks in it. All of us, clapping because we're left with no other choice.

I feel so bad for Chloe because you can tell that she hates this with every ounce of her body. There's a part of me where for a brief second, really, so brief, it just passes through me, I appreciate my own mother. Where I appreciate her for all of her feminist bullshit. For all of her preaching about living a single and free life. For all of her parties and her boyfriends and her friends coming in from Morocco and drinking too much wine, prancing around in their cliché caftans and waking me up at three in the morning because they're fighting about politics.

My mom is nothing like Chloe Orbach's. In all of her worst mothering, as much as I've often hated her, underneath it all, she's magnificent. She does a coconut oil hair mask every Sunday to make sure her hair doesn't frizz. She doesn't believe in heavy eye makeup, just a bold red lip. She isn't afraid of her age and doesn't try to cover up sun spots with massive amounts of foundation. Chloe Orbach's looks like she's wearing a Halloween mask. You could cut a knife through her blush.

My mother isn't an American beauty like Chloe Orbach's once was. My mother is still growing into her beauty, and I know that not just because people stare at her at the market, or because I hear men and women telling her how beautiful she looks, but because I can see it myself. When the sunlight hits her, when she sweeps her hair away from her face, or even when she drinks coffee in one of her caftans, she isn't trying for anyone, and that is the most beautiful part about her.

No one says anything for a couple of seconds, and Chloe's mom does a big goodbye wave like she's on a float in a parade with her little athletic minions following her out.

Keke, military daughter Keke, turns to me. "That was awkward."

■ ■ ■

I get home and my mom's in bed watching an old movie, *Moonstruck*. She's watched it a million times. She once admitted that she wished someone would sweep her off her feet and take her to bed like Nicholas Cage did with Cher. "This is what centuries of the patriarchy will do to you," she told me.

I hear Olympia Dukakis, who plays Cher's mother, screaming at her, "You got a love bite on your neck. He's coming back this morning, what's the matter with you? Your life's going down the toilet!"

My mother's laughing as I lean in and give her a kiss on the cheek. She puts the movie on pause. Cher can wait. She turns her head to me in shock.

"What on earth did I do to deserve that?"

"I just love you sometimes, okay?" I say. "Is that okay?"

"You love me *sometimes*?" she says, tears in her eyes. "Yes, it's perfect."

Chapter 10

IT'S SUNDAY late afternoon, and I'm still exhausted from the game yesterday. All I want to do is hide in bed, but Jadis wants me to come to her house. Just to swim. They leave the pool's heater on until New Year's Day because her mom says it's good to swim on New Year's Day to get the stench of the year off you. A new beginning. Then she closes it until summer.

Jadis says you hardly need any chlorine in the winter, so the water's got this freshness to it. Last year we swam after a big snowstorm, the steam streaming off the water. The diving board covered in five inches of snow, and we used old saucers to sled into the pool.

It's a beautiful thing, seeing that pink late September sky and the reflection of the trees turning red. Jadis says her mom keeps it open out of guilt, that this is her consolation prize since she's never home.

Just for a little while, she texts.

But I'm exhausted. My thighs are raw from slapping down

on them. My ribs burn from the baskets. My belly is sore from all of those tucks.

A slew of texts come in from Jadis.

Shade you can't say no

I miss you

Come on

So I go. I have to go.

■ ■ ■

Jadis's house is the biggest at the bottom of my street. Every other house is split-level like mine, all looking exactly the same in their row like a supermarket shelf. This whole area was a big stretch of farmland that got split up. Open and wild. A small white farmhouse with a rickety front porch. I'd go to the bottom of the street and watch the bulldozers take it down, my little hand in my mother's hand, as they built Jadis's house. "Nothing stays the same," my mom said. I was only ten years old.

Jadis came into my life when I turned eleven. She moved into her new, modern house down the street and I walked around it in awe, the cavernous ceilings, the skylights and arches. The paintings on the wall. We'd sit in her room and she'd play her father's records. He was a music arranger when he still lived with them. Always trying to make his own album, but ended up angry that he had to make other people look brilliant.

"My father is a mastermind," she told me once. "He's a musical genius." That was before he left her mother for a much younger musician. A woman Jadis's mother calls "The Wicked Ingenue."

Two weeks after her father left, Jadis took lighter fluid from the garage and knocked on my door. She told me that we were going to the school to play a trick on someone. Me and her on our bikes riding through the night. Two young girls shouldn't have been alone like that. We sat in the empty parking lot of the middle school. Jadis had her little backpack filled with lighter fluid, matches, and her math book. "I'm making a statement," she said.

There were a lot of pages in that math book. And she doused it with a healthy squirt of lighter fluid. A cop car drove by and saw the fire, peeled down into the middle school driveway, and called our moms. We both had Saturday detention for a month, and the principal said we were lucky we weren't suspended. All day sitting there wishing it was like *The Breakfast Club*, but it was just lonely. The desks at Saturday detention are crammed with boys who inspect their cuticles, dreaming about their phones.

When I get to Jadis's house, she's out back by the pool with her brother, Eddie, and some girl who introduces herself as Sunshine. She's really skinny and long and smiles at me as if there's not a care in the world. I don't know if Sunshine is her real name or not, but I wave, smile. Sunshine has a little kid who's in the pool in floaties. Eddie's always been a mystery to me. He's seems older than his years, being Jadis's stand-in parent while her mother traveled and her father disappeared with his new girlfriend. He practically raised her.

I've always had a little crush on Eddie, and tonight is no different. Seeing him with this beautiful hippie lady and her kid should make me want to throw up, but it makes him seem even hotter. Eddie would be a good father; I can see it in the way he's playing with this kid.

Jadis is stretching out on a dirty lounge chair watching Eddie and Sunshine splash around in the pool. She rips a long vape cloud that seems to go on forever. Like it came from one of those fog machines.

"Wow, getting good at that," I say, and sit down on the chair next to her.

"Been practicing a lot with Emma."

"You and Emma, sweet."

"My only issue with her is that she likes that minty vape and it makes me want to puke when we kiss." She smirks. Then, the vape cloud streaming from her lips, "See. We both have something new. You have cheering and I have Emma."

When Jadis would call me at camp to tell me about Emma, she'd joke that we'd have to find some boy for me, but she knew that wasn't going to happen. For one, I don't really trust boys. Call it daddy issues, call it what you want.

There was one boy, Jamie Shriver from Moonachie, who I met when I briefly worked at a vile clothing store in the mall. We'd talk about how the mall won't even be around in twenty years, that there will be these empty, decrepit buildings all over the country that people used to shop at. And people will point as they whiz by in their self-driving cars, *Oh, look, remember the mall?*

It was the way Jamie looked at me in his car one night. The way he ran his fingers through my hair. The way he gently touched my breasts. I shivered when he dropped me off, and it scared me. I had to break up with him before I fell in love.

She's not wrong: cheer is easier to commit to than a boy.

Jadis shows me two of her new tattoos, both of which she did on herself. A ghost and a fox.

"What's the fox symbolize?" I say.

"The fox? Oh, that's me," she says. Her confident Jadis grin. "I'm the fox."

Then there's a ghost. It's more crude. The lines blurred. A little sad ghost all by itself.

"And what about the ghost?"

"The ghost?" she says, her face lighting up, giggling. "Oh, that's you."

And she jumps in the water, hardly a splash. I kneel down at the side of the pool. One of the lights is out, the other one shining over her. A silver fish flying across the water. She comes up for air, breathing heavy. Resting her hands on the cement.

"I'm the ghost?" I say. "Thanks, Jadis."

She swears it's a joke. That it was easy to do and she was bored. "It's autumn. You know, Halloween-ish?"

But she's full of it. She did it to remind me that I untethered myself from her.

"So what are we doing?" she says. "Going for a drive? Doing a photo shoot in the grass with my ancient spotlight? Tarot cards? Ping-Pong at Sozo's?"

That eager need of hers. That hyper desire, to always be

moving, to always be creating. Talking. Swallowing people whole. I used to love that part of her. That insatiable side of her. That's when I'd follow her around like a puppy dog.

"I have an idea," I say. "Wanna do a stick and poke on me?"

She climbs out of the pool, water dripping. "Dead, I'm dead," she says, and sprawls out on the concrete waving her hand in front of her face, like she's a fainting Southern belle. "Shade Meyer, star cheerleader, is asking me for a stick and poke? Wake me up. Wake me up."

I pull her up from her death pose and wrap her up in a big towel, and we head into her bedroom. I'd rather go home and go to sleep, but Emma Scanlen or not, I know Jadis is lonely. I know me being so committed to cheer has been hard for her. I slam down a Diet Coke and open another one. Let out a raging belch that sounds like it came from the depths of my soul. She takes a few sips of hers and matches me.

"So what are we doing?" she says, bright-eyed.

"I want a cheerleader. A flying cheerleader."

As soon as I say it, I cover my face with my hands.

"You want a what?" she screeches. "No way. *No* fucking way, Shade!"

"I didn't say anything when you wanted that musical note on your leg, did I? Did I say, 'Jadis, one day you're gonna hate this because it's going to make you think of your dad'? I didn't try to talk you out of it, did I?"

Bringing him up feels below the belt, and her eyes gaze somewhere else, like she's picturing him.

"I shouldn't have said that. I'm sorry," I say.

"It's fine. You should have warned me about that," she says, and hops off the bed, shaking off the bad juju I invited in by mentioning her dad. "And anyway, I'm *me*. And you're *you*. People expect me to have tattoos that make no sense on my body."

"Oh, I'm not cool enough, not an artist enough, to put random tattoos on my body? Oh, I see how it is."

There's a pink pencil on her nightstand. It says *Love Is the Drug*. I stick the needle at the edge of the pencil, messily wrap the twine around it. I'm not as good as she is. But if I want a cheerleader, I can draw myself a cheerleader.

I grab the box of ink out of her dresser and keep wrapping the thread so the needle's stiff until she gives in.

"Put the thread down and tell me how this cheerleader's gonna look," she says. "If I'm going to draw a cheerleader, she's gotta look amazing."

And so I tell her how I've been thinking about flying since that day I saw Chloe Clarke going up, the way they tossed her up there. How she seemed so free. And they're lifting *me*, and I'm up there, solitary. So strong like a tree. It's a tingle that won't go away, like this dagger feeling deep inside and you have to squirm to make it disappear.

She blinks twice. "It sounds like love."

"Maybe it is," I say.

So she sketches something, and like magic, she's created a girl, a stringy doll thrown up in the air. Her hair completely covers her face, across her shoulders. Her limbs, lanky and thin, like mine. No muscles. No texture.

I stretch out across the bed and she slides one leg over my thigh, the other curled under her. She turns on the light next to her bed. A low-light lamp from the 1960s with a pink velvet tassel shade.

You have to wrap the tape around the edge of the eraser and then encase the needle in the thread so that it doesn't slide off. Especially around the top where the ink is going to be thick and full.

Stretching back on the bed, I pull down my sweats a little. She places her hand on my leg and pushes it to the side, so she can draw right into that soft spot above my hip bone. Just a squirt of alcohol on the cotton ball to wipe my hip clean, and then she presses the needle into my skin, diving down over and over again. Tiny little dots.

There's that tingling inside of me. They say that you get addicted to tattoos. That when you get one, you want to get more. That your body craves it. That rush of adrenaline. Your heart racing.

After about a hundred pokes, you get numb to it. I zone out, humming that song she's been singing, that low druggy tune, my skin on fire. Jadis wipes away the ink and the blood, and I breathe through the pinch of the needle, replaying my routine over and over in my mind.

"Open your eyes," Jadis says, and I come to. "Take a look."

I twist around from my dreamy haze, peek down at my flying girl.

Except she's not flying.

My red, blotchy skin. The girl is falling like a rag doll

plummeting from a tower after being tossed. She's down low in the air, her legs up high, her hands in a rising free motion. Her hair in her face because that's what happens when you drop—everything else flies up. Your legs, your arms, your hair. All of it.

"Jadis," I say, shaky. "She's falling. Not flying."

"What? No?" Jadis says. "She's flying. What are you talking about?"

My heart races. My hip throbbing, the pain seeping through like the needle is still in my skin.

Jadis looks at it, her smile turning into shock as she climbs over, sitting next to me instead of facing me.

"Oh shit," she says.

How could this have happened? How did my vision of this flying girl morph into a manifestation of everything I fear?

Crashing down into the ground. Falling.

And now she's on me forever.

"Handstands will definitely help this problem," Jadis says. "Just keep doing handstands and she'll be forever flying."

"It's not funny," I scream.

I stand, hike up my sweats. *Her* sweats. Feeling dizzy. I kneel down on the floor. Like I'm about to pass out.

"Did you do this on purpose? Were you trying to hurt me?"

How could I have trusted her? The girl who's against everything this team stands for. How could I have trusted her to ink me with a cheerleader?

"Trying to hurt you? What are you even talking about? You wanted this. *You* wanted a cheerleader," she says, scowling now. "What goes up must come down. Did that not occur to you?"

Her words sting. The tattoo stings. I just want to go home. My head pounding. The adrenaline rush. The Diet Cokes. All of it.

"It's like an omen or something. Like an albatross," I say.

"Shade, you're the only one who'll see her falling. Don't you understand? Everyone else will see her flying. You're the one person staring at her from that angle."

And it's so true isn't it? The irony of it all. That I'll never be able to get away from her. This image of a cheerleader, on her way down.

■ ■ ■

At home in my own bed. Staring at this tattoo. Inspecting it. I text Jadis.

I'm sorry I accused you of trying to hurt me.

Fine, she texts back.

Are you mad at me? I write.

No.

Then her last text of the night: *You need to understand. I gave you exactly what you wanted.*

I glimpse down at my new tattoo. Is it what I wanted? Is it?

Chapter
11

COACH IS RUNNING US like a drill sergeant on the new routine Monday morning so we can get our pyramid tight by homecoming.

I'm the weak link. My scorpion still isn't going well. I can load in, dig my foot into their clasped hands, and they can raise me up. But when I get up there to catch my foot in one hand, the whole thing falls apart, and I plummet through them.

"Chest up, dammit, Sasha, otherwise she's gonna collapse on top of you," Chloe Schmidt says. "Use those monster-ass shoulders of yours."

And me, I'm not crisp enough, I'm too sloppy.

"Arch that back, Meyer!" she barks. Or "Toes, toes, what's wrong with you? Toes!" Or "Look up, Shade, look up."

I'm too distracted to look up or point because every time Pri holds on to my hip, she rubs against my new stick and poke. It's not Pri's fault, she doesn't even know it's there. I'm wearing extra-high booty shorts to cover it, not the low-slung ones that we usually wear.

Why am I hiding it? For one, I don't want anyone seeing it until I can stop myself from colliding into Chloe Schmidt. Plus, if she saw it, she'd snicker and call me out for being a presumptuous bitch. That I'm a little ahead of myself for getting a flyer tattoo when I haven't even mastered anything else besides a baby basket.

I'm turning out to be quite possibly the worst cheerleader on the planet.

Pri counts. *One, two*, then I load in. Sasha pops her chest up, but it's too sudden, and I fall through them, landing on my ass. Again. We do it again. And again.

But it's not working. I wobble and then smash to the ground. Heads and shoulders and knees crashing into each other.

Chloe Orbach comes over, sees my frustration, and pulls me off to the side for a pep talk. "You're too worried about falling," she says.

"Isn't everyone worried about falling?" I say, out of breath.

She points to Chloe Clarke, who's on her fourth scorpion cradle in a row; probably a rib is going to fall out of her side. "That girl doesn't even think about falling. All she thinks about is flying." A sip of her kombucha, a crack of the neck. Chloe Orbach massaging out a knot in my upper spine.

I gaze around; the rest of the squad is staring at us. To bask in the sun of Chloe Orbach is to bask in the warmest glow, and I want it, I want her to transform my terrible attitude. I want to show her that I can really get up there on one leg and come down in their arms like a baby even though my ribs ache and even though Chloe Schmidt calls my transitions *lesser-than.* I want to deserve this sour kombucha.

"They're feeding off your energy, Shade," she says. "That's how it works when people look up to you."

■ ■ ■

My body is weak and my thighs are Jell-O when I get home, but I strap that band Chloe Orbach gave me around my legs. Hike my booty shorts above my hip so I don't have to see that girl sinking forever to the earth.

They're feeding off your energy, Chloe told me.

Because I'm a top girl now.

I pull harder on the leg band, clenching my teeth as I wince, tightening it. It's that wobbly weird feeling when you're not sure if your muscles can stand it. But I keep going, extend my leg out as far as it will go so I morph into something else.

Someone else.

■ ■ ■

The next day at practice, there's a shift, and it's like I'm loading onto metal pipes. Sasha and Pri, their bodies steel, unwavering. Me, six feet high in the air. Pri, her calm, instructive voice, counting. That left leg has got to come up. There it goes, left leg bent behind me. Right arm up, catching my foot in my hand.

"Lock that knee, Meyer," Chloe Schmidt growls under me. But her voice is an echoey blur.

I move forward into it, the searing in my inner thigh, balancing the weight of my entire body on one leg. I'm locked in. Top girl.

I look across to the upper field. The soccer boys watching from behind the fence. And then farther, to the trees, the slight mountain behind the golden leaves. The view from up top, it's spectacular.

They toss me up, and I land in their arms like a fucking baby.

Chloe Orbach runs across the field, hands outstretched, the rest of the girls running with her.

■ ■ ■

Later, Jadis comes over even though it's been a long day at practice and I'm still annoyed with her about the stick and poke. She climbs into my bed like she's done for years. Curls around her favorite pillow, the one with the real feathers.

"How's it going with cheer? Like, *really*, how is it?" This is the first time she sounds genuine. "How's the back-tuck basket scorpion pancake cobra going?"

I laugh because she always makes me laugh at her stupid cheer jokes.

She jumps up and bounces, my sore body just trying to hold on. And I notice she's wearing a silver bracelet with a turquoise bead that I've never seen before.

"Where did you get that?"

"Oh, this?" she says, jingling it over me. "Emma. Her mother does art therapy with beads or something. Very Southwest motif. Isn't it pretty?"

"You *hate* turquoise," I say.

"I'm trying new things, Shade," she says, her eyes lighting up. "What? You think you're the only one allowed to try something new?"

I don't say anything, change into my sweats while she dances to some banal song that everyone hates, but no one can stop singing because there are a million iterations of it all over social media. It's not like Jadis to know this dance, and she does it terribly. Her skinny pale arms and the way her black bob flops in her face make me smile.

"There's a homecoming dance after the game," I say.

She stops wiggling and stares me down. "Oh my god."

"And I'm supposed to go," I say.

"So go," she says flatly. "I'm not stopping you. I'm sure it's your duty as a cheerleader or something. You probably have to run in with the school mascot. Or maybe you'll be carried in on thrones."

The old me would never have gone to a homecoming game. The old me would have sat at home with Jadis protesting it.

Our antics flood back to me. That time when she and I learned how to put tampons in together. How we howled inside a public restroom at a movie theater. *Is it in? Is it all the way up there?* I screamed. *Push it in further! Push it all the way in!* Bowled over with laughter. A mother scolded us from outside the bathroom stall, annoyed. *Girls! There are children in here!*

Just the two of us, in our own backward world.

"Maybe you and Emma want to come? You know, with me to homecoming?"

She looks at me, horrified, then slides off my bed to the floor, gasping for breath as if she's convulsing. I crawl to the edge of the bed, my chin propped in my hands, and watch her.

"I'm dead. I'm literally dead," she says. "Put it on my tombstone. Died at the mere *suggestion* of the homecoming dance."

"Does this mean you'll go?" I say, and stretch my hand out, my pinkie to her, just like our matching stick and pokes. I'm not even mad about the falling girl tattoo anymore—at least not in this moment. At some point in the future, I'm sure I'll be furious about it. But right now, I miss how we used to be. All those feelings, that shared energy. That line we used to say: *Same person, different hair.*

She sits up from her death pose and stares at me. "Serious question. Why do you need me to go? If you have that whole team of yours? Why?"

"Because I want you to be there with me. I don't want everything to be so separate. I don't want *us* to be so separate."

"I will lose my entire reputation going to a homecoming dance with you," she says. "You know that, don't you? People expect *more* of me."

"Like who?" I laugh.

"The freshmen who vape in the first-floor bathroom, for instance. They need someone to look up to, with everyone quitting vaping these days," she says. "Pussies."

Her eyes move from my face to my arm, specifically my bicep. "Look at you. Those muscles you've gotten. What are you? The cheerleader Hulk?"

"Come on, Jadis. Is that a yes?"

She raises one of her eyebrows, and then a smirk. I can see the change in her eyes, a kind of defeat.

"Fine," she says. "I'll go . . . reluctantly."

And I jump up and down in front of her, wiggling back and forth, making her look me in the eye. I take her hand and twirl her around, one time, two times, three times, until I'm dizzy and exasperated.

"Enough!" she says, laughing, giving in to the moment. "You got yourself a date."

Chapter 12

"WANT A RIDE?"

It's after practice, and Chloe Orbach is waving me over. She's standing there in front of Chloe Schmidt's Jeep. Clean and sparkly and white. The ultimate cheerleader wagon. Her prize possession. And it feels so natural as I walk toward them—just three weeks ago I didn't even acknowledge the Three Chloes in the hallway. When Jadis and I would stand on the corner by the old farm, smoking cigarettes, we'd see her Jeep whiz by and we'd throw up our middle fingers at it.

"I can't give her a ride today," Chloe Schmidt says, major fish pout. "You know I have to go to the gym. My personal trainer's waiting for me. I told you this," she says, then turns to me. "Shade, if I give you a ride, I'm going completely out of my way and I'll be late." She actually seems sincere.

"No problem," I say.

"So she should walk home?" Chloe Orbach says. "Like you didn't work Shade hard enough this week? Like she didn't bust her ass with those baskets? And I didn't see her complain about it once. Not like you."

"He gets paid by the hour, Chloe," she says.

Chloe Orbach mocks her. *"He gets paid by the hour."*

This side of her reveals itself fast and furious. She glowers at Chloe Schmidt, waiting for her to crumble or cry.

"It's a commitment, Chloe. He wrote a cookbook!" she squeals.

"He wrote a cookbook," Chloe Orbach says, whining.

"Stop making fun of me."

"Oh, *poor* little Chloe. With her trainer and her chef and her Jeep that no one else is allowed to drive and her Instagram followers. Wah wah wah. She doesn't want anyone picking on her."

I'm uncomfortable with how Chloe Orbach is taunting her, but at the same time, I also get a lot of pleasure from it because not once has Chloe Schmidt offered me a lift home, and she has been riding me so hard at practice with no patience or empathy.

I think of what Chloe Clarke told me that day in school: *One minute Chloe Orbach will profess loyalty to you. And the next, she'll turn on you and cackle as blood seeps out of your crushed skull.*

"Well, this afternoon is fun and delightful," Chloe Clarke says sharply, and she hops in the passenger seat.

Chloe Schmidt's face is sour as she climbs in her Jeep and sinks behind the wheel.

"Really, it's okay. I don't need a ride," I say.

But Chloe Orbach grabs my hand. "You stay right here. You are *not* walking."

She snakes her way over to the driver's side and leans up against the door. "Tell the truth," Chloe Orbach says. "How many followers do you have now? Two hundred and fifty K? That's a lot of young girls. A lot of impressionable minds. A lot of girls with eating disorders. A lot of guys who dream of you at night, who get hard under the sheets—"

"Chloe, enough," Clarke says.

"What? Her followers know all about her viral *This is what my stomach looks like from all angles* TikTok, and how everyone should be #normalizenormalbodies and #body-acceptance and how body confident she is, but I find it curious that she didn't mention the liposuction she got over the summer because she couldn't get her thighs to stop touching. I wonder what they would say to that?" Orbach says.

Chloe Schmidt's mouth opens wide, and Chloe Orbach doesn't even look away.

"Where is this coming from?" Chloe Clarke barks.

"Unity. Isn't that what Coach preaches? Chloe here thinks she's above all that. She's entirely comfortable making one of our top girls walk home."

"I can't believe you," Chloe Schmidt seethes.

"Right back at you, bitch," Chloe Orbach says. Then she turns to Chloe Clarke. "To answer your question, let's just say I've been holding it in all week."

They all do *something*, these Instagram and TikTok girls.

You're morphing yourself into your own little Frankenstein every time you take a picture, getting that creamy filter on, massaging that angle so your chin doesn't look so weak. But to be a body-positive Instagrammer who secretly hates her body? Who gets liposuction and then doesn't come clean about it to her followers? These are secrets you tell your best friend in the middle of the night. The secrets you're ashamed of, that you don't even want to admit to yourself.

Maybe Chloe Schmidt is waiting for the right moment to tell her followers. Maybe she's working up to it. None of that matters.

What matters is that Chloe Orbach spilled classified information. In front of me.

Now, that's a betrayal. It's the cruelest thing.

Chloe Clarke turns to Chloe Schmidt and begs her to give me a ride. Just to end this. I still don't want a ride, but when Chloe Schmidt tells me to get in, I can't say no. Too much has already been sacrificed.

It's decided that Chloe Schmidt will drive me to Chloe Clarke's house and I'll walk from there. We jump in the Jeep, and she takes off before we can even sit. Chloe Orbach lets out a screech and a howl. As if she didn't just out her best friend. As if there wasn't some lingering threat that she may do it again, maybe publicly. Chloe Orbach whines for Chloe Schmidt to let it go. That she loves her. That she would never tell another soul. That she shouldn't be so sensitive.

I flash to Jadis. The way she tells me, "I'm just being honest."

Chloe Orbach's face, a wild smile like nothing even happened.

Chloe Schmidt scowls in the rearview mirror as she makes a sharp turn. Chloe Orbach holds on tight, laughing, and I'm the one who slides over, practically falling out of the Jeep. Chloe knocks right into me, my ribs smashing against the door. I groan because I'm already sore from the basket tosses.

I reach up to grip the outer rail so I can sit straight, and though I've been hiding it for the past few days in my high-rise booty shorts, the shifting has pushed down the fabric, and there she is, in full view. My new stick and poke.

My flying girl.

My falling girl.

I can feel my shorts sink further below my hip, this cheap elastic, and because I'm holding so tight to the frame, I can't pull them back up.

"Oh my god," Chloe says, scooting back to her side. "A new one? You got a new one, Shade?"

This ride is feverish, with Chloe Schmidt riding over sidewalks and hitting all the potholes.

"Shade, lift up your shirt."

"Stop, Chloe. I'm not lifting up my shirt."

Chloe Orbach slides over to me and pulls at my shorts, stretching them out so she can see the whole thing. I smack her hand away and push her back, knee her in the chest because she's practically on top of me like an impatient child, her hair blowing all over the place. But she's grabbing and reaching for me, not letting me go until my head smacks against the rail.

"Let me see!"

"What are you trying to look at?" Chloe Clarke turns around now from the passenger seat.

"Shade has a new tattoo. I want to see it," she screams, squeezing me still. "But she won't let me!"

"Honestly, Shade, don't you know already that Chloe always gets her way," Chloe Schmidt says, seething. "Haven't you figured that out already? Just show her the damn tattoo."

Chloe Orbach stands up, her hair through the wind, holding on to the top of the frame, and screams. Screams like someone is chasing her. Screams like she's in the middle of a nightmare. She's not even looking at me now. She's just grasping for air, screaming.

"I just want to see it!" Standing, riding the bumps and the road like she's surfing across some dangerous wave in the ocean. No fear in this one. No fear.

But I laugh, an uncomfortable laugh, a release, because here's Chloe Orbach, so wild, and it makes me want to stand up there and scream right along with her. Just let everything go and feel as breathless and as free.

"If you come down I'll show you," I say. "Just come down."

And she plops next to me, like a puppy, her face so close to mine. Her perfect eyebrows. The whites of her eyes. Her blonde hair everywhere. She doesn't even try to get it out of her face.

I stretch out my shorts so my hip is completely exposed. My

stomach in knots. She makes me so nervous. So I let her see it. My girl, my falling or flying girl. Whatever she is.

"Wow, I love it," she says. She says it with sincerity. "Who did this?"

"Jadis did it." Jadis. Who would hate me sharing this with Chloe Orbach. Just showing this to Chloe Orbach would make her nuts.

Chloe Clarke whines that she wants to see it too. She turns her body toward me. So I pull down my shorts again. Why not? It was my idea, wasn't it?

"Is she falling or flying?" Orbach says.

After the way I watched Chloe Orbach tear Chloe Schmidt apart, there's no way I'll ever admit to her how I really feel about this tattoo. That it makes me feel weak. That she's falling. That maybe, somewhere in the back of Jadis's mind, she wanted to hurt me.

"Oh, flying," I say, my voice solid. "She's definitely flying."

"Shade Meyer. The flyer!" and she grasps my thigh. "See! This girl's so dedicated she got herself a flyer tat. Because that girl wants more than a basket. She wants so many rotations that she pukes her brains out. Isn't that right, Shade?"

She's not wrong. That's what I want. At the very least I'd like to get ten feet up in that basket. Is that so much to ask?

"It's the most beautiful thing and you're going to be so beautiful doing it." She takes my arm and shakes it up and down. "I'm so excited, Shade. Aren't you excited? Say you're excited."

"I'm excited," I say, but it's flat. "I feel embarrassed."

"About what?"

"That I want this so badly."

Chloe stares at me, her eyes filling up. She grabs my hand, the Jeep banging up and down, sloshing over each bump. "You do not need permission to want something, Shade Meyer. If you want it, you take it. And if that's not enough, you take more." She goes on a rant about how girls are supposed to yearn for everything to be fair, that we're supposed to want everyone to play nice, and worse, *even worse*, she says, we're supposed to make all this niceness appear natural.

I look up quickly and feel Chloe Schmidt's hot eyes on me through the rearview mirror.

Chloe shakes me. "Say you're a flyer."

A rush rams through me from deep inside, up through my aching ribs, legs prickly, a full-body chill. "I'm a flyer!"

It's hard not to get caught up in Chloe's excitement. She assaults you with it until you give in. And she's not wrong. Top girls scream from the pinnacle. They're up there at the peak.

It's why I'm in this white Jeep with the Three Chloes. You don't just get here, bouncing in the back seat, by accident.

With the sun in front of us and the wind in my hair, I take my ponytail out and let it all fall around me, a smile exploding on my face.

"Let that hair go, girl!" Chloe Clarke says, and takes out her pony too, then reaches over the seat and snatches the elastic out of Chloe Schmidt's hair too. The whole thing, so damn free. Hair flapping everywhere. Like I'm part of something sweet and good. It feels like the kind of moment that's meant to be a greeting card, and I want to hold my breath to stay in it, because moments like this always fade.

Chloe Schmidt peels into Chloe Clarke's driveway. Slams the car into park.

"Chloe! Road rager!" Chloe Orbach screams. "Wow, get all that anger out! You'll burn even more calories and it's a success all around!"

"I told you I had an appointment," Chloe Schmidt shrieks. "How come you can't listen?"

Chloe Clarke hops out of the Jeep, and I'm right behind her. "Please don't kill each other," Clarke says, a heavy worry in her voice.

Then Chloe Schmidt hits the gas, goes in reverse, the tires squealing, beckoning out, and then they're gone.

◼ ◼ ◼

"What's going on between the two of them?" I say once they turn the corner.

Chloe tells me some of what I already know. That Chloe Schmidt's father died from cancer years ago. That her mother got remarried to someone who's fine in theory, but an asshole in real life. That her mother grounds her if she comes home a minute after midnight. Her mother is all gung-ho body positivity on the outside, but she's also the one who suggested Chloe get lipo this summer. Which she tells me I cannot say anything about.

"Chloe Orbach, as you just saw, loves to give her shit, you

know, just stick it to her," she says. "I used to think it was entertaining because of how hypocritical her online presence is, but now I just think it's manipulative."

"So why does she do it? Chloe Orbach, I mean."

"Why? Because she has a lot of envy."

"Chloe Schmidt's father died of cancer, how much envy can you have?"

"Orbach's father isn't exactly in her life either, so she doesn't see it that way," she says. "And I'm in the middle. I've talked to Chloe about it, but she just doesn't know when to stop." She looks away, then gives me the kind of face that makes it seem like she's said too much.

"Friendships are complicated," I say, thinking of Jadis.

"I love that girl and I'm loyal to her to the end. But it's not easy being her best friend. It's a job these days."

"Who, Chloe Schmidt?"

"No, but her too. Trust me," she says, and pauses. "I mean Chloe Orbach." She pauses again, stares off into the distance, seeming surprised that she even said it out loud.

She shakes her head, says she has to go. As I drift away from her front steps, she calls out to me. "Sometimes people push you into a corner, Shade. You just get pushed and pushed until you can't take it anymore. I've tried to talk to her about it. About all of this stuff, but she doesn't want to listen to me."

"What's that supposed to mean?"

"It means that our little cheer team isn't so perfect. It means there are deep flaws."

She opens the door to her house and turns back to me.

"I love them both, Shade," she says.

"I know," I tell her from the end of the driveway. "I know."

■ ■ ■

Walking up the driveway to my house, it's one of those beautiful nights at dusk when everything above you and in front of you turns a dusty rose. I get a text from Jadis.

Look at what one of your Chloes is posting.

I scroll through Instagram to find Chloe Schmidt, and she posted something from TikTok to her Instagram stories when she was supposed to be working out with her special coach. She's lip-synching to Alec Benjamin's song "The Knife in My Back."

I thought we were friends, but now we're enemies.

The TikTok is in black and white. Just a close-up of her face talking to the camera. Over a thousand likes.

The caption says: "I trusted you."

Trouble in paradise? Jadis texts.

She's too happy about it. And that irritates me. So I swipe my phone off.

Chapter 13

COACH WANTS a full out, which is equivalent to a dress rehearsal for a play. This means she wants the sharp details. The phony gestures. The head snaps. The toe points. Your smile, plastic. There's five more days until homecoming.

They lift Chloe Clarke and me on one leg on a count of five. Pri doesn't even shake anymore. She's got me in a vise. She and Schmidt hold steady, Sasha behind me, her hands wrapped around my ankle. I look across at Chloe, and our eyes meet. She gives me the cheer wink and nod. Chin up. I make a face like I'm going to puke.

She yells across at me. "You gotta do it back, Shade."

"But it's so cheesy," I moan.

I feel Sasha's arms shake behind me. "Don't you dare mess this up, Shade," Chloe Schmidt snaps, "or Coach'll make us do it again and I swear to god—"

So I wink and nod, an extra-wide smile on my face. It's so embarrassing, yet it comes so easy to me now.

Chloe Orbach counts *five, six, seven, eight* and Chloe and I move into our scorpions at the same time. Kicking my foot back so it meets my hand perfectly. Clockwork.

Now the cradle. All week I've been working on being strong in the air in my scorp, no buckling, but the cradle is harder. You have to trust your bases and your backspot aren't going to drop you, that they're going to toss you up enough so they have time to catch you on the landing. And I've landed it, but not on the same count with Chloe Clarke.

I keep my leg perfectly steady while Pri counts *one, two* and I pop, catapulting into the sky, up in the air, like slow motion, like I could fly all day.

"Point those toes, Shade," Coach roars. And I lock my legs, square my body, my arms clean and tight at my sides. My stomach drops the way it does when you're on a roller coaster. Slightly open at the catch, Sasha's arms bang underneath my armpits, and my ribs throb, yet none of it matters because I'm secure. I bounce to the ground, and we finish it off by waving like maniacs at the pretend crowd.

Chloe Clarke and I are in sync, like we've been doing this for years.

After the full out, Chloe Orbach feeds me sliced turkey and tells me that's the highest she's seen me fly.

"You're warriors," Coach says, clapping. "All of you should be proud of yourselves. Every single one of you."

■ ■ ■

"You look happy," my mother says that night as I'm rifling through the fridge for something that's not pasta. "Do you feel happy?"

"I do," I tell her. "It's weird. I didn't think just being on the cheer squad would make me feel good like this. It's hard to explain." And it *is* hard to explain, all that energy I have when I'm at practice, all that soreness at the end of the day. I crave it. I think about it at school, wanting to push myself, wanting to make the other girls proud. I feel, finally, part of something.

"It's called purpose, honey," she says. "You've found purpose."

My mother wants to know how Jadis is taking all this. That it must be hard for her.

I shrug. "Jadis has a girlfriend. Jadis has a lot of things. She's fine." I don't tell her how I really feel, like a rope's been cut between us. I cringe thinking about the homecoming dance, hoping it was the right move inviting her.

"All friendships have hills and valleys, Shade. It's perfectly normal," she says. "I've had my share of them. Esthere and I, there was a time when we weren't talking. It went on for about a year, actually."

But this irritates me because I hate when she inserts her opinion about everything, when she compares us, trying to tell me how similar we are.

If her life was different, maybe we wouldn't seem like such outcasts.

"Your friends are unstable. That's why you have drama with them," I snap. "I'm nothing like you."

It's an awful thing to say to my mother, I know I can be incredibly hard on her, and I wish I could take it back, but it's also true. If she lived some regular life and surrounded herself with some regular women who had jobs in an office, or if she had a friend who was an accountant or a lawyer, anything steady, then *maybe* I'd listen to her. But her friends have come in and out of our house for so long, with their beer breath and their affairs and their caftans and their lips stained with red wine.

She nods, tears in her eyes.

So I apologize, and she accepts it even though the truth is I don't want any of my friendships to have hills and valleys like hers do. I want my friendships to be steady, a plateau.

I don't want to be anything like her.

Chapter

14

THE NEXT DAY, another full out, all of us pushing ourselves hard, even little baby Zoey who's on Chloe Orbach's shoulders, straight and tight for the first time instead of hunched over like a terrified mouse. Zoey, who was scared of a back handspring on the first day, is now the center of our pyramid. Who would have thought?

After practice, Chloe Orbach and I fade away. She tells Chloe Schmidt to drive home without her. She doesn't mention the trainer, the #bodyconfidence, or the chef. She just says it matter of fact, "I'm walking home with Shade."

And you would think that Chloe Schmidt would be like, *Cool, please walk home with Shade.* That she would be happy about the break, but no, she gives her a hard time. Teasing her about walking home, how she's going to be a derelict, a streetwalker. How a blonde cheerleader like her is going to get snatched and tied up in someone's trunk. When none of that gets Chloe's attention, she keeps going. That she's doing it to get those extra steps in. That maybe someone ate too many Doritos last night.

"Mmmhmmm," Chloe Orbach says back to her, completely detached, and walks the other way.

Icing someone out is worse than a comeback. It's worse than tearing her apart. You can't work with someone who ices you out. You just have to take it. Chloe Schmidt slams the Jeep door with Chloe Clarke inside, her mouth twitching, a tic I've noticed when she's upset. And they drive away.

■ ■ ■

Chloe and I wander to the abandoned railroad tracks, neither of us wanting to go home. They haven't been used in the twenty years since they built the high-speed rail line that goes into New York City.

She knows about a crumbling emergency staircase behind someone's house, so we sneak through the yard, trying to hide behind a row of hedges. But an old guy comes out on to his back patio and yells at us for cutting though his yard.

"You kids! You can't just trespass like this every damn day. I'm calling the cops. That's it."

"Sorry, sir," Chloe yelps.

We climb down behind the house into a deep trench, just before the graffiti-tagged trestle, and graze through the overgrown grass sprouting its way between the wooden planks of the old track.

"I love this time right before homecoming," she says. "Before it gets dark at five o'clock. Right before the injuries. Before we all get burned out on practice."

We walk down the track on autopilot, kicking stones. Dusk lingers between the tree branches. Everything still green, the ivy climbing up the tree trunks hasn't turned brown yet.

"It used to be me and Chloe Schmidt, you know. We were the closest. Inseparable," she says.

I grunt. "I find that hard to believe."

"'Cause I'm such a bitch to her?"

"You could say that."

She grabs a dead branch from the ground, whips it into the air, and it lands in a pile of rubble. "I'm so tired of everyone these days. So bored from all the same bullshit. It makes me want to lash out, and then I just end up lashing out at her."

I have a flash of that night we crammed in her bedroom, how I saw through her. All those Chloé ads on her wall and how she so carefully pinned them up like an art installation. The way her mom treated her like a windup toy. She made that wall of Chloés because that's how she wants to see herself—beautiful, unbothered, and in control.

"This is going to sound weird, but I think I really started resenting Chloe after her dad died. And I wasn't even close with him, but everything changed."

"Why would you resent her after her dad died?" I say.

"Once he was gone, I spent every weekend at Chloe's, just me, Chloe, and her mom. She'd cook, make pancakes, we drew on the walls in her bedroom. Séances to try to talk to her dead dad. Dancing and gymnastics at his grave. I'd answer the phone at her house like I lived there," she says, as if she's so far away. "Her house was so big, so beautiful. It was around the same time my mother was getting married to the idiot who gets drunk in my basement. Then my mother got pregnant with those half-wit brats. Chloe's house was . . . I loved being there."

I try to picture Chloe Schmidt and Chloe Orbach bonding together, the two of them inseparable. It's hard to imagine, seeing how they are now.

"So what changed?"

"Well, Chloe's mother got remarried. The trainer came in, the Weight Watchers meetings, a personal chef who only cooked vegan." She angrily tugs a chunk of ivy off a tree until it snaps. "No more sleepovers because they had early morning workout times. The nanny got fired. Sometimes I'd get glimpses of the old Chloe when she'd come to my house and spray whipped cream in her mouth. Last time I was over there, her mother had just gotten a face-lift and with all those bruises, staring in the mirror, she was saying that the doctor didn't do enough and she'd need another one soon. Chloe's standing there going, 'Ma, let the swelling go down first before you book a second one.' But that's what happens when you have more money than God. You spend it on your face."

She tightly wraps the ivy around her arm, and it makes a dent in her skin. She loosens it and then ties it like a bracelet.

"Chloe Clarke moved into town around the time Chloe Schmidt's mother got married, and it became the three of us. It was like we were forever sealed because of our names."

Forever sealed. It sounds familiar. That's how it's always felt between me and Jadis. Lately I'm not so sure.

"I know Chloe and I say awful stuff to each other. But then we make up. And then it starts all over again. I guess you could say we're in an abusive relationship. Sometimes I think we need couples therapy. Or maybe we just need to break up for a little while. You know, a trial separation," she says. "I've said enough about me and Chloe. What about you and Jadis?"

"Jadis?" I say. "You'd have to tear us apart. There'd be blood."

"BFFs for life!" she squawks, and drifts over to the rail to do a couple of split leaps. She jumps off and sways in the tall meadow grass, humming that Lana Del Rey song. *"All I wanna do is get high by the beach, get high by the beach, get high."*

"Don't you love that song?" she says, throwing her head back, swaying more. "Isn't it so dreamy? Like you could just fall into it." She rocks her hips back and forth, swirling her arms up in the air.

I watch her in a trance for I don't know how long, beholden to her as she sings the same line over and over, all of it blurring, the meadow grass and her blonde hair, her fingers floating above her, until I hear a kid calling out from somewhere in the neighborhood above us, and I'm shook out of it. I turn away, embarrassed that I was riveted for so long.

"Shade. Shade. Shade," she says, and sits on a rock next to me. "What kind of name is Shade anyway?"

"It's my mother's version of poetry. She thought that she

was giving me a name that represented relief. You know, because where do you escape to when the sun is so hot?"

"Ahhhh, in the shade." Her face in awe with those pink and gold dots making her look so sweet, that big smile. "That is what you're like, Shade. Sweet relief."

She swirls her finger across the tattoo on my arm, the intertwined pinkies. My whole chest tightens, my breath quickening.

"Okay, let's talk about something serious," she says.

"What's that?"

"I want one of those tattoos," she says, and points to mine. "And I want one right now."

"I don't even have the stuff for it," I say. "It's all at Jadis's house."

She unzips her backpack and pulls out a gallon-size plastic bag. Inside, wrapped in white tissue paper, is a pack of needles, a bottle of ink, thread, and alcohol wipes.

"What? How did you know what to get?"

"YouTube. Duh." She's got this silly smile on her face. But she means it. She wants me to give her a stick and poke right here at the tracks.

Really, the person to call is Jadis. And the funny thing about Jadis is that if I called her, she would come right down here, through that old guy's yard, give him the finger, and then do a stick and poke on Chloe Orbach like it's no big deal.

But I don't want to share Chloe Orbach with Jadis. I don't want Jadis down here like she has some hold on Chloe forever, with her cheer critiques, talking over us and judging me for this, for being *one of them.* "It's going to bleed a little," I say. "Just so you know."

"You're so cute, Shade, taking care of me."

Chloe turns on her phone's flashlight and rests it up against a rock.

"I've only done a few of these," I say, my hand trembling.

"I intrinsically trust you," she says. She touches the edge of my nose with her finger like I'm her pet. She wants a little cheer bow on her thumb. A bow is two triangles and a circle in the middle. Of course I can do this.

I swab the needle with the alcohol pad. Tie it around the pencil with the thread. Looping it over and over. Dip it in black ink, then little sharp pokes, tracing the outline. I think about something Jadis said once, how when you tattoo someone you're taking a little bit of them and making them yours. I'm leaving a mark on Chloe's skin that'll be there forever, or at least until her mother finds out and makes her get it lasered off.

But for now, she's mine.

It only takes around twenty minutes, her breath in my hair as she watches me poke at her skin, her pink skin, the soft blonde hairs on her knuckles. Shaping that sweet bow, so innocent. Just two cheerleaders on abandoned tracks, doing jailhouse tattoos.

What could be more pure?

We both lie back on the gravel when I'm done. She's talking

really fast, and I get it because that's how it feels after you get a stick and poke, your nervous system pumping and your blood tingling. It's real dark now, the crickets chirping, and the sky is so clear that the stars, or satellites, whatever the hell they are, sparkle like glitter.

She starts telling me about an astrology class she took to get out of the house, away from her stepfather who is too careless to lock his liquor cabinet and away from her mother who wishes she was twenty-five again. Her mother who wishes she was her.

"Did you know that when we were in gymnastics together, my mother used to drone on about what a natural you were. Endlessly. It drove me absolutely bananas. *That Shade Meyer. What a natural.* Oh my god, I was so jealous of you. I wanted to kill you."

"You tormented me," I say. "I quit gymnastics because of you."

"Yeah, I know," she says, smugly, no remorse.

I sit up and face her. "So you *know* I quit because of you?"

"I wanted to be you," she says, twisting my curls. "So I had to destroy you."

She smirks, raises an eyebrow.

A thought flutters through me. Me as a twelve-year-old, helpless and mad on the ground after I fell off the balance beam. How I was terrified of her. How I hated her.

Now I want to be a good cheerleader for her. I want to be as good as her. I want to be better than all of them.

I think of that first day when I promised Jadis that nothing would change between us, but it was a lie. Everything's changed.

I've changed.

■   ■   ■

That night I dream about cheer. It's the same dream I've been having all week about stunting. Except this time I'm flying up in the air, toe touch, head whip, and then Chloe Orbach catches me in her arms. And I'm safe.

Chapter
15

JUST BEFORE the homecoming game Friday late afternoon. I stare in the mirror and I draw a *G* in black on my cheek. Glitter dotted under my eyebrows. Hair slicked back in a tight ponytail and that bow smack on top of my head. If Jadis saw me, she'd tell me that she doesn't recognize me. But I can see myself through all of this. Through the glitter. Through the heavy eye makeup. Through the uniform, tight across my now muscular body. My arms, cut. My stomach, flat. No more pooch. I do a horrible wink-and-nod head shake.

That girl in the mirror is me. Clean clap clean. I'm ready.

■ ■ ■

I walk out of my bathroom and my mother is waiting for me in the hall. "Well, look at you. Aren't you all gussied up?" she says, with a little twang in her voice.

"Gussied? What's that supposed to mean? It's my uniform, Mom." I can see what she thinks, that her daughter looks like one of those girls on those pageant shows on some obscure cable network. The kind of show where the mother feeds the kid Mountain Dew in a sippy cup and then dresses her up to look like a Miss America contestant.

"No, no. I didn't mean it like that. You look great, honey. You look like a . . . cheerleader," she says, and shockingly, it seems to be sincere.

"Cheerleading really should be considered a sport," I say, and I don't know why I'm so defensive. I guess because I have this pang of fleeting guilt that I'm not the kind of daughter who sails across the world in a boat by herself, single-handedly warring against climate change.

"I have no doubt that whatever you're doing out there is more strategic and more complicated than any of those games the masses consider sports."

I melt when she says it. I don't ever think I want her approval, but when I get it, it changes my world. I can feel the smile spread across my face, and I feel bad that I was so mean to her earlier in the week.

She gives me a kiss on the head. "I would give you a kiss on the cheek, but I don't want to mess up your makeup."

She takes her phone out and tells me to do my best cheer pose. So I lift my arms up into a high V then smile.

"I get a smile too?" she says. "Goodness."

I blush, because smiling for my mom is better than I thought it would be.

■ ■ ■

On the sidelines, we stretch out as the crowd fills up. Gretch passes around a glitter stick, her impenetrable positivity. I look up into the stands for Jadis because she told me she would be here, and I'm taken by the sea of faces. Little girls with their daddies, cramming into the bleachers, their bellies pressed up against the metal bar, staring at us with wide eyes. The moms wearing their FOOTBALL MOM sweatshirts in glitter with their thermoses filled with steaming hot cocoa. The college boys and their Solo cups, pointing, their heavy stares.

Chloe Orbach sidles up against me, playfully shoving her hip into mine, then wiggles her thumb at me, the one with the new bow that I tattooed on her the other night.

"I can't stop staring at it," she says, stroking it. "I had to hide it from my mother, of course. She'd have a shit fit. Look at her up there." She points at her mother, with her blonde hair, her perfect curling-iron curls, in her CHEER MOM sweatshirt, shaking her little metallic pom-pom.

"So fucking embarrassing," she says, and turns away.

I scan the stands again to see if I can find Jadis.

"Looking for your mom?" Chloe says.

"Oh, no," I say, and don't bother to tell her who I'm really searching for. "My mom doesn't do football games."

"Wow, you're so lucky."

We start with simple cheers. *We are the tower of power, above all the rest.* Easy stuff, waiting for people to get there.

Between cheers, Coach preaches: "Starve your distractions. Feed your focus."

How do you starve your distractions when that's all you have?

Then I see a girl with bright green hair, the color of grass, hopping up through the middle of the stands. I know without even seeing her face, it's Jadis.

Jadis with bright green hair.

She's up at the back. I can tell it's her by those bony shoulders, the fringe from the Japanese feather razor she bought online to cut wisps through her ends. Following behind her, Emma Scanlen, the two of them in all black, standing out between a sea of periwinkle-blue and white jerseys.

"What is she, the Green Goblin?" Chloe Schmidt mutters. She's next to me in the back line. She says it low enough so no one else hears her.

It's hard to react to a comment like this when the whole town is watching you. All of those faces up there in the bleachers. I want to walk away from her, switch positions, but I'm stuck in this spot.

"What is your problem?" I say.

"The moment you came on this team, you turned Chloe against me. That's my problem," she growls. "You. You're an interloper."

Something about her scares me. The way she looks at me so open-faced, with her hands still at her hips in cheerleader position. Her back straight up the way an animal does when they're threatened.

Chloe Orbach bellows: "On five, let's go!"

I'm rattled. Face front. Hands on hips. Fake smile. Chin up.

Ready, and!

Let's go!

Get fired up! Get fired up!

Let's go!

Everyone bounces around, clapping and waving to the crowd. That contagious cheer energy bubbling over. Then there's a few moments between cheers where we're supposed to face the crowd and keep everyone pumped and riled up.

Chloe Clarke swiftly turns to both of us. "What's going on?"

"Ask Chloe," I say. "She started a fight with me."

"I'm sick of it," she says to Chloe Clarke, "I'm sick of being blamed for everything." Tears in her eyes now, this look of despair like she really believes what she's saying.

Chloe Schmidt is *not* the girl I want to have an irrational argument with right now. The clock on the scoreboard says there's 8:56 left, so we're inching closer to halftime. This is the girl who, in about twenty minutes, is supposed to toss me ten feet in the air and then catch me in her arms.

"I'm sorry the two of you are having problems," I say to her. "But I promise you, I have nothing to do with it."

I can feel Coach giving us the death stare from her spot. Chloe Orbach already huffing toward us.

"What did you do?" Orbach says to Chloe Schmidt, her voice urgent. "Coach is gonna lose it."

"Me?" Schmidt squeals. *"Me?"*

"I think there's been a misunderstanding," I say.

It's not like I'm immune to jealousy. I've been jealous of Jadis and Emma. I know for certain that Jadis is jealous of Chloe Orbach. *Of course* Chloe Schmidt is going to feel territorial about me and Chloe Orbach too.

"You've been treating me like shit ever since Shade showed up on this team," Chloe Schmidt bursts out.

"If I hear one more word," Chloe Orbach snarls, her voice raised now, her finger in Chloe Schmidt's face, practically touching her nose.

"Both of you, calm down," Chloe Clarke says.

"Get your finger out of my face," Schmidt says. But then she notices the little bow I etched on to Chloe Orbach's finger and clutches her wrist.

"What the hell is this?" Schmidt turns to me, her face in fury. "You did this to her?" She whips back to Chloe Clarke. "*See?* See what I'm talking about?"

"I *begged* her for it," Chloe Orbach says, the words dripping off her tongue, and pries her hand away.

Chloe Schmidt runs her nails through her hair, scooping the bow off the crown of her head, tugging a few strands of hair with it.

"You want a bow? Here's a bow." And she chucks the bow so that it smacks Chloe Orbach right in the face.

There's a stunned silence between the four of us.

Coach storming over to us. The rest of the squad is watching. We've broken all the rules.

"*Poor* little Chloe," Chloe Orbach purrs. "*Insecure* little Chloe."

You can feel it between them, that a line had been drawn. That Chloe Schmidt, dumbfounded, the fury all over her face, is done. That there has been a break, a fissure that can't be repaired.

"I hate you, and I think you're evil," Chloe Schmidt says, and picks up her bow from the ground, clips it back in her ponytail.

"What on earth is this?" Coach says. "Are you arguing? At homecoming?" She glances at the clock. "With four minutes until your routine? You are a team, girls. Pull your shit together." I've never seen Coach mad like this. "Wave and smile or something, Jesus," she seethes.

On cue, the four of us turn to the crowd, yelling some form of *Go, Panthers!* Except for Chloe Schmidt, who shoves through a bewildered Sasha and Olivia, standing by herself.

"She threw a bow at me." Chloe Orbach callously shrugs. "She'll get over it."

■ ■ ■

Halftime and the band, the award-winning Groveton High School marching band, bleats out "Seven Nation Army," the sports anthem of all sports anthems. We wait on the sideline. Chloe Orbach grabs both mine and Chloe Clarke's hands, bouncing up and down to the drumbeat, like none of that even happened, just a few minutes ago. Like all of that rage was somehow normal.

"You didn't have to do that, you know," I say to Chloe over the music. "She seems kind of messed up."

The trumpets and drums thundering, everyone completely losing their minds in the stands, chanting, *Ohh, oh-OH-oh-oh ohhhh, ohhh.*

"Fuck her, let's dance." She rocks her hips to the clamoring trumpets, her hands on mine, tugging me into the music.

The band marches off, and all that bottled energy, all of that fear and excitement at the tips of our fingers, five weeks of practicing this routine, and it's finally here. Chloe Orbach yells, "Ready!" and we take the field.

I pray to the cheer gods that Chloe Schmidt is not going to purposely drop me. It's a terrifying and somewhat exhilarating feeling to have, putting all your trust in a girl who thinks you're responsible for her problems with her best friend.

I shake it off.

All eleven of us press our bodies into a huddle on the fifty-yard line, that glitter on our skin sparkling off the lights.

Chloe Orbach, with a big smile on her face as we breathe into each other, the air so hot inside that circle. She squats down to the ground, stares at us, then screams, her veins popping out of her neck, her eyes shut: "WHO ARE WE?"

We gaze down at her and yelp back:

"GROVETON!"

"WHO ARE WE?"

"GROVETON!"

Then one last call, one last fiery pump, her voice in its

shrieking, deep glory. "WHAT DO WE WANT?" And we all answer her, oblige, screaming back at the top of our lungs: "TO KICK IT!"

We pop up, our bodies bouncing wild, like a prison break. Chloe Orbach bolts into a cartwheel front handspring front handspring, and me right behind her in a cartwheel front tuck. In formation from mid-field, you can't see the crowd. You can't see the stands. All of it's a blur, a tornado of noise.

The dance music blares through the speakers, and on three, me, Zoey, and Chloe Orbach backflip across the grass. We run into a V shape, all of us sprouting out like wings from Chloe Orbach, who's front and center. In sync, everyone slams a toe touch, left hurdler, right hurdler, toe touch. Chloe Schmidt, Chloe Orbach, and Zoey pound into back handsprings. Kaitlyn, who never really could figure out the back handspring, cartwheels a few times.

I can hear the crowd louder now, pumped when Chloe Clarke and I lift into our scorps, my leg higher than I've ever stretched it, my fake smile, tossing my hair back. Pop up on three, I explode in the air, my body straight. Legs together. Perfect timing to that Yellow Claw song:

And now I'm falling, so promise that you'll catch me.

Boom! They hook me in the cradle, and Chloe Schmidt and I lock eyes just before they pop me up to standing.

"Don't even," she says.

We charge back into formation, arm swings, each row rotating so it looks like we're swimming. Or drowning.

Zoey's on Chloe Orbach's shoulders to hit our pyramid, and

Chloe Clarke and I tick tock up and hit our libs, legs out-stretched, Chloe Schmidt, Sasha, and Pri's gathered hands under me, and I pull up tight through my hips, lock it in, my arms up extending to the sky.

All those people clapping and cheering in the stands as we hold it. Coach is on the track springing up and down, electric.

As we run off the field, waving both arms high (because that's what you do when you're a cheerleader, these are not my rules), the white lights blazing above the bleachers, the sunset pressing the sky to orange. I scan the rows for that green hair again, hoping Jadis saw me. I shade my eyes from the sun, searching through faces in the crowd.

And there she is, that shining green streak between all of the blue and white, like a vision. I can feel that relief wash over me. She's so clear, a sparkling emerald. I wave to her, and her face comes into focus.

Jadis, completely still. Glaring at me.

Chapter 16

"I DON'T KNOW what face I made," Jadis is saying to me after the game, outside the stadium. "I have a resting bitch face. You know this about me."

"You were giving me a dirty look," I say. "I wasn't dreaming."

She pulls out her vape because it's become her security blanket, and maybe she's right. Maybe it's all in my head. Too many things happened today. My thoughts banging around. It's already dark out, and that early sundown is tiring me out.

"It was pretty cool. A lot of, what would you call it? Athleticism?" Emma says, shrugging, and yawns.

Emma couldn't care less.

"You didn't say anything about my hair," Jadis says. "I did it so you could see me through the crowd. I had to prove to you I was there. Prove to you that I watched every painful moment of it."

She starts bouncing and clapping, mocking me in a high-pitched voice: *"We are the tower of power . . . above all the rest . . ."* She throws her arms up in the air, her eyes sparkling, mugging. *"We are the tower of power . . . GHS!"*

Then back to her vape. A long exhale. *"Are* we the tower of power? Or do we just *think* we're the tower of power?"

"They lost," Emma says, "so I don't think they can consider themselves the tower of anything."

"Ah," I say, my heart fluttering. "So you *were* watching."

"I was watching."

Jadis throws her arm around me, and I'm relieved.

That's when I hear my name. Chloe Orbach in her low cheer voice. We stop and turn around to face the Three Chloes, and there's dread in my stomach, because they're so much worse together, fighting like deranged family members at Thanksgiving dinner.

I'm not even sure why they're together after what happened on the sideline, what's happened the past few weeks. The bow in Chloe's face. The *I hate you.* Words slung like they had no meaning.

Chloe Orbach snaps her gum. Blowing bubbles so big that they catch a pink translucent glow to them. She's wearing these ridiculous gold-rim glasses. Smoky lenses so that you can still see her eyes.

This is the *other* Chloe. Not the Chloe who I gave the stick and poke to at the abandoned tracks. This is the insecure Chloe who pasted pictures of glamorous women all over her bedroom, her name *Chloé Chloé Chloé* swirling around her. This is the Chloe who demands attention.

"Such a good stunter we have here," Chloe Orbach squeals, running up to me, clapping. "Did you catch it, Jadis? Did you see how great your girl has gotten?"

"I saw," Jadis says. "She was amazing."

"We really have to get going." I take Jadis's arm.

"Why so soon?" Jadis quickly says, her eyes trained on Chloe Orbach, like she's waiting for a collision. I think of how she posted on Instagram once after that singer got into a car accident. *But what was it like when you crashed through the car window? Did you watch the glass fly around your face?* It was such a gory thing to write.

She got slammed by the singer's fans, her little monsters or gremlins or kitty cats, whatever they called themselves. That she was a sadist. That she was insensitive. That she had forgotten that she was commenting on a real person's account.

When I asked her why she would write that, she was all, "What? You never wanted to see a car wreck in slow motion?"

And just like that, as if on cue, Chloe Orbach sucks on the tip of her thumb so that the bow, the stick and poke that I gave her, faces out center stage for Jadis to see.

That fucking bow.

Chloe gazes down at her thumb, sunglasses at the edge of her nose, and grins.

"Wow, look at you," Jadis says. "A new tattoo on your thumb."

"You like it?" Chloe says, a tormented glee in her voice. "Shade did it."

"It's no big deal," I say, but I sound guilty, like a husband caught cheating. "I didn't even think I could do it. I almost called you," I stammer.

Jadis stares at Chloe's thumb, nodding. She's trying to play it cool, but I know she's blowing up inside. This isn't how I wanted her to find out about this.

Once you give someone a tattoo, you own a little bit of them.

Jadis will see it as a betrayal.

"Some art historians say that tattooing in ancient Greece added value to women who were bought for marriage," Jadis says frankly.

Chloe grimaces and tells me that she'll see me later at the dance.

"Oh, I'll see you later too, Chloe," Jadis says.

All three of them stare at Jadis, pom-poms under their arms.

"That's right, ladies. See you at the homecoming dance. I'm going to be Shade's date. I'll wear my best black suit."

Chloe Schmidt rolls her eyes and walks away.

"Great," Chloe Orbach says cheerfully. Chloe Clarke by her side, awkwardly. "By the way, Jadis, I didn't mean to start anything about the tattoo. It was just a spur-of-the-moment thing. No harm meant."

"Of course not," Jadis says, her words dripping. Acid. "No harm taken."

"Well, we better catch up to her," Chloe Orbach says. "She's our ride home."

She jiggles her pom-poms at us, takes Chloe Clarke's hand,

and floats away, through the cars and the kids and the parents, and I realize it was a mistake to compartmentalize them the way I have. It would have been better if Jadis hung around cheer practice so Chloe Orbach could see that I had a best friend who wasn't going to be erased and so Chloe Schmidt would see I wasn't trying to splinter her little beloved trio.

But it's possible that it wouldn't have changed a single thing.

"Are we in an alternate universe?" Emma turns to Jadis. "Are you actually going to the homecoming dance?"

"Oh, Shade and I are going tomorrow," Jadis says. "I wouldn't miss it for the world."

"You egged them on," I say to her. "I tried to pull you away, but you had to stay, didn't you? You wanted something to happen."

"What are you afraid of, Shade?" she says, goading me. "Some friendship rivalry? Isn't that what we watched on that football field today? Two teams going at each other. Aren't we all competitors in this *little* game?"

I watch the Three Chloes in the distance, Chloe Schmidt walking quickly to her Jeep, Chloe Orbach and Chloe Clarke trailing.

"What's that line from *The Taming of the Shrew*? I would have challenged her to a battle of wits," Jadis cracks, so pleased with herself, "but I saw she was unarmed."

Chapter 17

SATURDAY NIGHT. Glowing paper lanterns hang from the gym rafters. Winter theme. Fake snow sprinkled all over the sides of the gym floor. Tiny white lights hang across one wall. A disco ball in a slow revolve in the middle of the stage. Blues and whites and pinks streak across the room.

Jadis looks fantastic in her suit. White shirt buttoned up to the top. Her green hair sparkles in the disco globe. She's too good for this school. "I have a surprise for you later. You're going to be so happy," she whispers to me as we walk in.

Surprises from Jadis make me nervous, but she seems to have cheered up since yesterday. Chloe Orbach profusely texted me last night asking me to forgive her because she knows she can be impossible.

Then there were the intersecting texts from Jadis who told me that she really wanted to be a peacemaker and not the instigator. That Emma, whose mother is a famous therapist, told her to open her mind to new friends and expose her *emo-shunnnns*, as Mariah Carey would put it.

Across the gym, the Three Chloes huddle in a corner next to an LED tree. All of them lit up in metallic and white. They hold court for a glut of freshmen who gather around their queen, Chloe Orbach. All the freshmen follow the unspoken rule: Wear a black body-con dress above the knee and white Converse sneakers to the homecoming dance or you'll be blocked at the door. If not blocked, then humiliated.

Zoey is the only freshman on our team and she hops over to me, so excited, so grateful I'm here. She squeals, grabbing my hands, and Jadis sneers, but I laugh. I've learned to appreciate enthusiasm.

"I'm sorry you have to wear that dress, Zo," I say, even though she looks beautiful, her locs down, framing her face.

But she does a twist, her little body contorting. "Are you kidding? I'm so comfortable in this. I can do a back handspring. Wanna see?"

"Yes, show us," Jadis says, in this evil tone.

"No, no, not now, Zoey. Not now," I say, and she smiles, then leaps over to someone else.

The black body-con dress and white sneakers is a long-standing tradition in this town. All the mothers know about it. Freshman girls buying up all the tiny black dresses weeks before the dance just to get to this moment. The only way to avoid it is to not go to the homecoming dance when you're a freshman, and sit in your bedroom watching *Heathers* two times in a row like Jadis and I did.

Chloe Orbach sees me and her face lights up. She inter-locks her fingers in mine as Chloe and Chloe follow her over to us.

This uneasy feeling floundering inside of me, the five of us together feels wrong.

I glance at Jadis, who I expect to be twitching beside me, but she waves her finger, her best witchy impression, calling us in closer, that come-hither look.

"Closer, Chloes," she says, her voice, reaching out to us so softly. "Closer, you adorable little cheerleaders. Don't be scared."

She pulls a tiny little pillbox from her pocket. The box says *Quaaludes* in gold letters.

Her giddy face, lit up from the disco lights. There are five colored tablets inside: blue, yellow, white, green, pink. I'm stunned. It's Molly.

I drag her away from the tight circle.

"You brought Molly to the homecoming dance?" I say. "What the hell are you doing?"

"I told you I had a surprise, Shade," she says. "What? You think I can deal with this shit sober?"

I look back at the three of them waiting with their mouths gaping.

"You need to play this cool, because your friends are watch-ing us," she says. "I'm opening my heart to them."

"This is your idea of opening your heart?" I know that they've tripped on Molly before, I heard them talking about it once. But to do something like this at a dance inside the school is a different kind of risk. "What makes you think they'll even do it?"

"Please, that little hellion Chloe Orbach? The one who convinced a total novice to give her a stick and poke on her thumb for anyone to see? I assumed she was up for anything."

The novice comment hurts, but I ignore it.

"Why didn't you even tell me that you planned this?"

"Why? Because you would have said that we couldn't possibly roll on Molly during the homecoming dance, like, *Oh my god, Jadis, I'm a cheerleader. Cheerleaders don't do that sort of thing*," she says in this baby voice. "But I think it'll be fun for all of us. Really, I mean that. I took Emma's advice."

Maybe she's right. Maybe it would be the kind of thing that gets everyone on the same page. No fighting. No bickering. No insults or jabs or snarks. Just all five of us on Molly. Equal footing, seeped in ecstasy. A big ol' love bomb.

We cluster in a tight circle. *Tighter*, I tell them. I don't want anyone hearing or seeing what we're doing.

Jadis opens up the little Quaaludes box.

Chloe Orbach squeals, hopping up and down.

"Is that Molly?" Chloe Clarke says.

"It is. You want to do it?" Jadis says, big smile. Her face has trouble written all over it.

"Is there one for all of us?" Chloe Schmidt smirks.

"Yes, little cheerleader, I bought this for all of us. There's only five. We can't share with the rest of your sorority. This is *our* little stash. Our little secret. Is that understood?"

"One for each of us?" Chloe Orbach says sweetly. "My gosh." And all that hardness melts.

I look over at Gretchen and Keke, their high morals, their steady hands. They'd be so disappointed.

Sweet freshman Zoey who just smoked pot for the first time last weekend, she told me. God, what about Pri and Olivia with their we-eat-dinner-every-night-together parents? They'd lock those girls up in their bedrooms for the rest of their lives if they witnessed this.

"I don't want to fight with you, Chloe," Jadis says, and it seems sincere. Mature, actually. "Or with *you*, Chloe, or with *you*, Chloe. Whether you believe that or not, it's true. I want what Shade wants. I want to be the supportive friend. I don't want any animosity."

I want to believe her, I really do.

"Oh my god, group hug," Chloe Orbach says, hopping up and down again. "We *have* to do a group hug." And the five of us smush into each other, our necks and faces with nowhere to go, arms and limbs and angles and sequins and hot breath, holding it for a minute that feels like forever until Chloe Schmidt says, "Okay, that's enough. Let's hit the bathroom and get our roll on. This dance is boring as fuck."

And then it's the five of us sauntering to the bathroom because it's so easy to fall in line behind Chloe Orbach.

The snap of her fingers. And just like that there's a plan to do Molly at the homecoming dance, which should feel outrageous and like a huge mistake, yet it relaxes me, and I'm not sure why. Maybe because everything leading up to this night has been so planned and so stressful, and there's been so much hard work for the past five weeks, that I'm happy to have something spontaneous. For a brief moment, I don't care anymore about being a cheerleader, or that we're at a dance or that the gym is teeming with teachers, or that Jadis and Chloe Orbach were locking horns yesterday. Because it's just one big mash of kids leaping up and down to shitty music.

The five of us, connected, slide past the freshman girls in their black body-con dresses and white sneakers, their skinny bodies like bats all waiting for something to happen.

We crowd into the accessible bathroom stall. The white-hot fluorescent lights of the bathroom make our faces look green.

"They all have different stamps," Jadis says. Chloe Clarke gets the star. Me, a heart. Chloe Schmidt, a bunny. Jadis takes the smiley face.

"And for you," Jadis says to Chloe Orbach. "The crown."

Chloe's whole face lights up. Her hands to her chest. "You seriously got this just for me? A crown?"

Jadis nods. "To new friends?" And she slips the Molly on her tongue.

"To new friends," Chloe says, closes her eyes and sticks her tongue out so that Jadis has to place it right there on her pink tip.

We step out of the stall, and the rest of the girls in the bathroom watch us like they want to be us. I would want that too.

Outside of the bathroom, Chloe Schmidt and Chloe Clarke

fetch Vitaminwater because that's what Chloe Orbach wants.

"Whatever Chloe wants, Chloe gets," Chloe Schmidt sings.

I take Jadis's hand. "Tell me everything is going to be fine."

"Shade. You anxious unicorn," she says, stroking my hair. "Everything's fine. We're gonna have fun. We're gonna roll. We're gonna set this boring hellhole of a place on fire. We're gonna dance with those girls and we're gonna bond. It's going to be great."

"You don't hate me?" I say.

She smiles in that awkward way, shaking her head. Love in her eyes. "I could never hate you."

Chapter
18

FIFTEEN MINUTES LATER and we're rolling on Molly. I've only done it once before with Jadis and we spent the whole night picking colorful trash from the street. This, with the music, the sweaty dance floor, the sea of kids—it sucks us in. The Three Chloes gulp down their Vitaminwaters but Jadis and I just go for regular water. That sugar taste is not what I want in my mouth. The first time Jadis and I did Molly, her brother told us to stay hydrated. Something about your brain frying.

Chloe Orbach takes both my hands in hers. Yells over the music. Grinds her hips into me. Jadis is on my left, and I take her hand in mine. *What a good idea*, I think, and maybe it's the drugs, or maybe it's just Jadis. She's always thinking ahead, and I never give her enough credit. Pinks and purples flash across the gym floor, Jadis's emerald hair shining in the white dotted light from the disco ball.

"Isn't it so beautiful?" Chloe says to me. And it is beautiful.

"The two of you, hold hands. It's gotta be this way," I say. "You can't have me without each other." Jadis and Chloe smile and swish to the music, and then something happens that I never expected. The two of them are dancing together like they've known each other forever. Like they can finish each other's sentences or walk the same way or text each other at the same moment the way you do when you're thinking about someone all the time. Their fingers touching and their eyes sparkling, and I wish it could be like this, always, the three of us.

The other two Chloes push their way into the circle, and we hold hands, our arms up in the air, bodies and hips touching and pulsing like we're in a celebratory ritual, our arms folding in and out, each of us rotating around the other. A witch's dance, the five of us in a trance, magic dazzling between us.

The music pumping harder and harder. Chloe Orbach wraps her hand around mine, then grasps Jadis's hand, dragging us in toward her until the three of us are shoulder to shoulder.

"I want tattoos. I want tattoos all over," she says, breathless, to Jadis. "I want flowers and hearts up my arms. Lilies and magnolias."

"What would your parents say?" Jadis says, laughing.

"My mother would be furious because she'd say I look like some anarchist cheerleader. Isn't that funny? An anarchist cheerleader like that Nirvana video with the girls and their tattoos cheering into the sky."

Chloe punches her arms in the air, dancing, then spins around and takes both Chloe Schmidt's and Chloe Clarke's hands.

"Dance with me," she screams over the music.

Chloe Clarke floats closer while Chloe Schmidt resists.

"Oh, Chloe, don't be so sad," Orbach says to Schmidt, her fingers reaching out to her. "What would we do without you, my love?" She squeezes Chloe Schmidt's cheeks.

Chloe Schmidt pushes her away lightly, really, just a little push, except Chloe Orbach wrenches back, wobbling. We all reach for her and right her back up to standing. But there's something wrong. She's blank, staring ahead. Her skin too pale, drained even under the disco lights.

"Let's get you some more water," I say. "Water will help everything." But then this look of dread comes over her, and she stumbles forward. Chloe Clarke and I catch her.

"You guys," Chloe Orbach says. "Something's not right, you guys." The room darker and smaller, and all of the music pumping too loud and too fast. She's falling in our arms, her feet loose underneath her.

"What's happening to me? I can't breathe," she's saying.

"Get her to the bathroom," Jadis says, panicking, and I put my bottle of water to her mouth, telling her to drink it, that tightness in my throat, that thud of reality that we're at the homecoming dance on Molly and the freshman girls in the black body-con dresses are starting to stare.

"I can't breathe," Chloe Orbach's saying again, and she swats the bottle away. Her body slips out of our hands, the weight of all of her dropping onto the gym floor, her body convulsing, jerking in ways I've never seen a body jerk. Her mouth sputtering, spitting, white bubbles of saliva coming out the sides.

Chloe Clarke is down beside her so fast, her eyes planted on Chloe Schmidt, screaming, "Chloe, what's happening? What's happening?" I drop down next to Chloe, our hands on her shoulders, holding her, calling to her, yelling her name. My whole body in a vibrating terror, I turn around and scream for help.

Someone takes hold of my arms and tugs me back. I think it's a teacher. Chloe's body so still on that gym floor and the disco balls lights spinning. Then Mrs. King, the nurse, her eyes wide and afraid, her face in Chloe Orbach's face, calling her name. "Chloe? Can you hear me?" Checking her pulse, yelling for the ambulance, her mouth on Chloe's mouth.

CPR. She's giving Chloe CPR.

Chloe Clarke screams over and over again, *Chloe, Chloe, Chloe.* Chloe Orbach's wild blonde hair spread all over the floor like a beautiful Instagram post with the lights dancing over her dress, Gretchen and Keke holding each other, the freshmen, all of them, shaking in each other's arms.

I turn to see Chloe Schmidt, who's standing there, frozen, no reaction, just flat, utter shock.

Teachers are screaming, *Put your phones away! Phones away!* Everyone circles around us with their phones in our faces like it's a fucking concert and my head is so heavy, like maybe I'll collapse. The room is spinning, flashes of light in front of me as the paramedics, two men and one woman, storm through while Mrs. King gives Chloe chest compressions.

Chloe Schmidt is next to me now, babbling, sobbing about Chloe Orbach being her best friend since kindergarten. *My best friend*, I hear her moaning. *My best friend.* Chloe Clarke wraps her arms around Schmidt. The music stops.

They lift Chloe into the stretcher. An EMT screams at us. "Girls! What did she take? What did she take?"

Jadis pinches my arm, so hard that it makes me squeal and tears run from my eyes.

"Girls, this is not a joke," the EMT yells again. "Did she take something? Did you see her take something?"

But no one says a thing. Just gasps, the words stuck in my throat. My mouth filled with fear.

■ ■ ■

The lights flip on, the searing light, my dilated pupils burning, so I shield my face with my arm, hiding from what's in front of me.

In the darkness behind my eyes, I'm in a place between now and then, and all I can see is Chloe's blonde hair, in waves across the gym. The lights blinking over her crystal-adorned dress.

Chapter 19

JADIS CLUTCHES my arm, whispers in my ear. "We have to go."

"Go? Where are we going?" I say, watching the EMTs roll Chloe out in a stretcher. Her limp body as they try to resuscitate her.

Chloe Clarke stares at me, tears washed down her face. I want to reach out to her, but I feel my whole life changing, a dark void, and she sinks into it. Her face so clear for that moment, and then she's gone.

Jadis is face-to-face with me now, her nose practically touching mine. Her voice calm and low. "We are walking out of here. Do you understand me, Shade?"

"We can't go anywhere. We have to stay to talk to the police. To tell them what happened."

"What's wrong with you? We're not telling the police anything. We're not waiting around for them."

"We have to," I say, breathless.

"Do you think her friends, those two Chloes, stuck around?"

Her voice, hot and worried, full of rage. "You think they're waiting for the police? They just ran out the door."

"Bullshit," I say. "I just saw Chloe Clarke, she was right there." But she's not there. I cover my eyes as the orange lights from outside crash through the doors.

"Do you see them here, Shade? Look around. They're gone."

I scan the gym. Neither Chloe is in sight.

Wasn't Chloe Schmidt crying just five minutes ago, or was it twenty minutes ago, or half an hour ago? Wasn't she crying, saying, *My best friend, my best friend*? Didn't I hear her saying that?

"Maybe they went to the hospital," I say. "Of course, that's where they went."

"Listen to me, Shade. I brought the Molly here. I gave it to them. And we all took it. And now Chloe Orbach is in an ambulance." She looks at me more sternly, more insistent. "So if we tell the police anything at all, they're going to bring us in. And those friends of hers, those two Chloes, they'll blame us for it. They'll say that it's our fault."

Our fault, Jadis says. *Our* fault?

It's always going to be Jadis and me fused together. Even if she was the one who brought the Molly to the dance. Even if I knew nothing about it.

To new friends, Chloe said.

"Chloe's going to be okay. It was an accident, Jadis. They know that."

"Oh, *do* they? Then where are they?" Jadis's eyes are darker than I've ever seen them. That deep anger.

"What are you saying, that it wasn't an accident?"

"I'm saying they're not here and that they knew to cut out quick and so should we." She pulls me even closer, a hard snap, my body into hers. Her mouth to my ear. "Time to go. *Now*."

Jadis's hand slides down into mine, and she walks me through the gym, between the kids and the teachers crying and the police walking in and the detectives and the principal.

We stroll out, like Chloe Orbach wasn't just on the floor convulsing. Like she wasn't getting CPR from the school nurse. Like the EMT didn't wheel her out. As we walk, I replay what she said to us right before she fell.

You guys. Something's not right.

Her face, that fear.

Jadis walks me through the metal door, and I snap into reality. The red, stinging glow of the cop cars, the fire trucks, the ambulance. When a seventeen-year-old collapses at the homecoming dance, when it's the captain of the cheer team, they all come.

The cold air bites into my shoulders. "How did this happen, Jadis?" Breath clouds flow out of my mouth, and I start to cry. "What if she's dead?" But Jadis doesn't answer me, she just keeps trudging. One hand in her pocket, the other gripping tight on to mine.

Last night, we were on that field. Everything planned so

carefully. Our cheer routine with such precision. The home-coming dance, I thought, would be some boring event. A head-ache at best. Shitty music and gawking boys. And now here I am, my mouth chattering in the cold. Chloe Orbach convuls-ing on the gym floor. EMTs knocking against her chest.

When we get around the corner past the cops, I throw up on someone's front lawn. Hot and violent, it spews out of me. I wipe my mouth with the back of my hand, and Jadis says nothing. We keep walking. We're two high school girls leaving a dance, like nothing happened.

Nothing is ever the way you think it'll be.

■ ■ ■

Around two in the morning I get a text from Zoey. Her mother's friend is an emergency room nurse at St. Joseph's.

My mom's friend doesn't think Chloe made it.

I don't answer her.

My mom's friend said a cheerleader died in the ER tonight. It has to be her right?

I don't answer.

I text Chloe Clarke the question I don't want an answer to.

Is she?

I cover my phone, shield the light from my face. The texts that come straggling in from Jadis from Zoey from the rest of the squad from whoever. I scroll and scroll until I see what I'm looking for. The text from Chloe Clarke.

Y

And my stomach cramps up, I bend over and gasp for air. It can't be. She must be lying. She must be saying this to me because of the Molly. Because she wants revenge.

Don't lie to me Chloe you're lying to me

Not lying

In this moment, when I want to tear my guts out, when everything in my room is a blur, I swipe through my phone to find her. She's in so many of my photos, smiling back at me, so alive, so vibrant. I don't know how I'll ever escape her.

Part

‖

Chapter 20

MEMORIALS START early on Sunday morning all over Instagram and Facebook, mostly from Chloe Schmidt, who makes collages of Chloe Orbach, documenting every moment they've spent together since second grade. Cheer camp. At the beach. Sharing virgin piña coladas in Miami. In sleeping bags. In Chloe Schmidt's Jeep with a big red bow around it. The pictures go on forever.

Chloe Clarke writes one thing. *I miss my friend.* And that's all.

A long thread of comments follows, and I don't feel like it's right to post anything.

Chloe Orbach is dead. I saw her convulse on the gym floor. I watched Jadis give her a tab of Molly with a crown stamped on it, and then twenty minutes later she was dead.

And for you, Jadis said, *the crown.*

She placed the tablet on Chloe Orbach's tongue. Like witchcraft.

Jadis frantically texts me, telling me we have to talk.

But I don't answer her. Every time my phone buzzes, I think about how it's my fault this happened. If I hadn't brought Jadis to the homecoming dance, there wouldn't have been any Molly. And Chloe Orbach wouldn't be dead.

Shade don't ghost me.

Shade where are you this is not a FUCKING game

Jadis is not someone you can escape. One time when my phone died and I was taking an extra-long shower, she showed up at my house, banging at my door, her face so vulnerable. Staring at me with my towel wrapped around me, and I laughed, I thought it was so sweet, all of that attention. But it wasn't sweet attention, was it? It was her insecurity. Her terror of being left alone.

If I text her back, it'll all come tumbling out, that it's my fault Chloe Orbach is dead. That it's *our* fault.

I keep thinking that I hear her banging on my door. I sneak into the hallway and whisper her name. *Jadis? Is that you?* But it's just a tree branch against my window.

■ ■ ■

On Monday, we're back to school. The superintendent sends an email that there will be extra counselors available to speak to. That we need to come together as a family. That we're all here to support Chloe Orbach's family and the cheerleading team, which has suffered this tragedy. Reporters are in the front of the building. A news crew that's been staked out since six o'clock in the morning, someone said. This story is gold for them. Head cheerleader dies at homecoming dance. This is the kind of story crime podcasts are made of.

■ ■ ■

After psychology, Jadis waits for me at the classroom door. Biting her nails, her green hair in her face.

She takes my hand in hers, her palm sweaty.

"I saw your two friends crying hysterically through the hallway. They're making a scene."

"Their best friend just died," I say. "How do you expect them to behave?"

"It's an act," she says, and rolls her eyes.

I turn her toward me and stop her in the hallway, whispering, "Aren't you just as upset? Just as devastated because we killed someone?"

Stop, she mouths, and puts her finger to her lips, pulls me to the locker wall.

"First of all, we didn't kill anyone. Get that out of your head. Secondly, Emma told me that all three of the Chloes were party girls. That she knows someone who sold Molly a few times to one of them."

This detail makes Jadis very happy, you can see that tingle in her eyes. Like she's made some connection that's absolved her from guilt.

"Of course they took it before, Jadis. It's not like their first time would be at the homecoming dance."

"Did it not cross your mind that she took something else before the dance? That the Molly had nothing to do with this?"

"I have to go to practice," I say.

"Oh, *practice*, right," she says. "Because practice is more important than everything else."

■ ■ ■

Coach tells us we're going to keep it light, and everyone lingers in the locker room, hardly talking. You can tell some of the younger girls like Zoey and Olivia don't know what to say or do. Their faces, their wide eyes, just looking at us for some kind of permission to speak, to laugh, to talk.

Chloe Clarke is already whimpering when I get in there. The saddest cheerleader you've ever seen. Big T-shirt and sweats. Hiding her whole body. Chloe Orbach would be mortified.

"Today? Why is she making us do this today?" Chloe sobs. "Cheer should be canceled for the rest of the season. That's all." Her head between her legs, sobbing. Keke wraps her arm around her. Olivia sinks down, kneels at her feet, rubbing her calves.

I can't get myself to sit with her. I can't even look at her. I feel so guilty for what happened that I can barely stand.

"I've never known anyone who died before," Sasha says. "It's just so real. This is going to define our lives forever. That's what my sister said."

Suddenly Chloe Schmidt comes bounding into the locker room. Her hyper energy taking over. "I have a great idea," she says, like she's high on something. Her voice running quick. Her words overlapping.

"We're going to make a huge blow-up poster of Chloe for the next game, one of those realistic ones so that she can look like she's in the picture with us. Or wait, maybe we can do a stand-up cardboard picture of her like a tribute. Or wait, we can go to yearbook and we'll tell them that we want an entire page dedicated to Chloe. All the pictures from cheer, the years she was a gymnast. Remember? Remember? I still have those pictures."

Her voice cracks, and she turns to me. "What about you, Shade? What's your plan?"

I can barely string a sentence together. I haven't slept in two nights. My brain is on fire for the terrible thing that I've done to my friend. I don't have a plan.

"I'd rather figure out what happened to her," I say. "Wouldn't you?"

"I think we know what happened to her—" Chloe Schmidt says snidely to me, then stops herself. "It could have been a heart condition. It could have been anything."

"I heard she took something," Kaitlyn, who can't do more than a cartwheel, says.

"You shouldn't spread gossip until you know the full story," I say. "None of you should."

Kaitlyn lowers her eyes, they all do.

"That's why we need a memorial. An over-the-top memorial. So people can remember how larger-than-life Chloe was. But, like, literally. Get it?"

You'd think Chloe Schmidt's only plan would be to go to the police, not create a life-sized poster of Chloe Orbach. I'm surprised she hasn't outed me right away or fed Jadis to the dogs yet.

"So, Shade?" she says. "What's your plan?"

"I don't have a plan," I say.

"It's weird that you have no thoughts about this," Chloe Schmidt says. "I'm sorry. It's just weird."

I have plenty of thoughts. Just none that I want to share with the whole squad right now. Nothing I want to share with her.

"It's called grief," I say to her.

"You can't press someone to grieve openly and publicly just because that's what you want," Zoey says. Little freshman Zoey.

"Please don't tell me about grief," Chloe snaps. She doesn't need to say any more. We all know what she's referring to. She's dealt with death firsthand.

Zoey apologizes. She's sorry that she forgot about Chloe's dad. Everyone is so sorry.

"All of you owe Chloe Orbach *everything*," Chloe Schmidt says. "All of you. Every single one of you got something out of being friends with her and being on this team with her. We are not letting her go down without a blaze of glory. Do you all understand me?"

■ ■ ■

After practice, I follow Chloe Clarke into the bathroom as everyone else is packing up. She's sitting in the stall crying, and I knock on the door. Tell her it's me.

I hear the lock turn, and she tells me to come in. I lean against the door as she sits on the toilet.

"Did the three of you do Molly a lot?" I say. "It doesn't matter if you did. I'm not judging. I just want to know. I just want to get something clear in my head."

"I only did it once before the dance," she says. "But Chloe and Chloe . . . a few more times than me."

Chloe Clarke tells me the reason they didn't stick around that night was because she was scared of being questioned by the police while she was still high. It was Chloe Schmidt's idea, that it would be a mistake to talk to anyone with their eyes dilated and with Molly still in their systems.

"See, that's why we have to go to the police," I say. "Because maybe she took something before the dance and we can explain to them what happened. We can tell them that we were scared—"

"We are not going to the police," she snaps. "Cheerleaders who want a National Honor Society Scholarship, who belong to Model UN and volunteer at the soup kitchen, don't turn themselves in to the police, Shade. Someone like you, maybe. But not someone like me."

"Someone like *me*?"

"Yeah, someone who doesn't have as much to lose."

The glint in her eye. She is dead serious.

"Really, Chloe? Is that how you see it? That I'm an expendable? That I can just go to jail or something? That I don't have anything to lose?"

These girls. Their entitlement. Their reputation is the only thing that matters. How cheer moms will see them. How Mommy will see them. How the town will see them.

"I sound like such a bitch, I'm sorry," she says, and I think part of her means it. "You don't know how messed up I am. You didn't lose your best friend like I did, Shade."

It's not fair for her to say that. She doesn't know about that night by the tracks, the way I pressed the needle in Chloe's skin. The way we talked to each other like we only existed for each other. How does *she* get to claim Chloe and I don't? She doesn't know how consumed I was by Chloe. How I'm still consumed, how when I was around Chloe Orbach, I wasn't in charge of myself.

I keep this locked up in my thoughts. Sharing it with her would mean giving up something that's mine. And I don't want to share.

"We were tight. She opened up to me about a lot." I say this gingerly. I know how vague it sounds.

"Look, I'm sure you two got close. But there are things you didn't know about Chloe," she says. She tells me how much Chloe was hurting. How much she hated her house, her mother, those brothers. That she had a harder life than any of us really knew. That she was always trying to mask how she really felt. Maybe that's why she was determined to get that stick and poke from me, even though, as Jadis said, I'm a novice. Because she wanted to be someone else.

"She had a lot of pain, Shade. And she could be really cruel because of it," she says, shaking her head. "She was envious of Chloe Schmidt. The chef. The personal trainer. The Jeep. Everything. She was tortured by it."

I think of what my mother once told me. That envy isn't jealousy. Envy is hate.

Chloe Schmidt knew how much Chloe Orbach envied her. But did she know how much she hated her?

Chapter
21

FOOTBALL PLAYERS sit on benches in front of the funeral home crying.

Inside, rows and rows of chairs. All of them filled. The room hot and crowded. A line snakes through the hallway with people waiting to pay respects to Chloe's family. Chloe's little brothers. Their sister will be a martyr now. The girl with the shrine of beautiful Chloés all over her bedroom. All the stages of Chloe in a slide show. A wonderful friend, big sister, dedicated daughter. Baby Chloe. Innocent Chloe.

And then, the biggest picture of them all. The golden-haired cheerleader. A towering image of her there with her blonde hair blowing in the wind, her perfectly white teeth sparkling. Just like the cardboard cutout that Chloe Schmidt talked about.

God, Chloe Orbach would have loved this funeral. She would have relished it.

I can see Chloe's mother's blonde hair bobbing in front of

her casket, Chloe's embalmed body just a few feet away. Jews don't do it this way, and I've never seen a dead body before. I'm scared to see Chloe like that. I don't know if I want to see what they've done to her.

Chloe Schmidt struts in like she owns the place in a black baby-doll dress with a white Peter Pan collar with cat whiskers embroidered onto it. Her thighs glistening like she just shaved and oiled them. Lips in a peach hue I've never seen. All of her hair down, unbrushed and wild. Not at all like the girl I saw babbling about losing her best friend in the gym that night.

I hold on to the laminated card of Chloe's face, smiling, a poem on the back. Something about rainbows and sunshine and when I see you again. A child isn't supposed to go before their parent.

Keke gets in line behind me and I smile, the two of us stuck in this long hallway together. I'm glad to see her among these faces of sad strangers.

Chloe Schmidt holds court way up ahead, kissing strangers young and old like she's part of a wedding receiving line. Like she's part of Chloe Orbach's family. I guess when you've known each other for so long, that's what happens. You meet the cousins and aunts and the uncles, and they all feel like they know you because they watched you grow up.

"I have a weird question to ask you," I say to Keke. "What were the Three Chloes like before I got on the team? Like, last year?"

"Trios are a problem," she says. "There's always someone left out. Two against one."

"I knew they were fighting recently," I say.

"It wasn't just recently. It had been going on since last year," Keke says. "Did you know they were attacking each other in their Instagram stories?"

"I knew," I told her.

"They were always posting cryptic messages like *I told you so.* Or *You're pathetic.* But everyone knew they were talking about each other."

Once, in the beginning of the year, Keke saw Chloe Schmidt crying after school in the locker room, and Chloe broke down to her, saying she felt so betrayed. That everyone could see what Chloe Orbach was posting and everyone knew that it was about her.

"She was just so devastated, saying she felt publicly humiliated. Saying that I didn't know what it was like to be friends with someone like . . ." Keke looks around and mouths *Chloe Orbach.* "That she just liked to lift people up and then break people apart. It made me so sad to hear it. That wasn't the girl I knew."

"What did you say to her?"

"I told her that sometimes friendships need a break. But she was shocked that I would even suggest that. She went on and on about how she couldn't just *stop* being friends with her. That it didn't work that way."

I never thought I'd relate to Chloe Schmidt, but hearing that, that she couldn't just stop being friends, I understood exactly what she meant.

"Chloe was tough," Keke says, whispering. "I'm not gonna

lie. It's not every day that you get a junior who fights to be captain when you have two seniors on the team."

She tells me about Chloe Orbach's campaign over the summer. Gretch and Keke were going to be co-captains because they were seniors and that's just the way they did it. But Chloe didn't like that. She complained to Coach. She said there should be an application. She wasn't mean about it, Keke says, but she was forceful, argued it like a case.

Keke tells me Chloe made a tryout packet with requirements, with essay questions. With an open form about how to improve school spirit. With *thirty-seven* leadership questions, like: *Do you hold yourself accountable? How do you plan to keep each squad member motivated? What accomplishments are you most proud of?*

"It had a fundraising plan, okay?" Keke says, and rolls her eyes, shakes her head. "Me and Gretch, we were going to be seniors. Do you think either of us wanted that kind of responsibility? I had SAT and ACT tests to study for, plus I have a job. Gretchen works at the pharmacy. It's not like either of us could just go home after cheer and make fundraising plans. We decided that if this girl wants captain so bad then we'd let her have it. Who was going to stop a driving force like that?"

"What happened to all the packets after she became captain?" I say. "I just had to sign my name on a line to get on the team. It wasn't exactly difficult."

"I saw them in the recycling bin after practice one day, I guess it was before the janitor came, and I couldn't believe it. But what could I say? I wanted Coach to think I was a team player. So I shut my mouth," she says. "Once Chloe became captain, she became top dog. She made up all the rules."

■ ■ ■

As I get closer to the casket, to Chloe's family, I hear people saying that she looks so beautiful. *Look at her, that gorgeous face.* I can't imagine a corpse being beautiful. If they think she looks beautiful now, they didn't see Chloe Orbach in the flesh. They didn't see her on the field. Those muscular thighs. That fresh face, the translucent skin, always glowing. Vibrant. Alive. Pushing me to push myself. The way she commanded us. The way she wanted more.

People are telling her mother, *Sit, you're going to pass out. You need to sit.* But she's fighting all of them. "I'm going to stand until this is over, until every last person who has come to say goodbye to my daughter is gone," she says. Finally, it's my turn, and I shake her hand because I don't know what else to do. Her hand is soft and lifeless.

"I'm so sorry," I say, thinking that she can see through me to what happened that night. The flashing lights. The purple glow. The tablets with the crown and the star and the heart. Like candy. Deathly candy. Chloe collapsing. *Focus, Shade. Focus.*

She stares at me with vacant eyes. Deep blue circles.

"I'm very sorry for your loss. Chloe was a really special person," I say. It comes out so unnaturally.

She smiles at me, her face robotic-looking. Her lips quivering. Her hands on mine.

"The police are going through her bedroom," Chloe's mother says. "Right after the funeral. Can you believe it? My little girl. They're asking so many questions. Can't they leave her in peace?"

It's as if she isn't even saying it to me. She's just speaking to the gods or the heavens or whoever decides that a teenage girl is supposed to be unnaturally taken away from her mother.

"And then there's the toxicology report," she says. "It'll take some time, they told me. My husband has some pull at the police department, so we won't have to wait as long as most people. Just a few weeks. Have you talked to the police yet?"

"Me? No." The whole night in a flashback. Me and Jadis running out of the gym. Sirens, swirling lights. Chloe and Chloe just gone. The teacher screaming, *Put your phones away*.

"I know they want to talk to the girls on the squad," she says, her hand gripped around my wrist. "Anything you can tell them, anything at all to help us. To give us a clue of what happened to my baby."

I shake her off, really yank my hand away, and she stares at me until three women Chloe's mother's age swoop in and embrace her. I become just another mourner in line.

Jadis was right. I never should have gone up there to talk to her.

The shock of what they'll find.

The women wail, grateful that it wasn't their daughter. "Sylvia, can you believe it?" Chloe's mother says. "My little girl. My little girl."

I turn to the casket because that's what I'm supposed to do. Stand or kneel in front of it. Say a prayer for Chloe. It's all white, the casket pristine. A white shiny box and white roses. The smell so overwhelming, so floral, so much jasmine, like someone spritzed a mall kiosk perfume everywhere. I may pass out.

I force myself to stand there and look down at her. Her perfect skin, her blonde hair, draped over her shoulders. Her cheeks and her eyelashes so sweet and young and innocent. Sleeping Beauty. Chloe doesn't look dead. She looks like a statue, and her face, her resting, calm face, looks remarkably like the Chloé ads she covered her room with. Flawless, sleeping, forever young.

I can't get rid of this feeling, that I'm responsible for her death. How long will I feel this way? Forever? Will I rewind and pause on that night eternally?

Her hands are clasped over each other, and there it is, the bow that I tattooed on her thumb. They tried to cover it up with makeup so no one else would see it. But I can see the outline. I'm so surprised to see it that I gasp, and I close my mouth tight so that I don't let any other noises out.

That reminder of the two of us that night at the abandoned tracks. The ivy around her wrist. The overgrown grass brushing against our hands. Her hair floating around her face as I gave her the stick and poke.

And now she's here like this. Forever.

■ ■ ■

When I get home, my mom is in her bedroom crying. I can hear her from the hallway. Her night table is littered with takeout Chinese food. A pile of lo mein half-eaten in a bowl. Her head is lowered over her knees. I stand there quietly for a minute until she sees me. Her face is wet and streaked with tears.

"Why are you crying, Mom?"

"I've been thinking about you having to go to a funeral today. About what happened to your friend Chloe Orbach, and it's heartbreaking." She holds in a cry, just to let a few more words out. "I would die if anything happened to you, Shade. I would just die."

She's such a good friend to all of these lost women and men who traipse in and out of our house. Making time for all of their readings or gallery openings or their performance art.

"You didn't even come to any of my games, so save your bullshit for someone else. Say what you want about Chloe Orbach's mom, but at least she showed up."

It's like I stabbed her through the heart. Her mouth agape.

"Shade, why are you being so mean?"

"Don't look at me like that, Mom," I say. "Do you know

that other girls' parents come to the games and cheer their daughters on? They take photos and post them on Facebook. They make CHEER MOM shirts with a horrific bedazzle tool. Sparkling rhinestones. And you?" I say, shoving the bowl of noodles from the side of her bed on the floor. "You just sit here smoking weed and eating lo mein."

She stutters, wiping her tears away, and I start to walk out, telling her that I have to be somewhere.

"Wait, Shade," she says. "So you're telling me that smoking weed and eating Chinese food makes me a bad person? Are you kidding me?"

"You're missing the point."

"I am proud of you, Shade. I'm always proud of you."

"Right, if I joined the feminist club. Or if I was the director of the school play or if I was out protesting somewhere or volunteering at the library. But a *cheerleader*, oh my goodness, how shallow. How old-fashioned and misogynist."

"I never said that, Shade." And she gets out of bed and down on her knees so she can pick up the noodles. Her face looking up at me, shedding tears. "I love you and I love anything you do. I'm sorry, okay? I'll come to the games. I don't know how to get a ticket . . ."

"It's a high school football game, Mom! Listen to you. You can travel around the world, you can meet all sorts of artists and bring them back to our house, and you can't figure out how to go to a fucking high school football game?"

I look around her room. All the artwork from Tibet. All of the paintings from a gallery in London. The Henry Taylor signed poster of Michelle Obama. I want to tear it all off her walls and light it on fire.

It used to be that I liked hiding everything from her. My secret life with Jadis was beyond her reach because the two of us were so isolated, whispering in my bedroom or smoking on the corner or sinking to the bottom of her pool. I'm used to avoiding her and her disappearing on me.

Now she's paying attention, and I'm supposed to be guilty for my explosions.

I want her to fight back, to punish me or something. The way the cheer moms would do with their kids, the way any mom would do. There would be rules. Limits. Wouldn't there be?

She's still on the floor picking up the lo mein, telling me that she loves me and that she's sorry. She knows I'm taking it out on her because my friend just died, she says.

It's fine, I tell her. I'm sorry for making a mess. Maybe she's right and I'm taking it out on her.

I could see all of a sudden that she was, in fact, acting like a mom would act. That she was like all the other moms in that way—she was scared of losing me.

Chapter 22

I ASK JADIS to pick me up after practice. I tell her it's to talk about the funeral, but it's really because I want her to know what Chloe Orbach's mother said about the police and the toxicology report. It doesn't feel right to me to put that in text. Call me paranoid.

We sit in the middle of the parking lot, idling, her looking around, watching for something.

"We could have talked about this last night if I had slept over," she says. She hasn't slept over in a few days. Maybe it's been a week. Everything has been a blur since that night. The truth is, I don't want her breathing in my neck, cuddling into my hip. I don't want her body hanging across mine right now. I'm too unsettled by her.

When I'm around her, I feel that twitching, that discomfort. There's an empty space between us, and I don't know what to put there.

In the side mirror I see Chloe and Chloe stroll to Chloe Schmidt's Jeep.

Then, suddenly, Jadis throws the car into reverse, riding backward in the parking lot. She quickly brakes, her tires squealing so that she blocks Chloe's car in.

"Jadis, what—?" I say.

"Those bitches don't want to talk to us. I'm going to make them talk."

I'm not going to lie. Part of me admires it. Only Jadis would have this kind of moxie.

"Hey! What the hell do you think you're doing?" Chloe Schmidt says in Jadis's window.

"Both of you get in the back seat," Jadis says. "We're going for a drive."

"Are you insane?" Chloe Schmidt says. "We're not going for a drive with you."

"Unless you're talking to the police and telling them everything, then you need to get in the car so we can talk," Jadis says.

"Oh, how do you know that we haven't already talked to the police and told them everything?" Chloe Schmidt says.

"Because you wouldn't have run out of the gym that night. That's how I know."

■ ■ ■

The four of us in the car, Jadis peels out of the parking lot.

Slow down, I tell her, *we don't want to get pulled over*. But there's no getting through to her right now. I can see the way she's clutching the wheel, her head jutting forward.

Jadis drives up the hill through the barren trees, up to Barbour Hill, along the rocky cliffs. The gravel kicks up under the tires as we pass under the evergreens. I roll down the window and try to catch my breath. Behind me in the side mirror I can see Chloe Clarke clutching on to herself, like if she let go, she'd break apart.

"So what do you want to talk about?" Chloe Schmidt says, peeling off her varsity jacket, then rolling her lip gloss all over her already shimmering lips.

"Were you somewhere before the dance?" Jadis asks her.

"We were at my house getting ready and then we went to the dance," she says. "What does it matter to you?"

"It matters because we don't trust either one of you," Jadis says.

Chloe Clarke shakes her head and starts crying. "I don't want to be in this car with you. You're scaring me. All of you."

I reach through the seat for her hand to comfort her, but Chloe Schmidt swats me away.

"We're friends," I say, pleading with all of them. "We just need to figure this out, but we have to do it together."

Except we're not friends. Our common denominator was Chloe Orbach, and she's gone.

"Before we get all chummy," Jadis says, "let's remember why we are in my car, okay?"

"Oh, I remember," Chloe Schmidt says. "We're here because Chloe is dead. Oh, and that's right, because you gave her a tablet of Molly with a crown on it specifically for her. Oh, and then she died."

Jadis doesn't say anything because what can she say? There's no denying that she did give her the crown. This conversation is going to get uglier.

"Look, we don't know what happened. One minute we were dancing, the next minute Chloe fell to the ground," I say, trying to stay calm. "We need to have the same story."

"It's called *telling the truth*," Chloe Clarke says, her voice cracking. "And the truth is that Jadis got the Molly. That we all took it. And something happened to her. That's the truth."

"Oh, so you want to tell the truth about taking Molly at the school dance? Really?" I say. "You want to get kicked off of cheer for doing illegal drugs? We'll get expelled from school too."

I hate every word that came out of my mouth and I hate saying it to Chloe Clarke, so angry like that, because she doesn't deserve it. But we're stuck with each other now and we need solutions.

Chloe Clarke starts to shake, really shake, sobbing, her head over her knees. Schmidt rubs her back, tries to calm her down, but there's no calming her.

"Where did you get the Molly?" Chloe Schmidt says to Jadis, smacking at the back of her seat. "That's what I would like to know."

"Don't ask me that question," Jadis says.

"It's a simple question!" Schmidt says, and all I can hear is Chloe Clarke wailing over and over that Chloe didn't deserve this and that she's gonna puke.

"Pull over," I'm saying to Jadis. "Pull over!"

The car screeches to the side of the road. Chloe Clarke's face is flushed in fear. I follow her out, feeling shaky myself. Hands on my knees and try to catch my breath. We're toward the top now, and you can see old houses in the woods below, the turrets peeking up through the trees. The tracks cutting down below it all, the ones where I tattooed the bow on Chloe's thumb.

I intrinsically trust you. That's what she said to me.

"I want go to home," Chloe Clarke says. "I want to get out of here and go home."

I hear Chloe Schmidt jumbling through the bag in the car to get her phone.

"I just want to make sure we're all clear," Jadis says. "That our stories all match up."

But we haven't gotten anywhere. Nothing matches up. Nothing is clear.

Chloe Clarke walks down the gravel road and I trail her, begging her to stop and talk to me.

She tells me that she's been running the scenario over and over in her head. That she's been trying to talk to Chloe Orbach in her dreams, asking her what happened to her.

I hear Chloe Schmidt and Jadis bickering in the car behind us. Something about the definition of a true friend.

"I know Jadis and you are like this, Shade," Chloe says,

crossing her middle and index fingers over each other. "And I know that no one wants to believe that best friends can do horrible things. But don't you want to know?"

"Know *what?*"

"It's so obvious, Shade. Where did she get the Molly?"

■ ■ ■

The ride back is quiet. Endless. The sky dark and empty. Jadis drops them off in the school parking lot and speeds away. Her reckless driving; I clutch on to the car handle. I think of the days leading up to Jadis getting her license, six months ahead of me. It was one of the most exciting times of my life. We were so eager for that license. It was the key to everything, the key to our freedom. Taking road trips. Cruising around Groveton. Going to concerts without having to ask our mostly absent mothers for a ride. Having to worry about them not remembering to pick us up.

But now I hate driving with her. She drives too fast, looking for trouble. All I want to do is crawl out of this car and get away from her.

Where did she get the Molly?

If Jadis just came clean to me about this, then we'd have something. We'd have some explanation at least. We'd have a story. But to keep it a secret, to insist on not telling even *me?* Why?

We pass a thick row of those electrical towers. The empty field around them.

"I hate Groveton. I hate all these towers and all of these condos and I can't wait to get out of here," Jadis says.

"I didn't know this was going to turn into a Bruce Springsteen song," I say, trying to crack a joke.

"You know I think Bruce Springsteen is an overhyped old man, so I don't even know what that's in reference to."

I sigh deeply.

I turn to her, my whole body. "I need to hear it from you, Jadis. Where did you get the Molly?"

"Oh my god!" she says, and slams her hands against the steering wheel. "I already told you that I got the Molly from a good source. Stop questioning me. You sound like them."

"Don't you see that you've set yourself up to be the bad guy here? The jealous best friend who cuts the cheerleader's Molly with something lethal. They write TV shows about this, Jadis," I say. "So if you could just explain—"

"I was trying to do a nice thing, Shade. I really was. I saw how much fun you were having with them and I just wanted to be part of that, get wrapped up in that like you were. Represent that other side of you. That wilder side. That independent side . . ."

But then she trails off. I'm not sure if she stops because what she's saying is bullshit or because she sees I don't care. I rest my head on the glass. I just feel tired.

■ ■ ■

In the shower, the water running over my face, replaying what Jadis said to me in the car. That she got the Molly from a good source. *Source.* It's cryptic and unlike her. She doesn't keep secrets like that from me, not anything this big, this important. At least she didn't use to. Maybe that's my fault.

Just like all of this is my fault.

I dream that night that Jadis cuts me open and splits me in half. That she's doing a stick and poke of a heart pierced with an arrow on one side. On the other side, by my hip where my falling girl tattoo is, she scribbles something in black marker that I can't read. When I ask her what it says, she whispers in my ear.

"You can't get rid of me."

23

COACH WANTS ME to push my body more. It's been four days since Chloe's funeral, and I still feel in shock. Disconnected from everyone. She knows that Chloe was the one to do this for me, to motivate me. I know how Chloe made me want to be better, but I didn't realize that other people saw it too. I especially didn't think that Coach noticed it.

"You remind me of all the possibilities, Shade," she says. And it makes me want to cry.

The gym is filled with our bodies smacking against the mat. A squad of nice girls, sweet girls, jamming their hands against the ground, fighting against gravity, making our bodies aggressively twist and turn and hurt.

All for you.

Coach thinks if I have something to focus on, something new, that it'll be good for me. Since I have a tight back handspring, she wants me to try a standing full. A standing full is like a back tuck with a twist. You're fighting against everything your body wants to do, which is land. You're trying to fly in the air, stay up as long as you can to spin.

Zoey is the only other person besides Chloe Clarke on the team who can do a standing full. Her tiny little body whips through the air, and so she spots me so I can work on my back tuck. I power up and arch my back, pushing my whole body over, but it's a terrible landing. My whole body jolts forward, and I land on my knees.

Chloe Clarke calls over to me, "You can't tackle it like a back handspring. It's entirely different."

I'm surprised she even sees me, she's been in so much of her own private melancholy. "You're rotating too low. Remember, Shade. You're shooting up, like a rocket. Think of your trajectory." She stretches her arms straight up to the sky, those long fingers, then walks over to stretch my arms up. "This is where you want to go. Up. You need height first, then push your body over."

Zoey stares at her in awe. "How were you able to explain that? How did you know the exact way to say it?"

"Because I'm a flyer," Chloe says, that big ego coming to the surface again, that light in her eyes that I haven't seen in so long. "And I soar."

"I'm sorry about the car thing the other day. That wasn't my idea," I say to Chloe.

"You're very good at blaming things on other people, Shade," she says. "Maybe you should stop doing that."

■ ■ ■

Practice takes away the sting. It stops the flooding of thoughts about Chloe Orbach that invade my mind all day. All night. The thoughts about Jadis and how she just showed everyone that little pillbox without even telling me.

At home, I'm back in the same muddy place, sinking in all those thoughts.

Chloe Clarke's comment repeating itself. *You're very good at blaming things on other people.*

Who am I blaming?

The only person I blame right now is myself.

I turn on the television, and Chloe Orbach is right there, all over the news. A constant badgering. They love her. She is the perfect victim.

When I close my eyes, she's swaying in front of me, singing.

I obsessively scroll through all the memorial posts, searching for something, like I'm going to uncover something I haven't seen before. Something that will give me a clue to the nagging, terrifying thought, the one that hurts me most. That Jadis had something to do with her death.

I think of the four of us in the bathroom stall. How Jadis so eagerly placed the Molly right on Chloe's tongue. How satisfied she was.

Why was she so satisfied?

Would I be so satisfied to give a drug to someone Jadis befriended, someone who I saw as a threat? Someone who took her away from me? That's the difference between us. I'd welcome that person.

Wouldn't I?

Isn't that what I've done with Emma, welcome her?

Or would I let that person fly out into the void? Would I try to make my mark? Would I try to take a stand or make a statement? Would I try to hurt the person?

Would Jadis?

■ ■ ■

At practice two days later, I'm more incensed, maybe because I'm so determined to forget. To erase all the noise from my mind. I sprawl out in the middle of our pep talk circle that Coach has started doing because "it's good for our souls," and show them a video I have of a full up. You load in, then they pop you like a top in a 360 spin.

"Coach, you want us to push ourselves to do something new," I say. "So let's push ourselves."

"When do you want to work on this for?" Keke says.

"For the first game back," I say. That gives us about a week and a half.

I look over at Chloe Clarke because I know she's got a tight full up.

She nods. "Let's do it."

Coach works with Chloe Schmidt and Keke, both main bases, on the mechanics of the spin. Keke takes off one of her cheer shoes and hands it to Coach. She holds the shoe as if we're in it, as if they're working with an invisible flyer above them. They bend knees and dip at the same time.

Across the mat, Chloe Clarke and I practice spinning on one foot for the stunt. One white cheer sneaker off to really dig into that grip.

But the spinning makes me dizzy, and I fall over clumsily a few times.

"You have to look at one thing across the room. Focus on something," she says.

Looking at her now, how graceful she is, I see how she could easily go into competitive cheer. There's a show-pony component, sure, but it's also beautiful the way those girls point their toes, extending their limbs like there's no end.

"Do you think Chloe's mother saved those pictures that she put up in her room?" I say.

"The last time I was there, I didn't really want to ask her what she was going to do with all those pictures. Chloe's been going over there a lot more than me. She would know."

I glance over at Chloe Schmidt, who is practicing footholds for the full up with Pri and Olivia.

"Talking to her lately hasn't been that easy," I say.

"I think if people start taking responsibility for their actions, then maybe everyone would be a little less tense."

"What is that supposed to mean?" I say.

"You don't think you're at all responsible?"

That sinking in my chest again. My stomach curdling up.

"Of course I feel responsible," I say, whispering. "But it was an accident, Chloe. We all took the same tablet."

And only one of us OD'd. But I can't bring myself to say the words.

She spins a few more times, her leg locked. Then moves closer to me. Catching her breath. "Did you ask Jadis where she got it?"

"Of course I asked her," I say. But did she answer me? No. She didn't answer me at all.

Chloe Schmidt calls for a run-through, and we all get into place. Coach starts out with a *five, six, seven, eight* and on the *one, two* I load in, Chloe Schmidt first base on my right and Priyanka on my left. Olivia behind me.

Quickly they heave me up, and on *four* I'm supposed to spin on that right foot, except something is off and on *five* I come crashing down. My ass cheek slams on Chloe Schmidt's shoulders, and I slide through Olivia's hands. Schmidt huffs away, rolling her shoulder, muttering, *Sloppy bitch.* I hate working with her.

Next to me, Chloe Clarke goes up beautifully like she's done it a million times, and her bases crouch down on the *two, three.* She spins on the *four, five* and sticks it, both feet down, their hands wrapped around her ankles and shins on the *six, seven, eight.*

"If I was with Chloe instead of *her*, then maybe I wouldn't have a dislocated shoulder," Schmidt yells, running through the door. "I'm getting an ice pack."

It's unnerving.

"Don't listen to her," Chloe Clarke says. "She's still mad

about the car. She says you basically kidnapped us. I told her
that we were willing to get in. To do all of it, you know what
I mean?"

I nod, my tailbone burning from slamming into Schmidt's
shoulder.

■ ■ ■

The next day before lunch, Jadis barrels through people in the
hallway, then bashes her palm into my locker door.

"Those cunts."

She shows me a social media post. It's a photo of Jadis. The
caption reads: *Chloe knows what you did.*

"They posted a picture of me."

I grab the phone out of her hand. Scroll through. Another
photo. A drawing of a tablet with a crown on it. Everything
tightens up inside of me. I didn't think they'd come after her
like this. Chloe Schmidt maybe. But not Chloe Clarke.

"You have to stop them, Shade. They're going to get me in
deep trouble. I'm not kidding."

"There's no reason for you to get in trouble. You didn't do
anything, right? *We* didn't do anything. We took Molly together, that's all."

I say this to her hoping it'll feel open-ended. That she'll
give me something in response. Because I'm looking for some
kind of awful detail, because I have racing thoughts about
Jadis and what she's capable of.

"If the police ask us questions . . . and if they ask those two bitches why anyone might want to hurt Chloe Orbach, then who do you think they're going to point at? Isn't that what they implied in the car? Isn't that what they're announcing to everyone with that Instagram story?"

Her face is darker now, and she stands there, staring into me, zipping and unzipping her black hoodie, her jaw grinding like metal blades. So much rage that I don't know what's left of her. I don't know her at all.

"They're all against us," Jadis says. "You have to quit cheer or they're going to take us down. Don't you understand?"

My heart sinks. Jadis will often say things just to push for a reaction, but I wonder if this time she means it. If she thinks me quitting cheer—as if I even *would*—would somehow protect us from the tangled situation she's got us in.

"I'm not quitting cheer."

"Why not?"

"Because I love cheer," I say, and it's like I smacked her in the face. I don't even tell her the real feelings I have. That I have to keep going, that I want to keep going, for Chloe Orbach. That her voice drowns out my insecurities. That when I'm at cheer, it's the only thing that stops me from feeling so guilty about everything. About bringing Jadis to the dance. About joining the team. About having a careless mother who doesn't take any of these social nuances into consideration.

"What will it do if I quit cheer anyway?" I say. "How will it change anything?"

"You have a death wish," she says, and walks away.

Chapter 24

I'M SO TIRED. Practicing so hard this week. The strumming of Jadis's threats. The way the school feels like it's on fire with gossip about what happened to Chloe. So I work harder at practice, slamming my back tuck with Zoey until I hurt. The more I work it, the tighter I hold my core, the louder the sound of the pounding on the mat, the less my mind races.

I miss Chloe Orbach. She floats in my mind, the way she used to walk into cheer with her kombucha and her turkey and her arnica gel and take care of us.

The way she took care of me.

That blonde hair always flying behind her, I miss that. The way she embraced life. Fearless and wild-eyed, I'd always remember her that way. Like the way you see those posters of dead celebrities—forever beautiful and forever young. I shake her away.

In the locker room, changing, it's like she's waiting there for me, and I slip around the doorway searching for her. Nothing.

■ ■ ■

I go home and pound down on my standing full, falling into a stack of pillows. My body exhausted. If I just put my head down for a few seconds. For a few minutes.

Darkness. My phone buzzes next to me, and it's an hour later. I must have passed out, stretched across of the pillows on my floor.

The call says it's from Chloe Orbach.

My heart stops. I sit up quick, the room fuzzy, my head throbbing, and I grab the phone from the floor. "Hello?" I say, shaky.

On the phone, a cracked, broken voice. A woman.

"Shade? It's Chloe Orbach's mother. I'm sorry to bother you," she says.

Sit up, wipe my face, rub my eyes. Try to sound awake. "Hi, Mrs. Orbach."

"You know I'm not Mrs. Orbach. I'm Mrs. Amato. I'm remarried."

"Right, of course, I'm sorry—"

"Look, I'm just going to get to the point here. I'm calling people in my daughter's phone because I'm just having problems digesting all of this. Chloe Schmidt mentioned the night my daughter . . . the night she . . . And I just need answers, because this is just not my daughter. The police are suggesting drugs because her autopsy suggests it. Can you believe they cut open my little girl? She was perfectly healthy. I just need to understand. Maybe you can help me understand?"

"Of course, of course," I say. But what can I tell her? How do I explain her daughter to her? A girl living in her own house, and she didn't even know who she was. She didn't know that she winced that night when her mother made her cheer with her. Or that she was ashamed of where she lived. That Chloe Orbach wanted out of that old static mold her mother had formed around her and she was willing to go to all lengths to claw her way out of it.

"You have such an unusual name. Shade. People thought the name Chloe was unusual when I named her that, at least my family did. We didn't know it was one of the most popular names. And my god, how could I know that Chloe would be best friends with two other girls who had the same name?"

I hear her sniffling, her breath shortening, her voice groggy like she's been drinking.

"I never knew my daughter did any of that stuff. That's what they're saying, that she was taking something that night. They just don't know what. I never knew a thing about my daughter. I really thought I knew everything. How naive was I?"

"I don't know what to say, Mrs. Orbach . . . I mean, Mrs. Amato. I'm just so sorry."

"Chloe Schmidt, she's been so hurt by all of this. Poor Chloe. She calls me every day, do you know that? Sometimes she just comes over and sits in Chloe's room and cries. I've known her since she was in kindergarten. Just a little girl."

Chloe Schmidt calling her mother every day would piss Chloe Orbach off to no end. I wonder if she's doing it to torment Chloe in the afterlife. To give her a big *fuck you* now that she's dead. I imagine her rummaging through Chloe's room, fingering all those Chloé pictures, snuggling in her bed, trying on her clothes, seeing what she can borrow.

Who am I to say? Maybe it's everything that their friendship represented. All of that animosity disguised as love.

"I feel bad for my daughter's friends more than I do for my boys. My boys don't even seem to notice what's happened. I think in some way they think their sister is coming back. Anyway, Chloe Schmidt, she thinks maybe it's possible that someone did this to her. Is that possible? You hear about these rape drugs. That's what the police said too. That maybe someone gave her one of those roofies."

"A roofie? In her drink?" I say. "Chloe wasn't drinking."

My stomach turns, that acid coming up again. I don't say anything.

"She never had a heart problem before. She never had even a murmur. There'd have to be a reason. And so the detectives think that one of her friends could have accidentally given her something. Maybe you were one of those girls? Did you give her something and you're just scared to tell?"

I flash back to the bathroom. The way Jadis placed the queen's crown on Chloe's tongue.

"I didn't give her anything."

I say it like it's true. When I know I'm the one who got her into that bathroom stall with Jadis in the first place. She never would have been around Jadis, not twenty feet from Jadis, if it wasn't for me.

"Did you know my daughter had a tattoo? Someone gave her a tattoo on her thumb. A bow. The mortician tried to hide it, but I could still see it was there. Chloe Clarke told me it was one of her new friends. She was always getting different girls to come around, bringing them in to cheer. But a tattoo? That someone would carve that into her body in such a vile way? Why would she let someone do that to her?"

I wish I could tell her what a fun night we had doing that stick and poke. How excited Chloe was. That it had nothing to do with pain. That it had everything to do with joy. That we became so close, the two of us. She just wanted to be closer to me. And I wanted to be closer to her. How do you explain this? Chloe's mother will never understand. She'll always judge me for it.

"Did my daughter hate me?" she says, crying. It doesn't even seem that she's talking to me now. She could be talking to anyone. To God. To the clouds. The sky. Whoever took her daughter from her. "Is that why she would do this to me? Why she would leave me like this?"

Yelling in the background. Boys' voices. Chloe Orbach's brothers fighting, maybe. Screaming, and then a wail of agony.

"I have to go," she says, and hangs up just like that.

■ ■ ■

It's Saturday, and my mom has been gone since Thursday on a forest bath retreat. She and her friend are going to bathe themselves in the sounds of the forest, she told me. I almost told her that it's the dumbest thing I've ever heard, but I know I've been awful to her lately, so I shut up.

That afternoon I invite Zoey over because if I don't fill every hour, I think about Chloe. The guilt is all-consuming, and I can't turn it off. I play it over in my head, the way Jadis opened up that little pillbox in the middle of the gym, how Jadis placed that Molly on her tongue, how Chloe was all of a sudden on the floor, and how we passed through those gym doors into the night.

Zoey brings her gym mat, and we cover it with pillows. I'm going to flip myself into this thing until I can shake the images from the homecoming dance from my mind.

Over and over back tuck, then rotating my body while I'm up in the air, Zoey spotting me, then twisting into the standing full. I do it so many times, land on my hips until I'm limping.

I rest my face on the pillows, just for a minute. Just to stop for a few seconds.

"What do you think happened to Chloe?" she says. "I didn't want to ask you, but I feel like we're all just avoiding it."

I tell her to go first. I want to know what she thinks.

She tells me that three main conspiracy theories have blown up about Chloe Orbach's death, and they're circulating the freshman class.

1. There's a *cheer coup*. There's a widely circulated Tik-Tok that the squad wanted to get rid of Chloe because of some secret war.
2. It was revenge. On Instagram, somehow it got out about Chloe Orbach's wall of Chloés. The theory is that people hated her because she was a narcissist. All she cared about was herself. People got sick of her.
3. It was jealousy. On Facebook, someone posted copies of an article about a cheer mom in Texas who planned to kill her daughter's cheer rival. They think the murderer is hoping for a Netflix deal.

Surprisingly, no one mentions drugs.

"How did the wall of Chloés get out? Someone had to have taken a picture of it," I say. Could it have been one of the girls from the team?

"I don't know," she says softly. "People think it's weird that Gretchen and Keke are both seniors but Chloe Orbach got the captain's spot. You understand that Black girls get overlooked for these spots, don't you, Shade?"

I shake my head no.

"My mother warned me before I joined the team about this."

"About what?"

"Shade, Black girls aren't exactly rolled out the red carpet on mostly white cheer teams. We're policed, our hair is policed. I have a cousin in New Hampshire who was told to take her braids out if she wanted to be on the team."

"Did she?"

"No. But I wasn't sure if my locs were going to be an issue. Keke's family is military so she's probably been straightening her hair forever. Military folks are, you know, more conservative. My dad is white and so he gets super defensive. My mother had to tell him to stop making it about him." She laughs a little, but then a detached look comes over her face.

I know this look of detachment. It reminds me of the time I was working at a health food store and this guy Nate asked me to borrow five bucks for lunch. It wasn't so weird because we'd become friends.

When I told him I only had two dollars in my bag, he said, "Don't Jew me down."

I almost choked. "You know I'm Jewish, right?"

"You don't look Jewish," he said.

I wish I could say I'm completely surprised with what Zoey told me about Black cheerleaders and how she took it all in stride, but I'm not. I know from my own experience that bigotry leaves you a little dead inside.

"Anyway, it's fine," she says. "No one said a word to me about my hair."

Zoey closes her eyes for a second. I have more questions for her, ones that might make her feel uncomfortable, and so I keep my mouth shut.

"Chloe Orbach made me feel good about my hair right from the start, did I ever tell you that?"

"No," I say. "This is the first I'm hearing about any of this."

But I'm not surprised. Chloe Orbach was a lot of things to a lot of people.

"She was a good leader," Zoey says.

"She wasn't even supposed to be captain. Chloe was just more determined than Keke and Gretch," I say. And just like that the topic changes. I tell her what Keke said about the formal cheer captain application. How possessed she was. "You gave me everyone else's theories, but you didn't give me yours."

She hangs on to her thought for what feels like forever. I feel like she's waiting for me to tell her what to say.

"I think it was someone close to her," she finally says. "Someone sweet and nice. The kind of person who one minute you think they're an angel and the next minute they're carving up their best friend in the basement."

"I think you watch too many horror movies."

But isn't this already a horror movie? I overheard people saying that at the funeral home. Every parents' worst nightmare.

"What if I told you I knew what happened to her?" I say. It comes out quick, and I clear my throat from nerves.

Careful, Shade, I think. *You can't just confess to Zoey, as innocent and as trusting as her big brown eyes might seem, that Jadis, your best friend, slipped Chloe Orbach Molly that potentially killed her. She'll tell someone, then they'll tell the cops, and then your worst nightmares will come true.*

"I'd say you can't hold on to that kind of information. That's what I would say," she says, hesitating. "If you and Chloe are as close as you seemed, that you'd have to tell because it would eat you up inside."

She tries to take my hand, to comfort me I guess, but I'm beyond comforting. I hate myself for what I've done or, really, for what I haven't done. I hate myself for even opening my mouth this way to Zoey.

"I was just kidding," I say, and stand up, looking down at her. Shaking my hands out. "Obviously if I knew anything, I would go to the police. There's a million horrible scenarios of what could have happened to Chloe." I straighten my shoulders, pull in my lower belly like I'm holding on to a ball, just like Coach taught us. My abs tight. My body, armor.

I tell her to show me what these freshmen are posting, I tell her I want to see the lies. But she's scared. These are girls I don't follow on Instagram. They don't follow me.

"You can't say anything to them, Shade. They'd track it back to me. I'm the only freshman on the squad."

"Show me," I say.

She pulls up a TikTok from an account called Crime-s000lver. It has 11,000 likes.

A girl I've never seen before with long red hair pops up on the video. She's got a septum nose ring and a voice like death.

"What is a murder that happened in your town that you think everyone should know about?"

The redhead cuts out and is stitched with a more familiar face, a mousy girl from school who I've seen in the hall, but I don't know her name. Behind her flashes a picture of Chloe Orbach, vibrant smile, in the grass, pom-poms next to her ears. Chloe and her blonde hair. In her cheer outfit. That glow.

"This is Chloe Orbach. She died at the homecoming dance just two weeks ago, and no one knows what happened to her. Was she killed by her two best friends, also named Chloe?"

I almost fall to the floor.

The Three Chloes, arms over each other's shoulders, dash across the screen.

"Was it the two senior teammates, who were jealous of her?" the girl says.

Gretchen and Keke in a cheer pose.

"Or was it someone new on the team? Someone she was seen at the homecoming dance with?"

And there it is. A photo of me, one that someone took before my cheer life began. I recognize the photo from last year because it showed up in the yearbook. My curly hair wild and long. Walking through the hallway. Staring blankly at the camera.

The caption reads: *What do you think happened* 🕵️*?*

I slam Zoey's phone down, shuddering.

"Are they crazy? They can't post this." My heart thrumming, my voice breaking.

"Shade, there's more. Look at the comments."

She hands me back the phone, and I scroll down, but can only stomach reading the first few.

idk but this death doesn't sit right with me, one person says.

My respect for the cheerleaders, 📉

The seniors are sus

My guilt boils up, my body ringing with alarm because I know Gretchen and Keke have nothing to do with this. My brain not knowing where to go next. They don't deserve to get dragged into this mess because of me, because I insisted on bringing Jadis to the homecoming dance.

I text everyone on the squad about the video. Gretchen is friends with the mousy girl's older sister, and it disappears. But the damage is done.

This is what our classmates are thinking about us? Pri texts.

They're freshmen. They're not our classmates, Chloe Schmidt writes.

The video was practically viral you idiots, Keke texts. *You can't just make something disappear off the internet.*

She's right. It'll never disappear.

■ ■ ■

Late Sunday night, my mom is back from the forest bath. She stands there captivated in front of the TV and waves me in.

"I haven't seen television in three days," she says, groggy. "I flicked it on and there she was. It's about your friend."

All sixty-five inches of Chloe Orbach's face spread across the television, smiling and happy, like the ray of sunshine that she was.

"They just talked about a toxicology report," my mother says. "Did she do a lot of drugs, Shade?"

I watch my mother's face. Part of me wants to tell her everything. Would she drag me to the police? Would she force me to talk to them? Would she give me one of her little lectures about how the female friendships in our lives are the most important and that women are the only people we can count on?

"Should I be worried about you?"

"Now you want to worry about me, Mom? *Now?*" I say, grabbing the remote and flicking the news off. "It's a little late for that, don't you think?"

"Shade, you're so angry lately. You have to talk to me."

"You're right," I say. "I'm angry that my friend died. I'm angry that I don't know who my real friends are. I'm angry that I even joined this cheer team. And I hate freshmen."

I walk out of her room and slam my door.

■ ■ ■

This is all everyone wants to talk about at practice on Monday, the video and the news coverage.

"My mother is considering suing for defamation," Gretchen says, hysterical. "This is something a college can see and then decide that I'm too controversial."

"You seem more upset about the video than you do about Chloe actually being dead, Gretch," Chloe Schmidt says. "What's that about?"

Gretchen, the nicest pastry cupcake, barrels over to Chloe Schmidt, rasping, points to her. "You shut your mouth."

"Maybe Gretchen has something to hide?" Chloe Schmidt says, needling her.

Gretchen knocks shoulder to shoulder with Chloe Schmidt as she passes her.

Every one of us, watching each other now. Our minds not in the right place.

Mostly we have to be guarded around Chloe Schmidt. She's out for blood.

Coach strolls between us during our push-ups.

"Starve your distractions," she says, her favorite saying. "Feed your focus."

My hands on my bases' shoulders just about to go into the full up. Chloe Schmidt turns to me and says, ever so sweetly, "You're awfully quiet, Shade. Don't you have something to contribute to the conversation from before? I'm sure you have so many thoughts about it."

They lift me up and I spin, not quite stable, my hands everywhere.

Chloe and Pri cradle me under each foot, Sasha's hands wrap around my ankles. As I sway, Chloe Schmidt digs her nails down into the front meshy part of my cheer shoe. I wince and buckle.

"Ankles together, Shade!" Coach yells, and Chloe releases her grip, getting me back up straight.

"What the hell was that?" I say to her as they bring me down.

"What was *what?*"

"My toes," I say, "you dug your nails into my toes."

"Oh, I'm so sorry," she says, her teeth gritted, her fake concern, "but I don't want you to fall on top of me and break my neck."

"Composure, girls. Composure." Coach goes over it again, intense, Chloe Clarke and I standing side by side. "Spinning is easy, but your legs have to be tightly together. Squeeze your hips forward." She roughly adjusts my hips so my pelvis juts ahead. "Squeeze your butt cheeks tight."

"Like you can hold a pencil in there," Clarke whispers to me.

"The flyer is only one part of this," Coach says, then asks me to take my shoe off. She holds the white cheer shoe at eye level with Keke, who is Chloe Clarke's main base, and Chloe Schmidt. "The main base is responsible for the direction of the stunt. Do you understand me?" But she's looking directly at Chloe Schmidt.

"Even if my flyer is wobbling?" Schmidt asks. "It's still my fault?"

I could strangle her.

"Yes, even if your flyer is wobbling," she says. "The hardest job in the full up is on the main base."

Because the main base can't let go. She says it twice.

"This is about trust, girls," Coach says. "I know it's a big ask right now. I know we're all feeling vulnerable."

"See, Shade, you just have to trust me," Chloe says, sing-songy, as we wrap up. "I know you have trust issues. I know that must be hard for you."

I just want to slap her for everything. For talking to me

that way, for clawing my toes, for accusing Gretchen earlier in the locker room. What makes her think she can act like this to me? To Gretchen? To any of us? But I let her walk away. And the rage inside of her.

■ ■ ■

After practice I've got a slew of texts from Jadis. She saw the news program too, the article in the local paper. All the media coverage. I tell her about the TikTok, and she's quiet.

I'm sorry for saying this, she texts, *but I'm glad someone else is getting heat.*

There's a lull, no word from Jadis—the beast must be resting—until I get incoming rapid-fire texts around eleven o'clock at night. She can't sleep. She hasn't slept over in almost a week. *Please, Shade*, she begs me. Emma's mother shut her phone off for the night. *Please, Shade.* She needs someone to cuddle with her. She needs me the way it was. She got into a fight with Emma and she feels sad.

I'm not used to being second fiddle. I say yes.

When she gets to my house, the first thing she notices is the gym mat on the floor with the pillows.

"What's this for?"

"It's a tumbling stunt I'm working on for cheer."

"Ah, cheer, the great equalizer. The one thing that brought us all together. The cheerleaders, the non-cheerleaders, the freshman conspiracy theorists."

"I thought you were coming over here to sleep," I snap. "Not to give me a hard time."

"We sound like an old married couple. I play the snarky wife and you play the cranky husband."

"That's because we are." I don't know if that's an insult or a compliment.

■ ■ ■

Later in bed, she mentions what she's most worried about, which is the toxicology report. What it'll mean when it comes out. That the police are going to talk to us. They're going to look at the security cameras. How they're going to arrest her for murder. How she's going to get thrown in jail.

"Which is why this *source* is so important," I say.

"Oh, enough about the source," she says, and she smacks the blanket.

"Would it be someone I know? Someone like Eddie?"

"Eddie has nothing to do with this."

"Because if we just knew where you got it, we could prove the Molly wasn't what caused it."

She turns over and is so quiet for a while. And then so am I.

"What are you thinking, Shade?"

"When I close my eyes, I see her," I say. "I see her everywhere."

■ ■ ■

It's about one thirty in the morning, and Jadis is asleep. Her light snore used to be something I loved. Now I hate it. Now it wakes me up.

My eyes drift shut, and Chloe Orbach's in front of me, her body somehow intertwined with Jadis's. The two of them, a vape cloud, whirling around each other.

And then my phone flashes, the light shining in my eye. It's a text from Chloe Schmidt.

The truth shall set you free

Chapter 25

I TEXT EMMA in the morning asking her to meet me in the gym. I figure it's the one place Jadis would never see us. I ask her not to say anything.

We head to the top of the bleachers, the echo as we walk up the wooden planks. The gym so huge with no one in it. We sit at the top, the back row, and lean against the cold wall.

"So this is like your turf," she says.

"Yeah," I say. "I've pounded the mats here hard this year."

I think about all of the pep rallies I've dragged Jadis to. The basketball games to watch cheerleaders at halftime. How we'd sit up here, all the way at the top, and she'd file her nails while I'd be completely engaged in what was happening down on the floor. She never complained much about it. She would sit next to me taking selfies, doing TikToks, playing the part of a bored friend watching cheer.

And then there's the other memory of this place. The place Chloe Orbach died.

The memories, overtaking me.

"Did you hear what I said?" Emma says.

"No, I'm sorry."

"I used to think that you and Jadis were so different. I didn't understand how the two of you could even be friends," she says.

"Really? I always feel like Jadis and I are exactly alike." But I haven't felt like that for a long time.

"I don't know. You're so quiet and she's so loud. You seemed more introverted and she was kind of bouncing all over the place, friends with so many different people. Hanging out with that muscle-necked Dave Sozo, which, I'm sorry, but I don't understand that friendship."

"It's about the Ping-Pong," I say, smiling. "The Sylvia Plath too."

"Right," she says, rolling her eyes. "Plath and Ping-Pong. I was at his house twice last week."

Emma has both her parents living with her. She has a stable home life. She doesn't know what it means to want to escape all that loneliness. To always want to be somewhere else to fill up that void. Emma doesn't know what it's like to have a father who's disappeared and a mother who is hardly present and doesn't want to be present, like Jadis's mother. This is what Jadis and I have always bonded over. That we're each other's families.

"Is your mom gone all the time too, like her mom?" Emma says.

"No, she's not like Jadis's mom."

I don't even try to explain my mother and her art salons and forest baths to Emma or how my mother's motto is "I deserve to have my own life."

Jadis was my only constant.

"Do you hate your mom like Jadis hates her mother?"

The question makes me uncomfortable, and I want to change the subject. I don't hate my mother. I just wish she was someone else. I wish I was her priority.

I've seen the pictures on Instagram of Emma and her blonde mother, the two of them with their long straight hair vacationing in Belgium, skiing in the Alps or some other snowy mountain in Europe. She wouldn't understand what Jadis and I have been through. Anyway, there's a reason I asked her here.

"Did Jadis say anything to you leading up to that night?"

She seems stunned that I'm asking her this. "I mean . . . I don't know . . . like what?"

"Anything, Emma. Did she say anything to you?"

A janitor swings open the gym doors, the sound of it bouncing across the rafters and the cement walls. He looks up at us, and we say nothing. Then he walks back out.

"She said she was getting Molly."

"So you knew about the Molly then?" I say, annoyed.

This is one more thing that Jadis hasn't told me: that Emma knows. That it's not just a secret between me, Jadis, Chloe, and Chloe. It's a secret that includes Emma.

"I think she was really affected by what happened to Chloe Orbach," Emma says. "More than I realized."

"Like, what do you mean?"

She makes me promise not to say anything to Jadis. That she feels it would betray their trust. Isn't it already broken by meeting me here in the gym?

She tells me something that happened over the weekend. It was her sister's twenty-first birthday, and her parents had a whole party with a DJ, a friend from Brooklyn. Drinks. A caterer. Emma was hanging out with this DJ friend who she's known forever, and I can see where this story is going.

"A girl?" I ask.

"Yeah, but she's a friend. She was spinning and I was just standing next to her dancing. I even called Jadis over to dance with me. But she wouldn't. It isn't like her to be so insecure." Emma winces uncomfortably, like the words shouldn't even come out of her mouth. "She got really out of control."

Emma tells me that Jadis got drunk and started screaming nonsensical things. That Emma wasn't paying enough attention to her. That she didn't love her. That I didn't love her anymore. That no one loved her.

"That *I* didn't love her?" My skin shivers hearing this. This must have been why Jadis was so desperate to sleep over last night. I think of everything that I've been doing since the night of the dance, not going to the police, not telling them what Chloe Orbach took, how I've been protecting her. How I've been racking my brain to fill those blank spots about that night so that I can prove to Chloe and Chloe that the Molly wasn't the reason Chloe Orbach died. That Jadis had nothing to do with it.

Because she didn't. Right?

How does she not see that?

"That's what she said," Emma says, and shrugs. "You know how dramatic she can be. Especially when it comes to you."

"What does that mean?"

"Oh, come on, Shade. I don't want to say that Jadis is obsessed with you because that wouldn't be the right word, but how about . . . territorial. She always tells me that you guys are the same person."

I remember the day we first started saying that. It was last year. Jadis had slept over for a week, the longest she had holed up in my house. She didn't want to go home because Eddie was in Colorado and her mother was, of course, traveling.

My mother had a house full of people and they just finished some crappy reading from a friend's poetry chapbook. Jadis and I tried to stay out of their way, but how could you ignore the empty bottles of red wine and the adults lounging all over the living room floor when you were trying to just get some leftover pizza from the kitchen?

Then we walked in on some random couple having sex in my bathroom and I screamed at my mom in front of all her friends. Someone muttered that I was a brat and my mother told me to go to my room. That I was too uptight.

We went to the movies instead. The one about the best friends. "We're the same person, but with different hair."

I was more disgusted than Jadis. It was my mom and her careless friends, so flagrant. Jadis was more intrigued. We made a plan to run away. Like, really run away. We searched prices of train tickets and called her cousin out in Montauk, which seemed the farthest point away from where we were, stuck in my house with messy adults.

And I was ready to go, to get away from there, to piss my mother off and maybe scare her. Hide in some beach shack in Montauk and spend my days hiking the cold dunes, staring out into the Atlantic Ocean.

But I knew Jadis wouldn't go. Jadis, for all of her wild-child exterior, liked everything to stay the same. We stared at our full backpacks, and I told her I knew she wouldn't go through with it. That she would get homesick. And she crumpled to the floor crying and told me that it wasn't just that I knew her like the back of my hand, but that I *was* her hand.

"Then why can't you run away with me?" I said. "If it's good for me, wouldn't it be good for you too?"

"You always figure things out, Shade. You always have answers and solutions. We'll get there and you'll have studied the map, you'll do something practical like get a job at a coffee shop. You'll find a way to do school remote. You'll call your mom every night even though you say you hate her. I just walk behind you, clueless. Waiting for you to tell me everything's okay."

"You're wrong," I said. "I'm the one who follows you everywhere. I'm *your* shadow."

"You would think that about yourself, wouldn't you?" she said.

We didn't go to Montauk.

Emma gets up from the bleachers, that squeal of the seats

as she shifts on her feet. She squints, a sharp stare. She tells me she has to get to class.

"Did she say anything to you, Emma? About her plan to get the Molly? Where she got it from?" I say. "Did you know that she gave us each different ones with special stamps?"

She shakes her head. Tells me that Jadis didn't get into any details with her. "She wanted to make things right, that's all I know," she says. "Still, I find the whole thing so weird. How you and Jadis were holed up in the bathroom with the Three Chloes."

She's looking at me like this a question I'm supposed to answer. Not a statement.

"Why would it be weird?" I say. "I cheer with them. I cheered with Chloe Orbach. And Jadis was with me."

"Because Jadis knows a lot of people, but not any cheerleaders."

"Well, I'm a cheerleader," I say, reminding her.

"Yeah, you are," she says, as if it takes her breath away. "You really are, aren't you?"

■ ■ ■

Later in the day, after sixth period, I see Chloe and Chloe by a locker, hands flailing all over the place. I want to turn the other way to avoid them, especially Chloe Schmidt. But then I hear Chloe Clarke's voice. She's screeching.

"Fuck off, Chloe," she's saying. "You're going to hell."

I turn around like everyone else in the hallway does, because anytime there's a loud argument you can't help but look. Any kind of distraction from our banal school day is usually welcome, and I know it sounds terrible to be excited for something like this, to watch people fall apart, but this time it's different. Because it's Chloe and Chloe, they're a spectacle. If they make a scene, then it reminds people of that freshman conspiracy theory, the one we're all named in. Their very public fight will remind people we were all together that night.

I hear her again, telling Chloe Schmidt, *You're going to hell.* This is very different from *Go to hell*, and it makes me pause.

Go to hell is a demand. *You're going to hell* is a prediction.

Then someone starts chanting, "Fight, fight, fight," and that's when my whole body turns into shivers, and I want to escape, be far away from this violent tornado sucking everything up in its path. I scamper down a different corridor by the media room and sink to the floor until I can get my breath again.

Chapter 26

JADIS BEGS ME to come over for a swim on Thursday night. Though I'm exhausted, used up from the week, I force myself to go to see if she says anything about what happened at the homecoming dance.

When I'm not thinking about Chloe, I imagine Jadis plotting revenge, giddy with the power of tiny stamped tablets.

She's out back by the pool, wrapped up in a blanket next to the firepit, so snuggly and relaxed. The steam from the pool rises in the air. Her hair is a different color again. Lavender, because it represents tranquility. Because she needs peace, she says.

"So what's new at cheer?"

"Like you care," I snipe.

"That's the thing, I care more than you know," she says, the blanket unfurling around her. "So tell me. I'm legit curious."

"Fine," I say. "New stunts. Working on a full up and a standing full."

"Full around. Full down. Fall down. Standing full. Full full. Full of shit," she says, her eyes darting right into me.

Then there's silence between us, the two of us staring at each other. Her, twisting her hair.

"What's your problem tonight?" I ask.

"There aren't any problems," she says, then gets up and grabs some sticks to toss in the fire, the embers creeping into the darkness. She rips a vape cloud so long and so heavy that it looks like she's a scorching dragon.

She throws her blanket down to the ground. Takes off her big New Order T-shirt, just a bra and underwear underneath, and jumps in the pool. She comes up to the surface, her lavender hair peeping out.

"Before cheer, do you think we were codependent?" she asks me. "That's what Emma says."

"I didn't know Emma had opinions about our friendship," I say, and then a bolt of panic hits me, remembering what Emma told me. "Did you tell Emma anything about that night?"

"We all have to have someone to tell our secrets to, Shade," she says. "You have the cheerleaders. Well, one less now."

She doesn't even blink.

The hatred rolls off her so easily.

"That's fucking morbid, Jadis. So crude."

"To answer your question. No. Of course I didn't tell Emma," she says.

Lie. I know it's a lie because Emma already told me she knew.

"Come on, let's stop badgering each other. Come in already."

I strip down to my bra and underwear and melt into the pool, trying to remember why I'm here. It's to ask her about that night.

Steam rises above the surface, hovering through the pool lights. My thighs sink in the thickness of the water. All of it feels so good, over my limbs, my shoulders. I tumble in the deep end and press my head underwater, listening to it *blub blub blub* around my ears, until I hear Jadis singing that Lana Del Rey song.

"All I wanna do is get high by the beach, get high by the beach, get high . . ." The same words over and over. *"We . . . won't . . . survive."*

I swing my head up. Water dripping over my eyes and mouth. My heart almost stopping. The last time I heard this song, Chloe Orbach was singing it at the abandoned tracks.

"What?" she says. "You look like you've seen a ghost."

Is it that simple? *Maybe I have*, I want to tell her. Maybe she and Chloe are the same person and the joke's on me. Chloe. Jadis. It's like they've fit inside some kind of Russian doll where you just keep opening a new doll head and you get a clone of the next one. A Chloe. Or a Jadis. Over and over and always.

I dive down deep into the pool until my ears pop. That song repeating itself. Chloe Orbach haunting me everywhere.

I come up for air, breathing heavily, to see Eddie and two of his friends, Drew Lieber and Luke Kaplan, barrel through the gate. I would have been embarrassed any other time for these guys, or any guys, to see me in my bra and underwear, but I've been running around in a sports bra and booty shorts for the past two months, so it doesn't even faze me. Plus, I'm glad they're here to ease the tension between me and Jadis.

Eddie, Drew, and Lucas get down to their boxers and cannonball into the pool, splashing each other, then splashing us. It's so light and silly and fun, all that water in my face so that I forget everything, at war with the boys and laughing so hard that my chest is heaving.

"Come on, Shade. Show us some moves," Jadis says, that glow in her eyes. "Let's see some of those flips."

I'm not sure if she's doing this for me or for her own entertainment, but when the guys start chanting, *Shade, Shade, Shade*, I swim over to the ladder and climb up on the diving board. Lightly bounce up and down. Hands flat by my side. Clean.

I think of Chloe Orbach. What she would say. *Clean!* So I yell it out. "Clean!" I stampede down to the edge, take a deep bounce, flip, then straighten out my whole body, toes pointed as I touch the water, pike down. I hear them screaming even below. My body rushes down to the bottom of the pool, their muffled cheers above, and I push off like Supergirl, rocketing up to the surface, all of my energy recharged again.

My face emerging from the water. "Watch her fly!" Jadis screams.

"Backflip!" Eddie says. And then the four of them are cheering, but a backflip is for babies. A backflip is for amateurs. I can do my standing full here because landing isn't an issue. Two back handsprings and the twist, then right into the water. It all makes so much sense. So easy. I could do it in my sleep.

I start up between the lounge chairs, my wet feet flopping on the concrete. The cold air. I know my white underwear's see-through, my nipples push through my nude bra. They can all see it now, me on display. For the first time, really. And I know they're staring at me and somehow, I don't care. I have purpose. This is what I do. This is when I feel most like myself. My feet firm to the ground. I tingle from it. I drink it in.

I smack my hands against my thighs and take off, my body backflipping, my hands bouncing off the damp concrete, all of the energy going to that last twist, and I fly up and round my hips, twisting over, then straight down into the pool, their voices like a blur until I'm submerged in the water again, everything floating around me, and I stay down there for a second, my skin sparkling in the glow of the underwater pool light.

I propel up, above the fog, a deep breath, the water gushing over my face. I did it. I did that beast of a double back handspring full.

The guys are clapping, whistling and Jadis is right there on the side, her tiny little black bra and her black lace undies, capturing the whole thing on her phone.

I climb out of the pool and plow toward her. "What are you doing?" I say, snatching at the phone. She won't let me have it. She holds it above her head.

"Oh my god, relax, Shade. It's just a video."

"I don't want you posting that. Do you understand me?" I

walk closer to her again, swiping at the phone.

"Why not? You look amazing." she says, playing it, trying to show it to me. And I get a glance of myself, my body lit up by the glow of the pool light. "It's like an independent film from the nineties. We could write a whole book about this video. It's brilliant."

I see it in such a different way than her. I see it as a chaotic mess. Messy girls swimming. My nipples charging through my bra. The boys and their drooling faces, the way they clamor for a peek of anything.

Then I think about that mousy freshman's crime TikTok from last week with my face plastered in her video as one of the suspects.

"You have to delete it," I say. "Do you understand me?"

She stops. Her whole face changes. She shoves the phone under her towel.

"Please tell me what could possibly be wrong with this video? Is it because you're a cheerleader and cheerleaders don't do these things? And oooh, cheerleaders don't swim in their bra and panties with a bunch of boys in a pool? We already know that the girls on that team are not as sweet as they say. They do psychedelics at the homecoming dance, for fuck's sake."

She shouldn't be so cavalier. This isn't something I want my cheer team to see. Especially not now, just a few weeks after we buried the team captain. After we buried my friend.

"Don't you get it? I don't want to look like I'm—"

"What? Like you're having fun? Even though she's dead?"

She says *dead* as if she takes pleasure in it. Like it rolls off her tongue.

"My friend just died," I say. "Do you not understand this?"

Jadis's whole face collapses. "I guess I didn't want to believe that."

"Believe what?"

"That you were actually *friends* with her. You being a cheerleader? Sure. I could see you as a cheerleader. You could fake it, but hardly. You could work your ass off to do those moves or those stunts, whatever you call them. But to be *friends* with them. To call Chloe Orbach your friend?" Her lower lip quivering. Her eyes tearing up. "You said nothing would be different, but everything is different."

"That's what this is about? The cheerleading?"

"Yes, of course it's the cheerleading," she says, exasperated. "I should just put this video out into the world so that you can remember who you are. That you're Shade fucking Meyer who swims with her best friend in October. Who dances in her bra and underwear. Who doesn't give a shit about anything or anyone!"

In eighth grade we made a pact that we'd never leave each other alone. The two of us, sitting in my bed, white sheets wrapped around us. No matter who we loved, no matter who we committed to, we'd always be there for each other first.

I wrote her a letter last year: *Stay forever in my heart and I will hear you in a deep forest. I'll hear you from the corners of the earth. I'll hear you when you think of me.*

She wrapped up that letter and sewed a pocket for it and tucked it under her pillow. Said that she'd sleep with it every night.

I sit down on the lounge chair and look up at her. "What was your intention that night at the dance?" I say.

"My intention was to make nice with your friends, as you call them."

"Did you go there to do something else?"

There's an anxious pause, her mouth open.

"Like what?"

"Like to hurt someone?"

And there it is. I've finally said it. Something that I can't take back.

The boys splash around behind us, far away enough so I know they can't completely hear us. I hear Drew mumble, "Catfight." Of course that's what a bunch of guys would chalk it up to. A catfight. Every part of my body, shaking. Like I can't catch my breath, and all of the images, all of them from that night at the dance. The Molly that she gave Chloe Orbach. How excited she was to share it.

I feel dizzy, like I might fall down. Panic comes over me in flashes of heat. First my arms then my chest then my neck. Those images again, how Chloe Orbach opened her mouth and stuck her tongue out. How Jadis carefully placed it at the tip. It's like I brought a lamb to the slaughter. The heat rising up to my face now. My whole body, engulfed.

It's not the first time I thought she could be responsible.

But if I say it out loud, once I ask her, it would make it real.

"Did you want to hurt Chloe Orbach?" I say.

She reaches for the bag of Twizzlers, rips it open, and shoves one in her mouth, holding it between her lips like it's a cigarette.

"I see what those bitches are doing, you know," she says.

"Oh? What's that?"

"They're trying to get you to think I did this. They're trying to turn you against me. They're trying turn us against each other."

"Like I would let anyone do that to us."

"Wouldn't you though?" She looks up at me, chomps on her Twizzler. "Did I mention that I'm trying to stop vaping?"

"No, you didn't," I say.

"I'm trying to kick things that aren't good for me. I'm trying to get rid of toxic things in my life."

"Who even *are* you?" I say.

"Who is anyone?"

This game of hers, wordplay and dares, cryptic answers. It scares me, and I've had enough of it. She got what she wanted. A video that shows me reveling after my friend died. A denial of any wrongdoing.

■ ■ ■

I stumble out of Jadis's house, and she's following me down the barren street, calling after me, promising that she's going to delete the video or that she did delete the video. I don't even know what she's saying anymore. I can't think straight. The only thing in my mind, the only thing that I can even *see* is that Molly, the crown that she fed to Chloe Orbach.

I'm walking in the middle of the street like some lost straggler and she's behind me in the dark, begging me to turn around, to talk to her. How was she supposed to respond to that question: *Did you want to hurt Chloe Orbach?*

Maybe she's right, maybe it was ridiculous to ask her or to expect the truth.

Except it all breaks apart in this moment. I can feel it like a quick bite—our friendship will never be the same. Everything inside of me shuts off. I can't turn around and make it okay.

I stomp over the yellow lines on the road and leave her voice behind me.

"Shade, c'mon, Shade," she's calling. "They're doing this to us. They're putting the wedge between us."

But the feeling just gets worse. That feeling of sickness and dread, all of it piling up inside me.

That if Jadis did this, if she really gave Chloe Orbach something different than the rest of us, it wasn't to hurt Chloe Orbach. If she did it, if she did something so horrific, she did it to hurt me.

Jadis was so willing to go to that homecoming dance. She hardly needed convincing. Maybe it was because she had a plan all along.

If Chloe Orbach died that night because of some revenge fantasy that Jadis concocted, then I don't know how I'm going to live with myself.

Chapter
27

I WAIT FOR Chloe Clarke in the library during study hall the next day. I didn't want to talk to her at practice the day before. Too many people around. The library has sounds of its own. It's an old building, so the floors are wooden and creaky. The lights on the library desks, a greenish blue, everyone studying, pallid and ghostlike.

I'm reluctant to talk to Chloe, but I don't feel like I have another option. It's not as if I can talk to anyone else about this. And it feels like a volcano in my chest, hot and pulsing.

Madeline Steiner and Rory Green are just behind me. Rory and I were the only sixth graders in pre-algebra. I didn't even know I was good at math, but I tested high. Jadis tested high too. But she didn't want to be in a class with seventh graders. Too much pressure from the teachers. She'd rather get an A in an easy class and breeze through.

But then Rory and I started studying together, and Jadis hated that. Hated Rory. Every day it was something else, this assault on Rory Green. *Rory Green smells like tuna fish. Rory Green doesn't wear a bra. Rory Green is a know-it-all. Rory Green has yellow teeth.* She infiltrated my mind with so much negativity about Rory Green that I started to look at her that way. Why did Rory have to eat a tuna fish sandwich every day for lunch? Did she not brush her teeth? Why did she think she was always right?

"Those seventh graders are all stuck up," Jadis said, all-knowingly.

So I told my mother I hated the teacher. That being in a seventh-grade class made me nervous, that I was having anxiety attacks. That I didn't want to be a spectacle. She spoke to the guidance counselor and had me moved me out of the class. And I stopped talking to Rory Green. Pretended she didn't exist. Ghosted her when she texted me and ignored her in the hallway.

I hear them talking about me now. Rory and Madeline. The two of them best friends. They probably study together. They probably sleep with their phones next to their pillows saying goodnight a million times.

"I heard they're looking at the surveillance tapes," Madeline whispers.

"Shh. She's going to hear you," Rory says.

It's so obvious that they want me to hear them. They're not trying at all to be quiet.

"Murderer," Madeline hisses.

I turn to them and point my finger. My broken face glaring. I'm scarier than I've ever been.

"I can hear both of you," I say crisply. "Shut up."

Rory's face looks disappointed. That she had once thought so much of me. And now look at who I am, caught up in all this madness.

My mother would love a girl like Rory Green. In the feminist club. Focusing on her grades. Making sure she saves the planet. Raising money for small villages in Guatemala. Doing a clothing drive for women's shelters.

They sneer at me and stand up. They're not the kind of girls who want to fight. They're just the kind of girls who want to passively talk behind your back until you break. But I'm not the kind of girl who breaks so easily.

Chloe sits down just as they walk away.

"Why are we meeting here like this?" she says. "Isn't it bad enough that we're being scrutinized by #crimetok or whatever they want to call themselves?"

"Where else would you like to meet? A dark alley?"

I remember what Emma said to me earlier in the week, how she finds it weird that we were in the bathroom together doing Molly. Jadis and the cheerleaders. That's how people see me now. As one of them.

"When you think about what happened to Chloe, what do you imagine?"

"I think about a lot of things," she says. "I think it's not fair that she died. That she had her whole life ahead of her."

I tell Chloe what Rory and Madeline said about the surveillance tapes. I leave out the part about how they called me a murderer.

"So what?" Chloe says. "We were hanging out in the bathroom together. That's what friends do. They can't point the finger at us for that."

"I feel like I'm going crazy," I say, and then finally spit it out. "Do you think it's my fault?" I want her to absolve me. I want her to make it go away.

"No, I don't think it's your fault," she says, shaking her head.

We sit quiet for a moment, and I almost say it, part of me is dying to say it, just to release it, *I think Jadis might have killed her.* But I swallow the words until they're buried deep. This is not something I can say to Chloe, no matter what I believe.

"The cops came to my house. They had questions for me about that night," she says, leaning in closer to me. "There was a woman detective who looked like Jennifer Lopez. It was like she was there because she was trying to trick me. She said she used to be a cheerleader. A top girl like me."

"What did you tell her?"

But she doesn't answer my question. She picks at a nail, fixating on it until she pulls it back, and I watch her, wondering if she'll peel the whole thing off, it looks so painful. Those long nails of hers. I wrap my hand around her wrist. "Chloe, stop. You're going to make it bleed."

I almost stun myself after I say it. Isn't that what we do when we're surrounded by the unknowns? We pick and pick at something until it bleeds? Until it unearths itself?

"We have to hold it together until the toxicology report

comes out," I say. "That's all. We have to just wait. If we can hold on until then—"

"I don't know if I can, Shade. I can't take all this lying. Everything just feels worse instead of feeling better," she says. "I can't even decipher what's a lie and what's not. What's the truth?"

"What does Chloe Schmidt say?"

"You know what Chloe Schmidt says," and she sighs deeply pulling her hair away from her face. "She wants to tell the cops that Jadis gave us the Molly."

I think about the bullshit texts that Chloe Schmidt has sent me. *The truth shall set you free.*

"So why doesn't she?" I say. "What's stopping her?"

"I don't know," she says, and exhales. "At first she said it was because she didn't want to get me in trouble. Now she just keeps threatening it. I'm almost ready for her to just do it."

This terrifies me. The idea of Chloe Schmidt going to the police and throwing Jadis to the wolves.

"Chloe, it was an accident," I say. "It had to have been an accident. A horrible accident."

I shift in my chair, uncomfortable. I sound too desperate. Like I'm trying to convince myself, and aren't I?

"There are stories like this all the time. That someone couldn't handle a drug because they had an underlying condition. An allergic reaction. A blood clot. Something."

I'm reaching. I can feel myself reaching for anything. For some answer that'll make this all better. Something that will make Jadis not guilty. Something that will make it so Jadis, the person I once called my best friend, is not a murderer.

But there's nothing there.

Tears run down my cheeks, my body curls over, and I hide my face in my sweatshirt.

"I just feel so terrible. I just feel so responsible," I say.

Chloe stands up from her chair, and the legs squeak through the cavernous room. Everyone stares. She pulls her arm around my shoulder and walks me out of the library.

I sink down against the cool cement wall.

"It's not your fault, Shade," she says. "You're a good person. I promise you."

"How do you know though? You've known me for all of a few months," I say. And I've known Jadis forever.

"What do you do when you thought you knew someone like the back of your hand?" I say, quietly sobbing. Trying so hard to hold it in. Feeling so bare even in this empty hallway. "What happens then?"

■ ■ ■

Chloe walks with me to practice, which kind of surprises me, but I take it. We get there early and do laps together. Feet stomping the track, my body hearing that *thud thud thud*, meditating on it until Jadis's voice bangs its way back into my head.

They're doing this to us. They're putting the wedge between us.

And I run faster, pounding the track hard so my thighs are hot, so I can hear my breath in my ears. I run until I numb out the pain.

Tomorrow is the first game back, and my practice is rough, but I don't stop until I have that double back handspring full. Coach hugs me at the end of practice, telling me that she's so proud, and I'm stiff from her touch. If I let myself settle even for a second, this whole hard facade will melt away. I'll dissolve into a puddle.

Chapter
28

AT HOME that night, in my bed with a blue KT Tape up my calves. My eyes closed because I can't scroll through Instagram anymore. I hear the bell and some murmuring. A minute later, my mom knocks on the door.

With her is a short woman with muscles popping under her tight athletic shirt. A gun on her hip. She introduces herself as Detective De Leon. The cop that went to Chloe Clarke's house. She makes it real chummy first, tells me she was a cheerleader, just like she told Chloe.

"What spot are you?"

"Flyer," I say.

"Ah, me too. But we called flyers 'top girl' on my squad. We were really competitive. I saw a couple of fights between cheerleaders in my day," she says with a chuckle.

I don't laugh.

Detective Cheerleader leans against my wall. She tells me she knows how cheerleaders stick together. That this accident with Chloe Orbach must have been terrible for us. She knows we're all so devastated.

"I met with two of her other friends," she says. "Both Chloes. Ms. Clarke and Ms. Schmidt. It can get really confusing being friends with so many people with the same name. When I was your age, I had a lot of friends named Jennifer. We'd call them by their last initial. Jennifer W. Jennifer J. Jennifer S." She pulls out a notepad. "So what do you call these girls?"

"Just Chloe," I say.

My eyes blinking from being nervous, my jaw tightening.

"I heard you were with Chloe Orbach that night. Can I ask some questions just to understand what happened? I promise it won't be long."

I nod again, lick my lips. She wants to get an idea about Chloe. If she was happy. If she showed signs of depression. If she'd want to harm herself.

"Chloe was never depressed," I say. "Not that I knew of."

"I heard you were close with her. Were you dancing with her that night when she collapsed?"

"Yeah, we were all dancing," I say. Like it's no big deal. Girls dancing together. What could possibly be suspicious about that?

"Were you taking anything that night, Shade? Maybe you let off some steam, all that work you put into cheer? I remember those days. I know how much pressure it can be. Maybe you guys did something? Maybe you were experimenting with something. Like an illegal substance?"

I glance over at my mom, who is leaning against my dresser. How worried she must be.

I'm trying to control my breath, wondering what Chloe Clarke really told Detective Cheerleader. If she already gave us away, and everything she told me at the library was a lie. Wouldn't the detective have called me down to the station and made me fess up if that was the case? Isn't this just a ploy to get me to talk?

"I don't do drugs," I say. My voice as straight as I can make it. "I'm a cheerleader. That's strictly against the rules."

"Okay, but sometimes even cheerleaders need to let go. Sometimes cheerleaders need to unwind," she says. "And look, if that's the case, we don't want to get anyone in trouble. We just want to know what happened to your friend."

I don't say any more. I have to talk to Jadis first. Because if they're talking to me now, they're going to talk to her next.

"Do you think she was well liked on the team? I mean, she was the captain, but did people like her?"

"Everyone loved her," I say. I hold back what I really want to say, which is that she fought with some people. That her own best friends had issues with her. That she was like any other girl and she could sweep you up in her manic energy, but that she was also complicated.

"Who else was with you that night at the dance? You said there were a bunch of you dancing. You, Ms. Schmidt, Ms. Clarke. Who else?"

My heart stops.

"My friend Jadis. Jadis Braff."

"And is Jadis on the cheerleading team?"

I laugh. "No, she's not."

"Why is that funny?"

"It's just that Jadis is anything but a cheerleader."

She nods. Pausing. Waiting for me to say something else. But maybe I've said too much.

"How did Ms. Braff become friends with Ms. Orbach?"

"Through me," I say, telling her the biggest lie of them all. "We were all friends. We all became friends." It hurts my mouth to smile, but I do. I give my best cheer grin.

Because that's what I've been training all this time for. To fake it.

When Detective Cheerleader leaves, my mom calls a lawyer friend of hers who says not to answer any more questions from any cops whatsoever.

■ ■ ■

I text Jadis frantically, and she doesn't get back to me for about an hour. The fallout of our new relationship is that now she makes me wait. I almost call her out on it, but for what? That night I walked away from her, I sealed that. Me.

I want to shake her, make her listen to me. *Oh, Jadis, if I could just convince you to tell the truth!* What would it take?

We meet at the bottom of the street. Our regular spot. But nothing about this place feels good now.

"Why does it matter, anyway? You're so worried about me

ghosting you and instead you should be focusing on why those bitches are trying to frame me. *Your* teammates."

I tell her that the detective came to my house. That's why.

Jadis nods like she expected that, like this is all part of the plan.

"I'm going to ask you this one more time, Jadis," I say, pleading with her, drawing out my words. "Did you give the crown to Chloe for a certain reason?"

"A certain reason? Of course I gave it to her for a *certain reason*, Shade. I gave her the crown because she was the queen. At least to you. To the girls on your team. You think if I handed her the joker or the king or, let's see, what if I handed her one with SpongeBob fucking SquarePants. You think she would have taken it?"

It's almost as if Jadis had a sense about Chloe that I somehow missed. That while I was trying to impress her, do everything she asked of me, Jadis had studied her.

"She needed to know that I wasn't the jealous best friend. That I was okay with all this. That I wasn't left behind, wondering all the time what happened to my life and why I lost it to someone like Chloe Orbach."

I notice her new tattoo on her left arm.

It's the words *Believe In Me*.

Chapter 29

"**WE'RE GONNA DO** this for Chloe!" Keke yells in that military voice of hers.

In the locker room, getting ready for our first game since Chloe died.

Chloe and Chloe going through cheer moves in the mirror. Lining up like twins, each movement in sync.

Sasha and Pri practicing their hand placements for the full up.

I smear glitter over my cheeks like a zombie, thinking about Detective Cheerleader and her questions. Chloe Orbach, everywhere I turn. Over my shoulder watching me, I can feel her, tucking my hair back, straightening my posture, locking eyes. Those glowing eyes.

Zoey, effervescent Zoey, bounces over, and I'm startled. "You can do this, girl," she says, bubbly. Zoey is big on pep talk. Everything is: *You got this.* Or *Girl, we're gonna rock it. You're on fire.* It makes me laugh, how earnest she is.

If she only knew how bad things were. How defective I am. Chloe Schmidt strolls down the aisle toward me.

"Wonder if the Green Goblin will be here today? Cheering on her best friend from the stands."

"Her hair is lavender now, so there's that," I say flatly.

"Oh, really? Maybe she's trying to disguise herself?" she says. "Wonder why?" She struts away.

Zoey wraps her hand in mine and gives me a tug. It's like she's grown half an inch since the beginning of the season.

"Ignore her. She likes to torment people," she says. "Do you know that when I see her in the hall, she sticks her tongue out at me?"

"Her tongue?"

"Yeah, like playground stuff. At first, I was really annoyed. You know, who do you think you are? But then I was like, that's some second-grade bullshit. Next time she did it, I laughed her off and she stopped. Now she just ignores me. Which is fine."

I don't even know what to make of this story. I can't imagine why Chloe Schmidt would stick out her tongue at Zoey, the most innocent freshman there ever was. I remember what Zoey said to me that day when we were working the mat. Plus, I hate that it makes her feel like she wasn't welcome. But maybe that's the point. Chloe Schmidt's a bully. She likes to intimidate people.

This is the kind of antic I'd tell Jadis about. She'd want to pummel Chloe Schmidt. Drag her through gravel, or at least threaten to, for the way she talked to me earlier. She'd want to walk behind her slowly and taunt her about bullying a freshman. It takes everything I have not to text her about it.

But I can't text her because she's not mine anymore. And it's empty. I feel stripped bare.

■ ■ ■

Before the game, I follow Chloe Schmidt over to the big mirror where she's glossing her lips. It's not my place to be Zoey's savior, but I want Schmidt to know I see her.

"What are you looking at?" Schmidt says.

"You," I say. "I see your little games."

She snorts at me. "Stalker," she says, and pushes past me.

■ ■ ■

When we take the field, there's a standing ovation, and I hate it. I hate that they're clapping for us as if we've accomplished something by just showing up. It makes me want to scream at them.

A girl is dead. There's no reason to clap.

So many more people here now than a usual game. And for what? To watch us crash into the ground? To watch us fall apart without Chloe? To see if we're still a team? To witness crying cheerleaders? To see if we can make it through the game without grieving for our dead friend?

I look through the stands for a glimpse of her. I see Dave

Sozo slide in with Trey and a few of his friends, and my heart stops for a second, thinking Jadis is with him. But she's not.

We line up on the field, and Keke and Gretchen take the captain's spot. They give us a *READY, SET*, and we all get in a huddle and scream her name on three.

"CHLO-E! CHLO-E! CHLO-E!"

We're so loud that it reverberates through the stadium, and I hear people clapping, and it all becomes a buzz when the music starts. Zoey and I get into position for our two back handspring fulls. She smiles at me, that sweet Zoey smile. Was I ever so wholesome?

With all my might, I run backward into it, my body on autopilot, and I'm flipping so hard in the air, propelling myself up and then into the twist and I'm flying, soaring.

Land—boom—flat on my feet. No wobble.

Clap into position, abs tight. For the full up scorpion.

Sasha behind me, Chloe Schmidt on my right, and Pri on my left. I dig into their shoulders and load in, my feet up in the air, then my right foot in Chloe Schmidt's hand, and there's a deep sigh of relief because she doesn't claw me this time. Pri counts *five, six, seven, eight*. They push me up on *one, two* and I start to spin.

Three, I'm all the way around, 360.

Four, I keep spinning to the front, but I'm off balance. I feel Sasha's hands grasping on to my ankles, but I'm falling through. There's no bottom. No one has my right foot.

The main base can't let go.

I fall right into Pri, slide through her, and I can see her fear, Sasha's hands grasping at my thighs, as I land face-first into the turf.

A minute later, trying to stand up, and I wobble, that salty taste, those fake soil particles in my mouth, as I spit them out into my hand and it's red. It's blood.

Fuzzy voices.

Pri crying telling me she's so sorry, so sorry, she doesn't know what went wrong.

Zoey repeating that it's going to be okay, that I'm fine, I'm fine.

Keke says she's going to pinch my nose to stop the blood. Her hand is shaking as she reaches in.

Sasha is on the other side, keeping me still. "You slipped right through my hands, Shade," she says, full of upset. And I see Coach running toward me.

All the noise just one big echo chamber, like when you're at the dentist and they're about to fill a cavity and they give you that laughing gas. All you hear is nothing and everything. Nothing and everything.

"Shade, can you see?" Coach says, kneeling in front of me.

"I fell on my face, Coach. There was nothing under me. No ground."

I look up and there's two EMTs next to her, I'm not sure where they came from, and then I remember they're at every football game, and every school event. Just like how they were at the homecoming dance.

I flash back to that night at the dance. Chloe Orbach and

Jadis and me holding hands, dancing. And I start to cry, all of the blood and all of the tears, all of it running down my face.

"They were holding hands at the dance," I'm saying to Coach. "We were having so much fun. So much fun, Coach."

She pulls me close into her chest, shushing me like a baby.

■ ■ ■

They walk me off the field, the blood finally stops, but the EMTs tell me it might be a slight concussion. They want to do a test off the field. Can I walk? I can walk. The football players clapping for me. The spectators who came to watch a cheerleader fall got exactly what they wanted. Everyone in the stands clapping.

I turn to look for Chloe Clarke, and she's far back, trailing us. She and Chloe Schmidt, separate.

I pull away from Keke, who's got her arm under me, and march toward Chloe Schmidt. My hands shaking.

"You purposely dropped me," I say to her.

"What are you talking about?" Chloe Schmidt says. "You weren't rock-solid. That's why you fell."

Chloe Clarke places her hand around my waist. "Shade, it's okay."

"She let go of my foot," I say to Chloe Clarke, gasping, wiping the snot and blood from my nose. "She wasn't supposed to let go. That's the whole stunt. That's the whole thing."

And I realize, it rushes to me, that I've been looking at everything sideways.

I close my eyes, and those white splatters are everywhere. When I open them Chloe Schmidt, that gloss smeared over her puckered lips, the way she contours those cheeks. Like a monster, all of it is so clear.

"My hand was firm around the base of your foot," she says to me, in her calmest voice, her low gaze locked on me. "I would never do that. You need a concussion check."

Coach is calling my name, walking toward me. And I think about the way Chloe Orbach used to look at me, all of that hope in her face. All of that trust.

I moan out in pain, the throbbing in my head starts up, the field, the players, the stands blurry. The adrenaline did its thing and now it's leaving me high and dry.

"I don't feel good," I say to Chloe Clarke, who's still got me. She holds on tighter, until Coach is next to me again, her arm under me. EMTs rushing in, asking me if I remember what happened. Making me track their finger.

I trusted Chloe Schmidt. Rambling thoughts. Surges of Chloe Schmidt's Instagram. I mistook her for someone else. I mistook her for a good girl. I mistook her for Chloe Orbach.

I trusted her not to let go of that foot. She was my floor. And she dropped me.

■ ■ ■

My mother is home with me, sitting by my bed. I've got a concussion. The doctor told my mother he'd seen too many cheerleading injuries in the emergency room these days. The way I described the fall, I could have broken my neck. He saw a cheerleader just last week fall fifteen feet, he said. A chipped neck vertebra.

I'm going to look beat-up like I've been in a fight. And haven't I been? My mother has one of those ice masks, and the doctor said that's the best thing. I can't go back to cheer for at least a week, but I'm shaken now in a way that I haven't felt since I don't know when. Thinking that I never should have done this to begin with. That I should never have joined this team. All my doubts, taking over.

■ ■ ■

On get-well-soon duty, the squad files in on Sunday. Except Chloe Schmidt.

Chloe Clarke tells me it's because she thinks I'm mad at her. That I blame her for falling.

"Flyers fall, Shade," Chloe says after everyone else leaves. She lingers in my room. Sitting at the edge of my bed and painting my nails gold and blue.

I replay it over and over.

My fall wasn't a fall. It was a drop.

That's not what Chloe Schmidt says, of course. But why would my mind play tricks on me like that? She let go of my foot. And that's one thing a base doesn't do. Let go.

30

BY WEDNESDAY, my face is still puffy, but the black and blue under my eyes has morphed into a golden beet color. The headaches, coming and going.

Jadis texts me a few times while I'm home, but they're so vague.

Heard you took a bad fall. Hope you're feeling better.

As if she's talking to a stranger. I want to text her that Chloe Schmidt dropped me. That she did it on purpose, that I know she did. And I type it out, but then I delete it. What would Jadis say anyway? She'd skip down the street, giddy, singing, *I told ya so.*

In my bed staring at the wall since I'm supposed to be limited on my phone, I can't pinpoint what the feeling is until it hits me. I'm lonely for Jadis.

My mother trolls the hallway, passing my bedroom door like a caged animal, waiting for me to recover.

"Are you sure you're going to be okay to go to school?"

"I'm fine," I tell her.

Zoey texts me like a little baby chick telling me that she misses me. That she can't wait for me to come back. Even though the doctor said I could look at a computer screen, it seems to make my headaches worse.

She says the freshman conspiracy theories are more fired up since my fall.

They say the team is cursed, she texts.

She says that someone talked about how I walked off the field with blood running down my face like a vampire.

They say the cheerleaders are terrifying.

I don't disagree.

■ ■ ■

I get into school late. My doctor's note is broad and will get me out of anything. I wait for Chloe Clarke by her locker, my head down, AirPods jammed in my ears, stares from people passing by me. Music drowns out meaningless hallway gossip, and I lift my eyes when I see her in front of me.

"Shade?" Chloe says. She stares at me like I have two heads. "You look horrible. Are you sure you should be back? Do you need to go to the nurse?"

But I cut her off. I don't need the nurse. I need her to be truthful with me.

The images of me sliding through Pri's arms and onto the turf are all tangled up with flashes of the homecoming dance, of Chloe Orbach, Jadis, and me pulsing under the disco ball.

I need answers about Chloe Schmidt.

"I have one question for you," I say, a deep worry in the pit of my stomach. "Did Chloe tell you what happened during the game?"

"We've been over this, Shade," she says. "Something went wrong with your foot, your placement. You didn't squeeze your legs together enough. Cheerleaders fall all the time."

"According to *her*."

"You have to stop thinking that Chloe is against you. She's got an issue with your friend Jadis—not you. And I don't have to explain to you why."

I pretend not to feel that shiver. I pretend her answer is enough. That I'm satisfied with her explanation. But so many excuses for one person, I wonder if Chloe Clarke even believes it herself.

■ ■ ■

My heart beating so hard, I go to Coach's office. It's not anything special. Just a small room right off the gym. She shares it with the volleyball coach. The field hockey coach and the girls' lacrosse coach share another office next door.

Boys' soccer has its own coach's office.

Football has its own coach's office.

You can say girls run the world all you want, but until I see a female coach with her own office, I don't believe it.

I lurk by the door. She's watching something on her computer, her hands clenched like she's practicing a routine. They stay in your head, routines. Those moves, stifling all your thoughts.

I knock lightly on the door and she smiles when she sees me, then that concerned look I'm familiar with. My swollen face. She waves me in.

"I thought you were coming back to school tomorrow?" she says, and tells me to take a seat.

"I got antsy at home. My mother's hovering over me. I'm not used to it." As long as I'm taking it slow, Coach says, motherly.

"I'm watching regionals from another squad down in Florida," she says. "As a team, we've come so far. I think we can really do some of these stunts. Once you've recovered, of course. Come see."

I scoot next to her and she pulls her dark hair behind her ears, straight as a pin. That perfect hair. Not one strand out of place. Her shoulders firm and dense. I'm so slight compared to her. I've worked my body so hard these past few months, but I don't know that I'll ever look as strong as her.

"I'm so excited for you to get back to your stunts, Shade. I have this great idea where you and Chloe can do a full up, then a scorpion double down. Maybe we get one of the boys from the gymnastics team to be a base. Get our pyramid solid, really show off what we have."

"Coach, I have to talk to you about something."

"You don't think you're ready? Because of that fall?" she says, her face sinking.

"No, I want to get back up there again," I say, and then a deep exhale. "Did you take video of the cheer that day? You know, our first game back? I want to see what I did wrong." I don't say the truth, that I want to see what Chloe Schmidt didn't do.

"Oh?" she says, surprised. "No, I haven't seen a video of it, but think it was just a matter of your legs being a little too far apart. Your ankles have to be sealed shut."

"Are you sure, Coach? Like, are you one hundred percent sure?" I say, my hands sweating. I rub them across my jeans.

"Well, that's what Chloe Schmidt told me. She was right under you. So she would know."

"Because you asked her to walk you through it? You asked her exactly what happened?"

Coach lingers on that question. Then her hand to her chin, thinking.

"I'm not sure how it came up, now that you mention it. We were talking about what happened, we were going over the stunt, and Chloe mentioned it. That your legs weren't tight enough, that your ankles weren't locked, that you didn't feel secure," she says.

Coach thinks Zoey's mother filmed it on her phone. She doesn't know if it's too far away for us to really see each step of it, but she'll ask.

I know she's not going to want to go down this road with me. Coach's job isn't to suspect anything. Coach's job is to put all of her faith in her girls.

I thank her. Assure her that I'll be back at practice next week as soon as the doctor gives the go-ahead.

"There are strong girls on this team. Big personalities. I know Chloe Orbach was one of those people. And I know how close the two of you got in such a short period of time," she says. "You've come such a long way, Shade. You've done so much since you've been on this team. You've added so much to who we are. I hope you know that."

Coach, our mama bear, gushing. Wanting to believe the best in us.

"Thanks, Coach."

"Just remember that you came on this team only having done gymnastics for a few years when you were eleven or twelve. Girls like Chloe Clarke, Chloe Orbach, and Chloe Schmidt, these girls have been going to cheer camps and conditioning practices for years. They know exact holds and positions. They know the technicalities. Tumbling. And even with all of that, mistakes can happen."

"I know, Coach," I say. "I know."

■　■　■

Right away, I text Pri to find out what class she's in. History on the upper level. I tell her to get a pass and meet me in the hallway, but when I run up there, she's still at her desk. I have to wave to get her attention, and she politely asks for the pass and slinks out.

"We're doing test prep, Shade, I can't be out here," she says.

"Listen to me," I say, out of breath. "Do you remember exactly how I fell?"

"How you fell at the game?"

"Yes, technically. What happened? What went wrong?"

"Honestly, Shade," she says, kind of mumbling. "I would never want to put the blame on anyone."

Of course not, I tell her. *Of course* we won't do that.

Let it out, I want to scream.

"We went over it with Coach. Because Chloe Schmidt was going on and on about how she saw your legs spread apart and wanted me to back her up on that detail, but I didn't see anything like that. I was looking right at your body because I have to let go of you for that split second while you spin. I know you're not a base, and I know being a flyer is terrifying. But so is basing, trust me. You're responsible for so much. You have to understand in that stunt, my job is to attack your ankle and cup your left foot."

She starts to tear up, wiping the wetness away from those long black lashes.

"Oh, Pri."

"I remember thinking that your body looked so tight. It was clear you were going to hit it. But then the next thing I knew, you lost your footing on your right side and I couldn't catch you." She lowers her head, sniffling. "I'm so sorry I couldn't catch you, Shade. I've been dreaming about you falling for the past three nights." Her head collapses in her hands, and she lets out a sob.

I stroke her soft hair, her head on my shoulder, and stare down the long empty hallway. It was so clear: Something happened at the game. I haven't been imagining it.

"It's not your fault, Pri," I say, hugging her. The back of my throat tightening. "It's not your fault at all."

Chapter 31

I RUN OUT of school and start to walk home through the light snow. The wet flakes on my face, meshing with my tears. I grunt as I walk, holding in all that pain, my head pounding now.

An older man with jeans and suspenders salts his front walk.

"Shouldn't someone your age be in school?" he says.

I keep trudging along, and he mutters something about kids these days.

I'm at my front door, and the key is jammed in the handle. The snow gets heavier, and I kick at the door.

My heart's beating so hard that it feels like it's going to thump out of my chest. I'm remembering the way Chloe Orbach tormented Chloe Schmidt in her Jeep that day after practice. When she blabbed about how Chloe Schmidt got liposuction and lied to her followers. That was a stab of betrayal, wasn't it? Not only did she bring it up—but she did it in front of me.

Then Chloe Schmidt branded me as an *interloper* at the homecoming game.

If you're Chloe Schmidt, you'd want revenge. You'd want to hit back.

Chloe Schmidt hated me. I don't need video of the game to know what she did. I can picture the whole thing blazing through my mind. Falling with no ground under me. Crashing into Priyanka because Chloe Schmidt didn't have my foot. I remember it clearly, don't I?

Her hand wasn't there.

What did the doctor say after I described the fall? I could have broken my neck.

If Chloe Schmidt could do that to me so recklessly, what else could she do? All those tears for Chloe Orbach, she even camped out in Chloe's bedroom. *My best friend*, she cried. *My best friend.* Could it all have been a show?

All this time I kept thinking it was Jadis who did something to Chloe Orbach. I accused her of it. But what if it wasn't?

I sink down to my knees. I can't stop the tears from pouring out. I hold my arm over my face and scream. My muffled cries.

My mother flings open the door. "What is it, Shade? What happened? Why are you home?" My hair is all wet from the snow, my nose full of snot. I can't stop crying. I can't stop crying. I can't even get the words out because I don't have any words.

What would the words be? That I had it all wrong? That I thought maybe for a minute that Jadis killed Chloe Orbach? How could I have even thought that about her?

My mom peels my hair from my wet face, holding me tightly and rocking me.

■ ■ ■

Thirty minutes later, I'm in bed, calmer because my mom gave me half an Ativan. Pills are my mother's answer to everything.

My body shakes as she rubs my back, but slowly, carefully, my mind is untangling. The Ativan doing its job. It's not like a sleeping pill where it knocks you out. It makes you drowsy, but mostly, it makes you not care. Someone could come in and take you in a white van and lock you up in a cellar and you'd say, *Uh-huh.*

Or if someone suggested that your best friend tried to kill the captain of the cheerleading team, you might shrug. I can see why people get addicted to this stuff, because you don't feel.

I start to fade out, my eyes shutting, then I hear my mother calling me.

"Shade?" my mother says, still sitting there on the side of my bed like she used to when I was little. "Where did you get this awful mat? It smells like feet."

■ ■ ■

Numb, but awake, a buzz comes through my phone about an hour later. It's an alert for Chloe Orbach. I had set it to pop up multiple times a day, but most of them are nothing. They're all Chloe Schmidt being quoted, saying how she misses her best friend. How detectives are working on the investigations. Montages of Chloe Orbach and how her life was taken too soon.

This one is different. My neck and chest tightening up as I read it.

> Chloe Orbach, the Groveton cheerleader who died last month at the homecoming dance, had Xanax, MDMA, also known as "Molly," and fentanyl in her system, according to a toxicology report released by the Passaic County Medical Examiner's office. In a statement provided, Ms. Orbach's family said they plan to investigate how Ms. Orbach obtained the drugs that led to her death.

Xanax, MDMA, and fentanyl.

My whole belly, acidic, stabbing pains through my ribs. I look out my window, focus on something concrete, the gray sky. The bare trees like skeletons.

I go right to Instagram. Because that's where Chloe Schmidt shares her most intimate secrets.

I swipe past the reels of her and her personal chef, the two of them in her massive kitchen, the kind of kitchen that I'm sure Chloe Orbach would have wanted. The one that any one of us would want. Chloe's mother and her newly tightened face strolling in and out, tasting her daughter's creations. Kissing her daughter and leaving. Just the whole thing perfectly adorable.

No update yet about the toxicology report.

And then I see that she has a new story. It was posted seconds ago.

In big white letters against a fuchsia background: *If anyone thinks they're better than me or thinks they can break me and Chloe apart, I have news for you: You can't.*

Break them apart *how*?

Chloe Schmidt, my god, what are you thinking?

Then another story appears, connected to the first. Just a picture of Chloe Clarke and Chloe Schmidt with their arms around each other, two all-American girls, cheerleaders, best friends forever and ever. Except the picture had been cut on one side; someone else's arm and head had been there. The wisps of blonde hair make it obvious who it was.

She cut Chloe Orbach out of the picture.

Just cut her out like she didn't even exist.

I take my finger off the screen and try to go back to the first slide to take a screenshot, but then the whole thing is gone.

Just like that. Poof.

■ ■ ■

I sneak out of my house, because my mother keeps wanting to tend to me. She's certainly had enough practice from all her unstable friends. I don't want her to know I'm gone.

Down at the bottom of my block, that spot where Jadis and I meet. I run into the field, throwing my hands down into the frozen ground, that light dust of snow and sharp meadow grass pressing into my palms. I do it again and again, tossing my body backward. I'm dizzy and I know I shouldn't be doing this. Staggering across the field. I should pay attention to an injury, not ignore it, not tumble on rock-solid earth without a spotter. Blame the Ativan. My mind's detached, but my body wants to ride hard.

Feed your focus, Coach always says, but what if you don't know what your focus is?

Go. I clap, shiver, squeezing my palms together. Double back handspring, down on the ground, and I rise up again. Smoky breath whisking from my mouth. Step back, inhale. Soar straight up in the air like a fucking bird with wings and twist my hips, knee across my body, flip over and land on my feet. I stumble, but I don't fall.

I scroll through my contacts in the dark. Who do I call, who do I call? I hit Chloe Clarke's number. It can't be text, I need words from her. I know she won't answer, but I dial again and again, piling up all of those missed calls. *Don't ignore me, Chloe. Don't you dare.*

Trudge back up my street, and my phone buzzes in the quiet night.

"Chloe?" I say, breathless, standing still.

"It's not a good look for you, being a stalker."

"Did you see the tox report? Did you see what else was in her system? Xanax and fentanyl," I say, a car whizzing by. My fingers freezing, holding my phone tight against my ear.

"Where are you? Sounds like you're on a road. Aren't you supposed to be home resting?"

"When did she take the Xanax, Chloe?"

I hear her mumbling something to her mom, that she's not hungry. *I'll eat later, Mom. I love you too. Yes, I promise, every-thing's fine*, I hear her say. This dangerous game of pretend that we've been playing. First trickling in, then swooping its wings around us.

"You don't understand, Shade. Chloe Schmidt's mother has a pharmacy in her bathroom. And so we were at Chloe Schmidt's house before the dance," she says softly. "We all took a little Xan, just to take the edge off. Chloe and Chloe were fighting, and it was my idea. It was a bottle right there on her mother's vanity, so I opened it up and split it up into quarters. Anyway, I thought it would relax us for a minute. All that meanness, I couldn't take it anymore."

This is the first I'm hearing about Xanax, even though I asked her multiple times if Chloe took anything before the dance.

"A quarter of a tab of Xanax isn't going to kill someone," I say to her.

"You don't know that," she says, shaky. "Together with the Molly. You don't know that."

"Okay, so let me get this straight. You think *you* killed her?" I say this in disbelief. Like she can't be serious.

"Read the toxicology report, Shade! That's one of the rea-sons we didn't want to go to the police. Because of the Xanax."

Back at the library that day, Miss Perfect Cheerleader swore up and down she left the gym after Chloe Orbach col-lapsed because she was saving face, because a cheerleader and an honor student would *never ever do* Molly.

Now she's telling me it's because of the Xanax.

"That's why Schmidt's been covering for me. She's been protecting me since it was my idea to steal the Xanax. Because I feel responsible for rummaging through her mom's stuff."

Chloe Schmidt, my oh-so-loyal base who was supposed to keep me from crashing into the turf? She's been *protecting* Chloe Clarke?

"Because we would do anything for each other," Clarke says. "Anything."

I think about what Chloe Schmidt wrote on her Instagram today. *If anyone thinks they're better than me or thinks they can break me and Chloe apart, I have news for you: You can't.*

That was a message meant for me. She must have known, or had some idea, that Chloe Clarke was going to spill it about the Xanax. That she had too much guilt to hold it back any longer.

The post was a warning for me to back off. But to back off from what?

Would Chloe Schmidt's mother have fentanyl in her bathroom? It's possible. That day at the tracks, Chloe Orbach told me that Schmidt's mother recently had a face-lift. Between the face-lift and the liposuction, a "pharmacy," according to Chloe Clarke, I'm sure she's got enough pills to anesthetize a large animal. Rich people can always get their hands on strong drugs.

It makes me want to scream for doubting Jadis the way I did.

I know I can't convince Chloe of anything in this moment; her loyalty to Chloe Schmidt is too strong. You can't penetrate best friends like that. Not when they're in cover-up mode. The two of them, they've had practice constructing lies to teachers, coaches, boys, and parents for years.

Until I can put all this together, I need her to think that I'm coming from a compassionate place. Isn't that what my mom likes to say: *Find compassion, Shade.*

I do feel sorry for Chloe Clarke. All that posturing for so long. All that pressure will make you do stupid things. Like turn your back on the truth.

Part

III

Chapter

32

FOR EVERYTHING that I can't stand about my mother, for all of her trips and her opinions and her friends floating in and out, she gives people chances and understands people. I know she feels that sometimes you have to look deep into what people are capable of.

I need my mother to tell me that Jadis has nothing to do with this.

She'll set me straight about Jadis. She'll tell me that our friendship hit a bump. That Jadis has her own long list of problems that has nothing to do with me, that has nothing to do with Chloe Orbach's death. Nothing at all.

■ ■ ■

I don't expect to see her doing her fish face in her bathroom mirror, dabbing blush on her round cheeks. Next to her, my hair so similar to hers, my cheekbones and my eye shape. I don't usually see the similarity, but I can't look away from it tonight. Even with my face flushed from the cold, with my mind wild.

"You're going out?" I say.

She glances at me funny. "Sienna called me last-minute. She has a ticket to that jazz club in Newark. I wasn't going to leave you, but I went in your room and you weren't there," she says.

"I needed some fresh air," I say. "You could have texted me if you wanted me to come home."

"You could have told me you were going," she says, sounding hurt. "I didn't want to seem like a nag."

"I wouldn't mind if you sounded like a nag once in a while. You'd sound like a mom."

She kisses my forehead, then turns to the mirror, doing the fish face and prune lips. I sidle up next to her and make the same fish face. It's become a joke between us, and anyone who knows her.

I need to get to the point before it's time for her to leave. I can see her being antsy already. Another swipe of the blush, another pass of mascara.

"I'm glad you're feeling better," she says. She must read my need to talk, because she leans against the sink. "So what's up?"

"Does something have to be *up* for me to come in here and talk to you?"

"Usually, you only come to talk to me because I've done something wrong. Usually, you're not talking to me at all."

"I'm sorry, Mom. I'm sorry that I've been taking it out on you."

"Oh?" she says. "I didn't expect you to say that."

"I've been going through some things. Things between me and Jadis have been . . . hard."

"I figured it had gotten complicated once you started cheer." She sprays a frizz tamer in her hair and scrunches. Fish face. Scrunch. Fish face. Scrunch.

"Mom, do you think Jadis is a good friend?"

"Jadis?" she says. "Jadis is very loyal."

"That doesn't answer my question."

"Well, this isn't a secret. But Jadis has a lot of problems. She comes from a family of neglect. And when someone has too many problems, it's not easy for them to be a good friend because they're only worried about surviving," she says. "And I love Jadis. She's spent so much time here. She came with us on that Jersey Shore vacation. When your grandmother was alive, you brought her to Florida. She's seen it all. But she's been different this past year. She's been distant."

"Distant? Because I joined cheer?"

"There's that. But for a while now, it seems like there's something else that's on her mind. That she's not present."

My mother sprays her wrist with a musky cologne, then washes it off. Itching her nose from the smell.

"You're with her all the time. You don't see this? I mean, you girls draw those tattoos up and down your body. And, Jesus, hopefully you're sterilizing those needles. I've never said anything because I know it wouldn't make a difference, but you can get diseases."

"Of course we're sterilizing the needles. It's a whole process, Mom. And they're not up and down my body. It's a few tattoos."

"One day you're going to ask me to take you to get them lasered off and it's going to hurt like hell. I'll remember this conversation then," she says, her voice rising, her anxiety, always the anxiety boiling up inside and releasing itself in a fury. "Do you think other mothers ignore when their daughters come home with a tattoo? Because I guarantee that they don't. I wish you would appreciate me."

"You're the one who always says to me that you want me to make my own decisions, even if they're not the decisions you agree with. So please, explain," I say.

She files the brushes back in the glass jar on her counter. The perfume smacking up against all of the other tiny bottles that she's collected. She must get so bored here, waiting for me to grow up so she can start her life and travel with her friends.

She closes her eyes. "Why did you come in here, Shade? What can I help you with?"

"I need to talk to you. Like, really need to talk to you."

So she sits on the toilet. Smooths out her silk skirt. Fixes her bangles so they lie flat on her wrist.

"Do you think Jadis would do something bad? Like, do you think she's capable of something?" I say.

"Capable of what?"

"Do you think she's capable of hurting someone?"

"She's a screwed-up girl, Shade. Her mother is in and out

of the country, and before that, she was in rehab. Her father left her for that younger woman. She only has that brother of hers. And you. You're all she has. So do I think she's capable of hurting someone?"

She stands up and stares into the mirror again like there's going to be an answer for her there. I can't read her hesitation. She goes back to the routine. Fish face. Wipes off blush with a cotton ball. Dabs more blush on.

"Just say what you're going to say," I tell her.

"I wondered how she was going to tolerate you joining cheer, to be quite honest. How she would cope with that new friendship of yours. How you were always whispering on the phone to Chloe Orbach. Three can be a crowd."

"We weren't three though."

"Not to *you*, you weren't. But come on, Shade. You're a smart girl. I'm sure Jadis felt like she was sharing you, and I know she's not great at that," she says. "Most friends aren't."

My mother tells me how she used to worry when Jadis and I were younger. She reminds me how Jadis didn't like it when I had another friend over. She pouted and cried and carried on when she and I weren't in the same class together. And when we were in the same class, she wrote the teacher letters about why she should sit next to me.

"Don't you remember all that? It was the two of you constantly in your own world, mostly of her doing. You—I think you would have made other friends, opened yourself up a little if it wasn't for her. Jadis wanted to be so close to you that sometimes it scared me. Even her mother thought it was weird. She said something to me one day about Jadis being obsessed with you. For a little while I thought it was cute, but then I started wondering if it was healthy. She wanted so much ownership over you. And you didn't seem to mind."

I remember those times. And I remember liking it. You learn to rely on your friends when your parents aren't around. Jadis and I had so much to share. Dads off somewhere living some bohemian life. Self-absorbed moms with flaws like Band-Aids, out there in the open for everyone to see their barely patched-together lives. We fell into each other so easily. I remember a time when we first walked home from school together and I was at her house, the two of us on her bed.

I asked her when her father would be home because back then I was scared of dads. That's what happens when you don't have a father in the house, you hear the noise of a bellowing man and you want to hide. But she laughed when I asked her.

"There's no dad here for miles," she said like she was in a Western movie, and cracked a smile.

Jadis was mine and I was hers. If I felt lost, she'd find me. She was the person I could look through crowds of people for, and there she'd be, right there, staring back at me.

"Well, she was my best friend, Mom. It felt good." *Was*, I hear myself say. Was.

"I know. I know it feels good to be wanted that way. To be the object of someone's affection," she says. "But when you went to cheerleading, I was relieved. Do you know why? Because you seemed happy cheerleading. And it gave you a little space from Jadis."

"Wait, *what?*" Silence. This isn't something she's ever said or even alluded to.

"Cheerleading has been good for you," she says slowly. "It helped give you another focus. So you had something else in your life. Other people in your life. Something other than her. I love Jadis, I do. But it's been nice to see you smile."

"You know those smiles are fake, Mom," I say. "That's part of the routine. They force me to do that, so I practice it around the house. It's a show."

"Okay, then," she says. "If smiling is so painful, then why do you keep going back? Why have you worked so hard?"

Smiling is an exercise in willpower, a muscle I work, just like my triceps or my quads. All of it came together as part of putting myself on. Of making myself into someone I wasn't, this girl who could fly, who could smile on command. Who could throw her body into twists and flips. The discipline of it. It's all part of the uniform. The whole performance.

I don't tell her that I dream about it.

Her phone buzzes. It's her ride. "I can cancel, really, honey. Do you need me to stay home?"

"Do I need you to stay home?" I laugh, surprised.

"What's so funny? I've been taking care of you since you got your concussion, haven't I? I'd stay home if you wanted me to."

"I don't think you've ever asked me that question."

"Oh, I see. This is when you start telling me I'm the worst mother ever. Trust me, there are worse mothers. Just look them up on the internet. You'll find them."

She pops a mint, shoves a lipstick and the blush in a little beaded bag. "I thought we were really connecting. I thought you were finally going to forgive me for all of my wrongdoings, or at least what you *perceive* as my wrongdoings. No one ever said I was perfect, Shade."

I take her hand. Her soft hand. Her veins large and pulsing. Her skin so different from mine. Older.

"I didn't mean it like that. I'm sorry," I say. "Go ahead and do your thing. Catch your ride. I'm fine."

I'm not at all fine. I want her to stay, but I don't know how to ask her.

She holds my face with her hands. "You only need this," she says, and touches my head with her finger. "And this," and softly touches my heart with her other finger. "But mostly you have to open your eyes, Shade. You have to see that some of these girls, their motivations are different than yours."

"What's that mean?"

"It means that not everyone does the right thing. And sometimes people who have anger toward someone else, they use it in a dangerous way."

"Mom, you never answered me," I say. "Do you think Jadis is capable of hurting someone?"

"Only herself, honey. Only herself."

I drift into my bedroom and I stare at my tattoo that Jadis branded me with. Of the girl falling. The girl flying. She said it was me, but I don't know anymore. Maybe she drew herself.

33

THE NEXT DAY I search for Jadis in school, scanning above the heads in the hallway for her lavender hair. Checking our old spot by the first-floor bathroom, near the music room, outside the cafeteria before lunch. Instead I find Emma by the media center, staring into her phone like it's a deep ocean and she's trying to see to the bottom.

"She won't come to school," Emma says. "And I can't force her. She doesn't care if she fails out. They can't make her go. She's seventeen."

"Did she tell you why?" I say.

"Did she have to?" Emma says. "She's scared of those Chloes and she's freaked out by the toxicology report."

I feel bad that Emma's mixed up in this. Her face, so confused.

"You're supposed to be the person who knows her the best, Shade. I'm surprised you can't understand this," she says. "I'm surprised you don't know the effect your little fight had on her."

"She told you about it?"

"Of course she told me. I'm her girlfriend."

■ ■ ■

After school, I stand in front of Jadis's house until I can get the courage to ring the bell. Jadis is the only real answer to this puzzle. I have to know where she got the Molly. The thoughts that blare through my mind are terrifying, and I'm not sure how she'll react to me being here, especially after everything. She might not care what I have to say.

Maybe I shouldn't be at her front door. Maybe I don't deserve to be.

I ring the bell a few times, then start banging on the door. She opens it up, shocked to see me.

"What are you doing here?" she says slyly.

"I need to know what happened that night," I say. "I need to know where you got the Molly. And I want the truth. I need to know everything."

We sit in her bedroom like we used to when we were kids. On the floor, her shag rug, the door closed behind us. I can hear Eddie and his friends downstairs playing music. The strumming of the guitar, beating of drums, so heavy I can hardly think. Part of me feels like nothing has even changed. Like we're back to the same old thing.

But she looks like she hasn't eaten in days. The way she bends over, with that stomach, a deep cavity. The bags under her eyes. She lights up her vape, pressing it hard into her mouth, and exhales.

"Why do you have to know where I got it? Tell me that at least?" she says, so timid. More vulnerable than I've seen Jadis in so long.

How do I answer that question? *Because you're scaring me, Jadis. Because even I thought you might have killed Chloe. Because I want to clear your name.*

I tell her it's the only way to prove that what Chloe and Chloe say isn't true. It's the only way out of this. We have to go straight to the center. I tell her about the Xanax, how they took some before the dance. We have to wash ourselves clean.

"We lied to the police, Jadis," I say, pleading with her. "They came to my house. They're going to come to your house soon. How far can we possibly take this?"

She finally lets it out. That she got the Molly from Eddie's friend Sunshine. The woman that night at the pool. The night she gave me the cheerleader tattoo.

"The lady with the kid?" I say.

"Don't be so judgmental, Shade. Not everyone has perfect lives in the suburbs like we do."

"Since when do we have perfect lives?" I say.

"Someone always has it worse than you. Trust me," she says, her eyes looking away.

Jadis explains that Sunshine was a chemistry major at MIT. That she wanted to be like Walter White in *Breaking*

Bad and started making her own Molly, just selling enough to pay for college, but then she got rich off it, and then she got pregnant. That she still makes very small batches. She only sells it to people she knows so she can keep track of it.

"Is this real? Are you joking?" I say. "MIT?"

"Not a joke at all. She's sort of like an artist. Like a drug artist slash scientist or something."

If there really is a drug artist slash scientist or whatever behind this, then we have to talk to her. So we can take control of this. So we don't sink deeper.

I tighten my voice. "We have to talk to her, Jadis."

"No no no no," Jadis says, pacing around her room now. "This is a small-batch dealer. She can't be traced back to it this way. I can't sell her out like that."

"If she's so responsible, she's going to want to know that someone died!"

"What are we going to say to her? *Was there fentanyl in this crown?*"

"Yes," I say. "We have to find out if something happened to that batch."

"You have to promise me, Shade, that you're not going to turn her over to the cops. Promise."

I know what she's saying. I remember what Detective Cheerleader told me that day in my bedroom. That they don't want anyone like me to get in trouble. That they just want to get the bad guys. Someone like Sunshine.

Jadis holds out her pinkie to me, and I glance at it. Why would she want to protect this woman over herself? Jadis goes on and on about how Sunshine is a good mother, that she just wants to put food on the table. She wants to take care of her kid. That she wants to be in charge of her life. Jadis makes me promise to go there without malice. That we can't push her into a corner.

Is it because this woman is so dedicated to her child that she would throw away her prestigious degree to become a drug cooker and a dealer?

Suddenly I get it. That's all Jadis wants, someone to put her first like that too.

"She's a mom, Shade. Don't you understand?"

I give Jadis my word. We're just going to talk to her. That's all.

■ ■ ■

Sunshine's house is a small, pink bungalow with creamy shutters. There's toys in the front yard and a little red baby toy car. It doesn't look like a drug dealer's house, and I guess that's the point. Jadis knocks, and Sunshine answers the door in a big fluffy robe, her hair in a tight bun, waving us in but telling us to keep our voices down because the baby is sleeping.

Jadis and I sink into her blue velvet couch. "We have a sensitive situation," Jadis says. She doesn't want to insult Sunshine. She's not saying there's something wrong with Sunshine's product. Her product is super clean and we had a good time on it, she says. Except something happened.

Sunshine is listening intently, nodding along.

"A friend of ours," Jadis says, and I can feel her holding it back, "OD'd."

"Wait," she says. "Stop."

"That's why we're here," I say. "Because we just wanted to know if there was any connection."

She glares at me. Stares at me up and down. "Who the fuck is this?"

"This is my best friend, Shade."

I remind her that we met briefly at Jadis's pool. But she doesn't remember me.

"Your name is *Shade*?"

I nod. I think a woman with the name Sunshine will appreciate that my name is Shade. I smile a little. Maybe we'll talk about names and how Sunshine is the opposite of Shade. How maybe we're supposed to be in each other's lives. I stare at her, my mind wandering to all of these places and then she snaps at me, her face in mine, right close to my nose. And I flinch.

"Are you a fucking narc, Shade?"

"Me? No, I'm a cheerleader." It just comes out like that. So gullible, so simple. I grunt-laugh like it's the funniest thing I could possibly say.

Sunshine doesn't laugh. She tells us to lift up our shirts. "I wanna see if you're wearing wires."

Jadis stands up and grabs at my arm, then strips off her shirt. She's wearing her black-and-white polka-dot bra, the one that used to be mine.

"Take off your shirt, Shade," she says. So I take mine off

too. Sunshine wants pants off to make sure there's no wire on our legs. And now I'm scared because even if she doesn't find a wire, will she beat the crap out of us? Does she know someone who will? The sweat at the back of my neck, and my head feeling hot. This is what she does for a living. She may look sweet, like a hippie throwback. She may live in a pink house and have a child, but she has to protect her business. Jesus, we were so naive to come here.

"Why does this chick have what's left of two black eyes?" Sunshine says to Jadis.

"She's a cheerleader. Really. She wasn't kidding. They do stunts. And she fell the other day during a game."

She looks back and forth between us, deciding if she believes this story.

We dump out our bags and our pockets. It's clear that we aren't wearing wires. She tells us to shut our phones off. That we've put her in a weird situation, and she's very sorry to hear about our friend, but she can't let anyone mess with her life, not now, not ever, especially because she has a kid. Do we understand? She's firm.

When she finally realizes that we're not taping her, she starts pacing. And we just watch her, back and forth, dragging her feet across her red-and-orange shag rug.

"Look," she says a few minutes later, as we're putting our clothes back on. "I don't know what happened to your friend. But I can tell you right now that I have nothing to do with it."

"How do you know for sure?" Jadis says.

"How do I know for sure?" she says, defensive, her voice

with a violent twang. "Because I made the crowns for my sister's bachelorette party. I made fifteen of them. Twelve of her friends took them. I took one and she took one. I sold you the fifteenth one. They were made in one batch. Do you understand what I'm saying to you? Whatever happened to that girl had nothing to do with that Molly."

She explains to us how you would hear about a bad batch. The police would be on it. There'd be word on the street. More than one person would be dead. "Whatever happened to that girl is tragic. But it's not connected to my stuff."

I'm grateful that she talked to us. That she told us the origin of the batch. She goes in the back room to get her daughter, who is adorable and pink-cheeked from her nap. She snuggles in her mother's neck. And for a second I forget where I am. I stare at the baby—I almost want to offer to babysit.

Except that's not why we're here. We're here on business. Sunshine opens the front door for us. She doesn't smile.

"Don't ever come here again." The seriousness of her statement, the point of her stare.

"I understand," Jadis says, looking stunned.

"No, I don't think you do. If I ever see you again, even by accident—" and she cuts herself off. "We are not friends and I don't know you."

■ ■ ■

Jadis and I are outside, and there's a crystal hanging from the corner of the house. The porch light catches it, and it reflects a pinkish hue across the window. It reminds me of the home-coming dance, the night Chloe died.

"Was she threatening you back there?" I say as we hustle to Jadis's car.

"Yeah, she was threatening me."

We slam the car doors, both of us jumpy. I take a few deep breaths. The most important thing is not how this woman spent her time in college concocting recipes to make Molly. We went there for answers. To prove that Jadis had nothing to do with what happened to Chloe.

I think about what the toxicology report said: fentanyl. How did fentanyl get into Chloe Orbach's system?

At the dance, before we took the Molly, she didn't seem wasted at all. Relaxed? Sure. But not sick. Not on the verge of OD'ing.

She had to have taken the fentanyl at some point during the dance. The night projects like a movie in my mind. Chloe wearing an A-line skirt, short and glittery. She was bright like a star. Everyone in a good mood. The Three Chloes and Jadis and I go into the stall at the same time. Details tumbling around in my brain, just knocking against itself. Fentanyl's fast acting. I can't find a place for when the fentanyl made its way into Chloe's system.

"How do we trust this woman?" I say. "How do we know what she says is real?"

"We've been through this! You stood there in your bra and panties, and she told you that the crown tablet was clean. With her baby in the next room. What else do you want?"

"I just don't understand why you didn't tell me," I plead. "Why you brought the Molly to the homecoming dance in the first place."

"For *you*," she says, slamming her hand on the wheel now, mad at me for not seeing what is so clear to her. "Don't you see that? I did it for you."

She grabs my arm, the one with the pinkies intertwined, and holds it up to my face. "This—you think this was a joke to me?"

I wrestle my arm away. "You wanted this to go on longer than it did, didn't you? You could have told me about Sunshine. You could have at least settled this between us."

And I see it now, the reason she held it all back. Because she was testing me in some sick way. She wanted to see if I'd turn against her. She wanted to see how loyal I really was. There's a terror in her face, and she crumples into her seat.

"What you don't understand, my sweet little Shade, is that this all started with Chloe Orbach and that bow. You just *had* to give it to her, didn't you? You had to take the only thing that was ours. They saw how much she meant to you. And then they made me a pawn."

"Whose pawn?" I say.

"The other two Chloes," she says, and gives me exaggerated air quotes. "Her best friends."

The way she says *best friends*. Like it's an insult she can't take back.

34

SOCIETY TELLS US girls are supposed to be lighthearted. We're not supposed to want to get to the top so desperately. We're not supposed to aspire to be better than everyone else. We're supposed to yearn for everything to be fair. For everyone to play nice. For everyone to get their fair shot. This is supposed to come naturally to us, they say; or at least we're supposed to make it *look* natural.

Coach called us a single unit. An army. At first I wondered what she meant. Who were we fighting? And then it all made sense.

Our bodies are our weapons.

When we're pushing against the ground for a higher bounce or pressing our feet into a base's shoulders or rotating, our bodies a tight aerial miracle, we're fighting against everything that gravity wants from us, which is to stay grounded. Everything about it is unnatural. When you're a cheerleader—but really when you're a flyer, a tumbler, a gymnast, a fucking trapeze artist—you're fighting against yourself.

■ ■ ■

On Friday I show up before practice just to hang out in the locker room. I need to see Chloe Schmidt in her element. Maybe she'll get sloppy.

When I walk in, they're all gathered together squawking about something of biblical proportions.

Keke heard that the cops are going to interview all the cheerleaders one by one.

Chloe Clarke is stretching, her long leg up against the locker. "I already talked to the cops," she says in a deadened tone.

"Really? What did you tell them?" Keke says.

"I told them the truth. The truth shall set you free," she says, glaring at Chloe Schmidt.

Except Chloe Schmidt doesn't seem to hear her. She stares at herself in the mirror, smacking her lip-glossed lips and getting that stance just right.

I'm not sure what I'm seeing here between them. I can't connect it.

"Just tell them what you saw," Schmidt says to the younger girls. The Court of Chloe. "Tell them who you saw Chloe dancing with. Tell them if you saw anything strange," she says, sounding like a drugged-up kindergarten teacher, her voice dripping in sweetness. Coaching them.

"For instance, if you saw a person that night who you wouldn't normally see with her, maybe someone out of the ordinary, make sure you tell the cops about *that* person."

Look at her. Prompting them to point their finger at Jadis. I will wring her neck.

Chloe Clarke slams her locker shut and walks out, passing me on the way. "What are you standing here for?" she says to me.

"I'm watching the show," I say. "She's an incredible performer. A flat-out liar."

I lurk in the doorway listening until Zoey sees me and squeals. My little freshman bunny, Zoey. She hops over and hugs me.

"None of you knew her like I did," Chloe Schmidt says, pulling the old *Chloe Orbach was my best friend* card trick. She sees me now, from across the room. She looks into the mirror and tightens her hair in a severe ponytail, perfectly slick. Not one hair out of place.

■ ■ ■

When everyone heads onto the field, I sneak into the bathroom to call Jadis and have her pick me up.

But I hear Zoey's little voice. "Shade, can I talk to you?" Zoey says.

She steps over to me, grimacing. She has something to tell me that she's scared to say in front of everyone else. She leans against one of the sinks and grips the edge.

She tells me that she made a collage of Chloe Orbach for both of the Chloes. She gave it to them while I was recovering. It was a cute collage of Chloe Orbach with pictures she took at practice, pictures online, pictures Zoey took with her instant camera.

"Remember that day when we were at Chloe Orbach's house and she had all of those Chloé magazine pictures? I just thought maybe her best friends would want something like that," she says. "I'm just trying to make them feel better. That's sort of what I do. It's a thing I'm working on with my therapist. Not being such a people pleaser."

That day at Chloe Orbach's house. How can I forget the torn-out magazine pictures, every single one with the word Chloé stamped across it? I shiver thinking about it, like it's something I had buried and now it's coming up through my mind, those words floating like clouds, CHLOÉ CHLOÉ CHLOÉ.

"And did they like it?"

"They were so floored. They loved it. Chloe Clarke cried, and I know she's so devastated," Zoey says. "But Chloe Schmidt. Wow. Something in her got turned on. Or turned up. She was oohing and squealing. It was the first time she was nice to me, even acknowledged me. It made me happy, you know?"

"It sounds nice," I say, but truthfully, it makes me cringe because I can tell it's a setup. She's about to break the story in two. She wouldn't have prefaced it with a promise of secrecy otherwise.

"You would think so, right?" Zoey says, shaky. "But then I went to the bathroom and Chloe Schmidt is sitting there on the locker room floor with the collage that I made in her lap, yanking pictures of Chloe, *as in Chloe Orbach*, off the page. I was shocked, of course, because, Jesus?"

"Did you say something?" My chest filling up with dread.

"I didn't know what to say. What could I say? I think she thought I left. She was in a daze, like as if she was alone, not in a locker room. I don't think anyone saw her but me, but it was so weird. Her just carefully, so hellishly ripping Chloe Orbach's face off."

I shudder thinking of Chloe on the floor that night at the homecoming dance. Chloe Schmidt's screeching voice. Chloe Clarke's blank stare.

"So I just watched her until she turned around and locked eyes with me. Then she said, 'I can't bear to look at pictures of Chloe right now.' And then she picked up her cheer bag, shoved the collage in it with all the scraps of pictures, and left."

All those pictures in Chloe's room. She wanted to be that girl in the magazines. And there was a part of her who thought she was that girl. It wasn't the way they looked, it was the life they had. So elegant and free.

"Shade, I didn't know what to do. I figured she'd text me or say something to me at practice, but nothing. And the two of them, they just keep standing there like we're against them or something."

"Against me and you?" I say.

"No. All of us."

■ ■ ■

Jadis is outside waiting for me. I tell her there's something I've been hiding and I'm not sure why.

"What is it?" she says, confused.

"It's about Chloe Schmidt."

"That psycho bitch? What detail could you possibly have left out about her?"

And I think about that. Really think about it. I don't care about Chloe Schmidt. I don't know why I didn't mention it to Jadis.

"She dropped me on purpose."

All that anger wells up inside me. Because it's been right there all along, and I've been too distracted by this bullshit idea that we were one army. That's why I didn't mention it.

But I think about what Zoey told me just thirty minutes ago. That they're against all of us. At least that's what Chloe Schmidt thought. That anyone who came into their circle was an outsider. That anyone who came into her circle already threatened her fragile relationship with Chloe.

She point-blank instructed the squad to tell the police if they saw Chloe Orbach dancing with someone who looked "out of the ordinary." She might as well have handed them a script: *Tell the cops you saw Chloe Orbach dancing with a girl with green hair and a black suit.*

She delivered Jadis to them on a platter.

Jadis's face brightens. A lightbulb inside goes off. She scrambles for her phone, swiping away at old texts until she finds what she's looking for.

She clicks on a video and turns it to face me.

It's us. The squad. The first game after Chloe Orbach's death. The day I fell.

"How? How did you get this?" I say, astounded.

It was passed on to her by her loyal, Sylvia Plath–loving, all-state wrestling champ of a friend, Dave Sozo.

Jadis told him how she felt uncomfortable going to that game. She didn't delve into details, but Sozo understood. He had her back and filmed our routine just for her. He got it all on camera. All of it.

"He said he knew I'd want to see it since I hadn't missed a game."

She and I huddle over the phone and pause just before my fall. Up I go. Pause. Spin all the way around.

"Pause," I say, breathless. "Zoom in."

"All I see are six hands," she says. "No one is going to be able to make sense of this."

■ ■ ■

Back at my house, we upload it to my computer and go over it step by step. I show her a video online, how the first base has her hand on the flyer's foot the whole time.

I zoom all the way in on Chloe Schmidt's hand, which should be cupped under my foot. It's fuzzy, but clear enough to see.

It's just not there.

As I fall, she doesn't even try to catch me. Her right arm lifeless, dragging. I topple down and crash into the ground.

"I could understand why she'd hate me," I say.

"Yeah, but why would she do something to Chloe Orbach?" Jadis says. "Why would she want to hurt her best friend?"

"Except they weren't best friends anymore," I say. "Chloe Orbach herself told me she felt like she and Schmidt were in an 'abusive' relationship. That they needed couples therapy. Those are the words she used. That they needed to break up."

"Well, that changes things," Jadis deadpans, and if I had to read the look on her face, it would say, *That could've been us.* "So Chloe Orbach was already separating from her at the beginning of the season, and you came into the picture like a perfect storm. The new flyer, the girl who gave Chloe Orbach a bow tattoo."

"It was more than that," I say. "Chloe Schmidt got lipo between her thighs, which is a big no-no in the body confidence Instagram world."

"So? Who cares."

"Well, Chloe Orbach brought it up . . . in front of me."

"Ohhhh," Jadis says. "So she gave Chloe Orbach fentanyl . . . How did she get the fentanyl? And how would she have gotten Chloe Orbach to take it at the dance?"

"Her mother has a bathroom full of pills," I say. "Access to anything."

We sit in silence digesting all of this, our cheerleading murder theory.

"Look what those bitches did to us," Jadis says.

Not just us. I think back to that day in the hallway with Chloe Orbach when I first wore my cheer uniform to school.

She and I were strolling, our hair intertwined, me wanting to be in a tough-girl gang with her.

"I don't think Chloe Clarke knew anything about it," I say. "I know she didn't. She wouldn't have admitted the thing about the Xanax otherwise."

But this doesn't matter to Jadis. They're all the same to her. One monster. Three heads.

"They did everything they could to break us apart, Chloe Orbach when she was alive and those two other Chloes after she died. And now look. They succeeded. You did nothing to stop it," she says. "And I'll tell you why, because this is what *you* wanted all along. I don't think someone could do this unless there was an opening for it. And you, my friend, *you* opened up the door."

"Because I signed up for cheer?"

"Ironically enough, cheer has nothing to do with it."

But didn't cheer have everything to do with it?

35

MY ALARM GOES off at six in the morning. My body sweating under my heavy blankets, Jadis curled up on the edge of the bed. Her lavender hair spilling across the pillow. I shake her lightly, then look out the window at the orange sun popping up through the trees. In the bathroom, I brush my teeth and hand the toothbrush to her. I swipe deodorant, and then she swipes. She rifles through my clothes to find something to wear. She sees my folded cheer sweater in the top drawer, pulls it out to inspect it, then shoves it back in.

We're coming over right now, I text Chloe Clarke.

Who's we?

Chloe Clarke comes right to the door when I text her. Hair messy, still in her pajamas. "What are you doing here?"

They were like this, Chloe and Chloe, that first day at cheer sign-ups, how one Chloe draped herself over another Chloe. It reminded me of me and Jadis, forever intertwined, unable to stop touching each other, feeding off of each other's energy.

"Why did you walk out of the locker room so quickly yesterday?" I say.

"I can't take it anymore, that's why. Because when something is rotten, you have to walk away from it," she says. "Is that why you're here? Because you want to tell me that I'm a terrible person. That I contributed to killing my best friend?"

I want to tell her everything about the fall, how I have a video of Chloe Schmidt letting go of my foot. Of the headless collage Zoey told me about. First I have to clear Jadis.

"Jadis didn't do it, Chloe," I say to her. "There wasn't any fentanyl in that Molly."

There's this long stare between us like she's trying to see through me, deep within me and what I'm trying to tell her.

"You have so much hope, Shade. You're such a good person, aren't you?" she says, and I think she's being earnest. "You're really good, you know that? You really see the good in people."

"What the fuck does that mean?" Jadis says, cutting her off. "Do you understand why we're here?"

I tell her it's time to go to the police. It's time we tell the truth. We have nothing to hide.

"It wasn't the Xanax," I say to her.

"I know," she says, her lips quivering.

"Oh my god, what do you know?" Jadis says.

"What happened that night at the dance, Chloe? I'm begging you."

"She made it so hard for me, always in the middle of the two of them like that. Constantly having to pick a side. Do you know how many nights I had to listen to Chloe Schmidt cry over her? How wounded she was? Chloe first putting her on a pedestal, then icing her out for days."

If Chloe lived long enough, would she have done that to me too? Would it have been inevitable? I can't help but think it.

"Did you see her do something?"

"I saw her shaking that Vitaminwater up a little too hard and maybe I saw her slip something in there. I don't know, Shade. I kept telling myself that I was seeing things. But the more time went on, I kept asking myself how this could be possible?" she says, her eyes wide, unblinking, her voice in tatters, barely able to get it out.

"When it was just the three of us, Chloe Schmidt used to make these threats in passing. Like, *I'm gonna spike that bitch with Xanax*. She said it so many times that it became her go-to insult. So I didn't take it seriously. There was so much drama between them. You say things like that sometimes. Like *I hate her*. Or *I never want to talk to her again*. Don't you?"

I nod my head. I knew it to be true, to never want to talk to your best friend again. To threaten something like that.

Jadis and I glance at each other. Jadis looks away first.

"Chloe Schmidt had a sweet craving because she had been on such a strict diet—no sugar allowed. So I wondered about it because, you know, Vitaminwater is full of sugar. But I let it go because it was a weird night. Homecoming. All of that attention and applause. The adrenaline still racing. And then on top of it, the Molly. That was the biggest surprise," she says. "She dumped fentanyl powder in the Vitaminwater. Just a little bit of powder, enough to knock her out. Not to kill her, she swore to me. Never to kill her."

It was that moment after we took the Molly, when they skipped off. *Whatever Chloe wants, Chloe gets*, Chloe Schmidt sang.

"How long did you know about this?"

"Last night," she says. "She told me the details late last night."

Chloe turns to look at Jadis. "When you gave us all the Molly, that's when she knew her plan would work."

All this time, Chloe Schmidt was trying to get me to believe that Jadis had something to do with it. I doubted my own best friend, questioned all of Jadis's motives. Everything that Jadis did, every move she made, fueled more doubt.

And I bought it.

The manipulation of it all. Those times that Chloe Schmidt cried about losing her best friend. The way Chloe's mother told me that Chloe Schmidt was spending so much time at her house, that she just wanted to be closer to Chloe, her scent, her memories. And then those girls in school, whispering that I was a murderer. How she tried to shake my confidence, how she let me fall to the turf. Me, six feet up in the air, spinning in a full circle, and she lets go. It takes my breath away.

"She told me she didn't want to kill her—just wanted to make her tumble a little so she could pick her back up again. She wanted to humiliate her the way she had been humiliated."

Except you don't make someone *tumble* with fentanyl. You crush them.

I think about the way Chloe Schmidt strutted into that funeral with that little black dress, the way she bossed everyone around at practice, the way she went after me. The way she went after Jadis.

I can hear her Jeep raging down the dead street. I know it's her Jeep. I know it.

"You texted her that we were here?" I say.

"She's my best friend," Chloe says, blankly. "What was I supposed to do?"

Chloe Schmidt races past the recycling bins until she stops short in front of Chloe's driveway. Slams her Jeep door and marches over like she's going to knock us down, just barrel right into us.

I have as much adrenaline as she has, and I meet her at the street and shove her back, my flat palms against her broad shoulders.

"I saw a video of our routine," I shout at her wildly, my voice deep and ragged. "I saw you let go of my foot. What do you think Coach will say when I show it to her?" I feel everything stiffening in my body. As if what she did to me was the worst of it.

In a low voice it comes to me. "What did you do to Chloe Orbach?"

"What did *I* do to her? What did I do that she hadn't already done to me?" she says, struggling to get away from me, but I have a lock hold on her forearm. Her voice lower and shaky, like she's transported somewhere else.

"Do you know when I got my Jeep, the first place I went was to Chloe Orbach's house. It was so warm, a perfect night to be outside and ride around with the top down. That shitty little house of hers on the hill. My Jeep was like a goddamn carriage coming to save her. I walked up the crumbling staircase. The bottom of the front door covered in mold. She said her mother had to fire the housekeeper because they couldn't afford her anymore. There was never a housekeeper to begin with."

Her mouth grimacing, shaking.

"The first thing she said? *Give me the keys, bitch.* Of course I was like, *You're not driving my Jeep, Chloe. Are you insane?* Oh, but you know Chloe Orbach. She pissed all over everything, like a territorial wolf. *Aren't best friends supposed to share everything?* she said. Wasn't everything that was mine hers? Did it have to be the Jeep too? I bought that Jeep with the money my father left me before he died. And she *knew* that. Wasn't it enough that I had given her that lapis heart and diamond necklace from that jewelry influencer on Instagram? Wasn't it enough that she came to all of my cooking classes? That I gave her half the Lululemon leggings my mother bought for me? That she spent all of middle school living in my house? Nothing was enough."

The heart-shaped necklace with the diamonds. I told her how pretty I thought it was in the hallway one day and she blew it off, rolling her eyes. *Thank Instagram.*

"She kept pushing me about the Jeep. Pushing and pushing, and I kept telling her to stop as I clutched the keys in my hand. She ripped the keys away from me and threw them into the street, cackling.

"She gave me that good cheer pivot that you know she had, and she said to me: *I hope you fucking crash.*"

Chloe Schmidt gets quiet, real quiet. Her eyes down. I think she forgets that we're even there.

"I could have torn her apart right there, told her she was a user or told her to get her father to buy her a Jeep of her own. But, oh, that's right. She doesn't have a father. Just a drunken joke of a stepfather with his two barrel-headed sons. At least I knew what it was like to have a father who loved me and left me something. Not like her, who had nothing except for a cringey cheerleader mother."

"Why are you telling us this, Chloe?" I say.

"Because I want *you* to know. I want all of you to know what kind of friend I was to her. How much I put up with. And through all of it, I was still her best friend. Her most loyal friend."

The anger back in Chloe Schmidt's face again, so much more anger than I've seen before. A flush of fury, and she swings her arm out of my grip.

"You killed your best friend and you tried to put it on me," Jadis is saying, growling. She follows Chloe Schmidt to the Jeep, so close to her, so filled with rage, that I wonder if she's going to hit her.

"Because she was mean to you? Because she threw your keys in the dirt? Because she bullied you? Because she said something horrible to you that she couldn't take back?" Jadis says. "Why?"

"Because I didn't like her," Chloe says. "Sometimes it's as simple as that."

An alarm inside of me sets off, the tragedy of it all sinking in, that Chloe Schmidt murdered Chloe Orbach.

Chloe hops in her Jeep, backs out of the driveway, and peels away.

Chloe Clarke buries her face in her hands and screams, a terrible scream filled with loss. I try to soothe, to shush Chloe, but there's no cork for this devastation. And I want to wrap my arms around her, I want to tell her that it's going to be okay, because that's what you do in this sort of situation, when you're watching someone hysterical like this, so fragile. When there are no other words.

While we wait for the police, Chloe's mom paces inside, on the phone with a lawyer. I can hear her sobbing.

36

CHEERLEADER KILLS BEST FRIEND AT HOMECOMING DANCE

On Saturday, November 7, high school cheerleader Chloe Schmidt was supposed to rally the home team at the Groveton Panthers' football game.

Instead of cheering, Schmidt was arrested for murder.

Yesterday, Schmidt pled guilty to drugging her best friend, cheer captain Chloe Orbach, with fentanyl, an opioid that is 50 to 100 times more potent than morphine. Schmidt, Orbach, and three other friends, all minors, took MDMA, also known on the street as Molly or ecstasy, at the homecoming dance.

"We are devastated about the senseless death of Chloe Orbach," said Jonie Verinza, Groveton High School principal. "We do not condone any use of illegal drugs or alcoholic substances during school functions."

A source close to Schmidt told *The Groveton Post* that she and Orbach had been fighting for months. "Their relationship was explosive," the source said. "They were on the verge of a breakup, which Chloe couldn't handle. "

Suffice it to say that most friendship breakups do not end in murder. And it has the town asking: Why would a teenage girl kill her best friend?

"That's the million-dollar question," sociologist Stacia Karols, a professor at New York University, said. "But the real question is, what happened in their friendship that caused Ms. Schmidt to resort to this kind of brutality?"

When you add together teenage hormones, a developing brain, and genetics, you are dealing with an explosive mix.

Friendship breakups can be a trigger for erratic behavior, Karols said. Because as common as friendship breakups between women are, they're also taboo. They're humiliating, according to Karols.

"No one really wants to admit that they've fallen out with their friend," she explained. "Because breakups between women go against all of women's ingrained social and emotional tendencies. Female friendships are the glue that keeps society together."

Studies show that when men are dealing with

stress, they go into a "fight or flight" mode. Women retreat and they run to their friends. But if the friendship is the cause of the stress—who do you turn to?

Francesca Mironda, PhD, a clinical psychologist who specializes in adolescent codependency, theorized that it is possible that Schmidt and Orbach had a classic codependent relationship that went wrong. The American Psychological Association describes codependency "as an unhealthy devotion to a relationship at the cost of one's personal and psychological needs."

In a codependent romantic relationship or a platonic friendship, one person can lose themselves in the other person, ignoring their own feelings.

"Eventually you need that friend to need you. And if that disappears, then it can be soul-crushing to the relationship," Dr. Mironda said. "It's impossible to say why Ms. Schmidt did what she did, but based on the evidence, based on her cold response to police, it seems that there was an element of rejection. It's possible that Ms. Schmidt no longer felt needed, that she was no longer cared for in the way that she had once been."

"My heart is absolutely broken," Groveton cheerleading coach Demi Alvarado said. "All of my girls are tough, resilient athletes. But it is going to take a long time for us to heal from this. Maybe we never will."

■ ■ ■

Two weeks into this and noise from the media doesn't stop. All the newspapers. National newspapers picked up the story. Crime podcasts. Everyone asked the same question. How could a girl just decide to kill her best friend? Couldn't she just stop talking to her? Couldn't she tell her that she didn't want to be friends anymore?

It's so much more complicated than that.

I'm not making excuses for Chloe Schmidt, but there was very much an all-or-nothing mentality around Chloe Orbach. When she fluttered around you, she encompassed you. She didn't let you go. I don't know what it was like for Chloe Schmidt to slowly lose that over time, but I imagine it was devastating.

Jadis says she's a sociopath.

They're saying in the comments that Chloe could get life in prison with parole after fifteen years. I scroll through all the comments, reading opinions people have from across the globe about this horror. A girl who kills her best friend. Someone writes that they'll wait until she's eighteen to try her so they can stick her in women's prison. That she doesn't deserve to be in juvy.

I try to imagine Chloe Schmidt in prison with grown women. How she'd fall asleep every night crying, fantasizing about her white Jeep, about her Instagram account and the way her life used to be.

■ ■ ■

Jadis's mother is taking a temporary leave from work that'll extend through the holidays. She's scared something is going to happen to Jadis. Taking Molly at the homecoming dance was the thing that finally got Jadis's mother's attention. I'm not sure why that was the final straw, but it was.

Jadis is going to an artsy boarding school up in Vermont after winter break. A place where she can be herself, where she can draw, her mother says. But we both know it's more than that. It's a place where other people can look after her.

■ ■ ■

I walk down to Jadis's house, my feet crunching over frozen leaves. Her mom decided to cover up the pool earlier than New Year's. When we asked her why, she said, "Too much has been left uncertain. We should start to follow some rules and close the pool in September like normal people. We don't always need to stand out, do we?"

The pool is covered up with a big black casing. The lounge chairs, except for two old ones, are all put away. There's nothing more depressing than a pool off-season. Makes you think back about what was and how it's all dead now.

"Did I tell you my mom invited my aunt and her husband over for Thanksgiving? My cousins who I haven't seen in two years are coming too."

"Wow, she's taking this let's-be-a-family kick seriously," I say.

"Yeah," Jadis says, her mind gazing somewhere else. "My

new therapist told her we should have family dinners. And also I talked about you today."

"Oh? What did you tell her?"

"Well, she asked me if I was mad at you for joining cheer. I explained to her that I wasn't mad about the cheer itself. It was really about me being mad that you wanted to do something without me. It was like you broke up with me, but you didn't tell me. You just kept pretending that everything was fine between us even though it wasn't at all."

I want to deny it, tell her it's not true. That I didn't break up with her. But in a way, I did. I did break up with her and I didn't know it either.

"I'm sorry, Jadis. I'm sorry for everything." And I am. I'm sorry for getting her wrapped up in the Three Chloes. I'm sorry for dragging her into this mess. I'm sorry that she thought she had to bring something like Molly to the dance to make me happy. I'm not sure if I could have done anything differently though. If I had, what would it had been?

"Why are you sorry? Sorry for having wants and desires? For making new friends? You shouldn't feel sorry for that," she says. "Just say it, Shade. You felt trapped in our friendship."

Jadis shakes her head. Takes out her vape. Draws in heavy and releases the smoke, and it's like a double cloud mixed in with her breath.

"That's not it at all," I say, and I want to cry, that clenched feeling in the back of my throat. With my finger, I hover over those two pinkies tattooed on her forearm. "That's what you thought. But that's not what happened. I just wanted to be . . .

myself." I say, and I can hardly get the words out. I don't know what about that is so difficult to convey. That I wanted to be completely enmeshed with her, inseparable as we'd been for so long. No ending, no beginning.

But I wanted to be me too.

■ ■ ■

Chloe Orbach's death and Chloe Schmidt's arrest put the future of the whole squad into question. Just before Thanksgiving, parents came out in droves to a school board meeting, protesting about cheer saying it was an old-fashioned, outdated cult. Not even a real sport. No protection for the girls. No real goal except to cheer for the boys. And now this. One cheerleader killed another one? Her motive so shallow and unclear.

"What kinds of girls are we raising?" one mother said. "The hypersexuality of their uniforms is offensive."

That's only how it looks from the outside. People didn't understand the drive of the team and how hard we worked. We lifted each other up and gave each other hope. What other sport could you say that about? Where a team stands on the sidelines trying to bring aspiration and optimism to a crowd of screaming fans?

The football moms showed up at the school board meeting to support the cheer moms and the squad. Altogether, about thirty of them spoke, many of them with CHEER MOM bedazzled on their sweatshirts, each of them starting their speeches with: *What is this country turning to? How could you imagine a town without cheerleaders?*

The biggest surprise: My mother was on the side of the football moms. Imagine *my mother*, on the side of the football moms?

I heard her talking on the phone one night to a friend. "Cheer saved Shade's life. I know that sounds bizarre after everything that happened. But it gave her something to live for, something to work toward."

In the end, they decided not to disband the team. It made no sense to punish future cheerleaders for what had happened in the past.

■　■　■

I start going to therapy in January, after Jadis leaves for school. When I tell the therapist I feel numb, she says you don't feel trauma until years later sometimes. So we talk about boundaries with friendships. What it means not to bleed into other people. Or for them to bleed into you. I tell her I don't know what that means. That I'm desperate to learn.

I tell her I still think I'm going to see Chloe Orbach, somewhere on the street, or around the corner in school. She said eventually, that goes away. I don't know if I want it to.

■　■　■

Jadis sends me letters from Vermont. They have her signature doodles all over them and look just like her stick and pokes, but on paper. She says writing letters is healthier than texting. Not as much instant gratification. She says that Emma's going to visit her in February, but that it's a long way away. She doesn't ask me to come.

Jadis writes that she's working with an art therapist to channel that yearning she has to draw on her skin. She says it's an urge that's hard to escape. But she's working on it.

It'll never be the same between us again. We used to blend into each other not too long ago. Those pinkies twisted on my arm, a forever reminder. But there's a clear delineation now. *Good luck at cheer*, she writes in one letter, and there's a sketch of a cheerleader, three bases lifting her in the air, her arms out in a V.

■ ■ ■

That night after I get the sketch, I dream that Jadis and Chloe Orbach are one person, morphing together, the two of them in a haze around a lake. I'm in the center of the lake, and they're still pulling me toward each of them. But I stay strong in the middle, not going either way. On someone's shoulders, above the water, my feet firmly planted. Then the shoulders become a rock, a boulder, and I'm standing there alone, without the tugging, completely balanced. There's a reflection below me. I see myself for the first time above it all.

Chapter
37

KEKE AND GRETCHEN are the new co-captains. It's their last year, and it's the start of basketball season. I smile thinking of Chloe Orbach and how she hijacked the captain's spot, that she wrestled it away from two seniors just with pure determination. But that was the power of Chloe Orbach. She could convince you of anything.

The bases are the heart of the team, Coach says when she makes the announcement. And I think about Chloe Schmidt, how someone like her could have been the heart of our team. How dangerous she was.

Everyone talks about whether Chloe Clarke is going to come back. That her mother is homeschooling her. That she got rid of her phone. No contact with the outside world. No way to get in touch with her. Zoey said she saw her running one day, or maybe it was someone else.

I didn't think the girls would want me on the team after everything that happened.

"We've survived so much together," Zoey says, her big weepy eyes. "Of course we want you."

It sounds so selfish, but I forget that they suffered too. I forget how this all affected them. They had their own experiences with the Three Chloes. They had their own brushes with the glow of Chloe Orbach. Everyone felt her loss, all those freshman conspiracy theories and how they dug into our souls, how she'd come skipping into practice with that manic energy or dancing with the band on the sidelines between cheers. We all hurt.

Over winter break we worked on some more complicated stunts, one where I would back handspring into their arms, they'd lift me up, and I'd spin. The technical word is back handspring full around. Gretch is my new main base and poor, sweet Gretch. First thing I did was kick her in the head. Everyone stood there with hands covering their mouths waiting for a Chloe Schmidt–like blowup.

But Gretch was completely calm. Nodded her head. Brushed herself off.

"Let's run it again."

■ ■ ■

My mother decides after the New Year that she's not going to have parties for a little while. That she needs to reassess her life and mine. That too many adults have influenced me in the wrong way, and she knows it's not great. She doesn't want to travel either, because she thinks I've been through a lot and she doesn't want me to be alone. Too much going on with all these girls and so much sadness. She wants to be around if I need her.

She won't budge on coming to one of my games. She can't bear to watch if I crash to the ground.

"I was thinking," she says, blushing, one night over ice cream sodas, "that maybe you could give me one of those stick and pokes." She rubs the edge of her wrist and smiles. "Maybe a little heart right here."

My whole face erupts, and I can't even look at her. I burst into laughter.

"What?" she says, defensive. "I'm too old to get a tattoo?"

"No, it's cute," I say, a certain calm over me. "It's really cute."

"Maybe you can get one too. Then we can both have a matching heart."

"To symbolize our love?" I say, snarky. But I think she means it.

"Yeah," she says, and takes a big slurping sip out of her ice cream soda. A little drips down the edge of her mouth.

And I think that would be nice. That would be really nice.

■ ■ ■

Basketball season has a different feel than football season. For one, there's no football moms with their little bullhorns and their pom-poms. Basketball moms don't wear BASKETBALL MOM sweatshirts. Basketball moms come to the game on their way home from work. They run into the gym, frazzled, just off the train with their leather tote bags and their trench coats and their big chunky glasses. They're always sitting behind us because that's the only place there's room in the stands when you're late.

Almost every game so far, I've heard a basketball mom taking a work call, saying, "I'm at my son's game. Let me get back to you?"

We roll out the mat during halftime, but there's not a lot of give to it. If I fall, I'm falling hard. These death-defying feats that we make look easy. One slip and I could crack my head open right there in front of all these kids. Teachers. Parents.

During halftime, after the pep band plays from the wooden bleachers, while the kids run in and out of the gym to the concession stand, with the mothers back on their calls to their clients or with their assistants, we cheer. The basketball spectators aren't as focused as they were during football games, and I'm grateful for it. We have room to be sloppier.

Zoey and Olivia double back handspring and then clap their way next to us. We try the new stunt for the first time. I back handspring and Gretch, Keke, and Olivia catch my legs, then lift me so that I can propel up above them, spin, and face forward again. I slide right into that scorpion, then a lib with one arm in the air.

Next to us, Sasha and Pri elevate Zoey, so that when I bend my right leg, Zoey can catch it, just below me, in her hand. Kaitlyn breezes in front of us with a double back handspring tuck.

It's our pyramid. It's lopsided and lanky, but it's ours. We get a slow clap from maybe nine people.

Gretchen counts, and on two, it's time for my double down. I fly up just enough to spin myself around, once, then twice, feeling the air across my face, my body so tight and held together, tight and hollow, me alone up there in the revolution, flying, flying, until I land in their arms like a baby.

At least that's what it looks like from the outside. My solid landing. Their forearms crashing against my ribs. The way they grunt when I thud into them, when they lift me high above.

We're not babies. We're not sweet.

We're nothing like you think we are.

And I've never felt more like myself.

ACKNOWLEDGMENTS

It's May 2021 as I write this, and most of all, I'm grateful to be alive. I'm grateful that my family is healthy and safe. This book was written deep in a pandemic, and if it feels like the world in this book is crumbling for these characters, that's because it was written and edited during the isolation, desolation, and fear we all experienced between 2020 and 2021.

I'd like to thank my editor, Julie Rosenberg, whose college cheer background made me look like a cheer pro. Julie, you made sure the cheer stunts in this book were *on point*, and I can't thank you enough for your edits and for getting me to drill down to what this book was really about: friendship. Thanks also to Emily Sylvan Kim for your tireless enthusiasm and guidance no matter how many times I call you in a panic. You are a friend, you are wise, and you are my saving grace.

The entire Razorbill and Penguin Teen team: thank you for your attention to detail and your razor-sharp focus on *The Falling Girls*. Casey McIntyre, Simone Roberts-Payne, Laura Blackwell, Krista Ahlberg, Felicity Vallence, Christina Colangelo, Tessa Meischeid, Bri Lockhart, Lyana Salcedo, Briana Wagner, James Akinaka, and Shannon Spann. To Sarah Maxwell for the most cryptic, stunning cover, which captured my girls in the most haunting way. To Samira Iravani for your beautiful design and, as always, for washing my book in pink. At MBC, my incredibly talented and ego-boosting publicist Megan Beatie.

I want to thank all of the cheerleaders out there: the elite leagues, the high school squads, the rec squads, the kids on the sidelines, and every single one of you who uploaded performances, practices, and instructional videos to YouTube, TikTok, and Instagram accounts. Special shout-out to the Instagram account Official Black Girls Cheer, which is one of my favorites. Though I was extremely lucky that my editor happened to be a college cheerleader, I studied y'all for this book!

Cheerleading has gotten much attention for its dangerous nature, which is something I touch on in the book. The National Center for Catastrophic Sport Injury Research (NCCSIR) found that the number of severe cheerleading injuries was second only to football injuries. While cheerleading has worked on lowering their concussion rates in recent years, concussions still make up 31 percent of injuries, according to the American Academy of Pediatrics. Watch just one episode of Netflix's *Cheer* and you'll be awestruck by the athletic and the no exaggeration—*death-defying* stunts that the squad members perform.

It leads me to the commonly asked question: Why isn't cheerleading recognized as a sport by the NCAA or by US federal Title IX guidelines? Title IX protections require all participants be treated equally and prohibits gender-based discrimination in sports.

Simply put: cheer is not taken as seriously as other sports because of societal structure and feminine tropes. Case in point: in January of this year, a member of the Northwestern cheerleading team filed a lawsuit against the university claiming she had been "groped, harassed and lifted" without her permission by intoxicated fans during university events. Yet she was *still* encouraged to mingle with potential donors for the university. *The New York Times* reported that after she and squad members detailed this harassment to the deputy athletic director, they were met with this response: "What did you expect as cheerleaders?"

Sexism and sexual harassment aren't the only problems in cheer; racism is as well. Erika Carter, who was a member of that same Northwestern team from 2016 to 2018, said that the coach threatened to cut Black cheerleaders from the team if they wore their hair naturally, *The Times* reported. Another offense: white cheerleaders were elevated above the Black cheerleaders so they could be the "face" of the team.

In a blog post for NYU's Cooper Squared, Cheyenne Leitch also pointed out the issue of racism in cheer, stating that there are significantly fewer Black women than white women involved in the sport, a problem that dates back to the 1960s, when "Black young women were fighting for and being denied acceptance onto cheerleading teams."

Take a look at *Bring It On*, the most iconic of all cheer movies, which was released in 2000, and tackled cultural appropriation long before it was a widely recognized issue. The main premise of the movie is that the white team, the San Diego Rancho Carne Toros, steals cheers from the Black team, the East Compton Clovers. The beauty of *Bring It On* is its political message, yes, but also how it focuses on the cheer-leaders' skills and performances rather than on sexist tropes.

I was a JV cheerleader in high school. Though my skills were limited to some tumbling and splits, I appreciated the stamina and practice that goes into sideline cheer. I had some basic gymnastic skills, and despite everyone around me being shocked that I was interested, I found myself drawn to the athleticism of cheer. Like Shade, I didn't quite fit in. And un-like Shade, I was a little too rebellious to fully commit. I was shy, I lacked confidence, I was depressed, I didn't like smiling, and I smoked too many cigarettes.

For *The Falling Girls*, I wanted to do something different: I wanted to dive into the unabashed commitment and determi-nation of these girls. Girls who took chances with their bodies, who dedicated their energy to the squad and bonded together from that determination.

While this book is about cheer, it was also loosely inspired by the murder of West Virginia teen Skylar Neese, who was only sixteen years old when her two best friends killed her. Anything I read about Skylar's death begged the same ques-tion: What would make two teenagers kill their best friend? When the police asked one of the killers why she did it, she answered: "We just didn't like her." For research, I'm indebted to the book *Pretty Little Killers* by Daleen Berry and Geoffrey C. Fuller as well as the *Elle* article "Trial by Twitter" by Holly Millea.

Like most women, I've had my share of friendship breakups. And yes, every teenage girl endures friendship battle scars. It's probably why I identified with the dark comedy *Heathers*, which came out when I was a senior in high school. I dug into that *Heathers*-inspired rage while writing *The Falling Girls*. Shade and Jadis are imperfect and messy, and I ache equally for both of them. I hope you know that you're not alone if you feel that you've grown apart from your best friend, or if she's grown apart from you. My mother always told me that friendships have hills and valleys and can often go through phases; while I didn't want to believe her at the time, she was absolutely right. You *can* come through the other side of a friendship breakup, with pain—yes, there is going to be lingering pain—but you can also find forgiveness and maybe understanding. And by that I mean understanding yourself.

I'm so thankful to have friends who support me through all of this, who talk me up, who love me up and lift me up. Thank you to my readers, helping me sift through the muck: Melissa Adler, Jessica Goodman, Sara Kaye, and Jodi Brooks. Thank you to all of the bookstagrammers, bloggers, vloggers, readers, librarians, authors, and independent booksellers who read and promoted and supported my debut, *Something Happened to Ali Greenleaf*, and got me here. Thank you, Kathleen Glasgow, Courtney Summers, and Amber Smith for your early and unwavering support.

To my humongous family, all the Krischers and all the Adlers, for your love, your support, and your shoulders to cry on. My children, Jake, and Elke, who I love and cherish—my life is nothing without you both. Lastly, I want to thank my husband, Andy. We held our family together after this dark year. I love you. Thank you for always making me laugh.